NEW DAWN,

NEW DAY

NEW DAWN TRILOGY

Book 1

By

A. K. Morgan

For Jo, my family and for my friends.

CONTENTS

CHAPTER 1

A Mission to the Stars

Captain Jonas Dean stands naked inside the sterile room. The Glasshouse, as it's been nicknamed by his medical team, is devoid of fixtures and fittings except for a small digital clock which is positioned over the glass cubicle's airlock door.

The clock strikes 2230 hours and the Europa Spaceprime Captain is in full pre-flight status at T-minus one hour and thirty minutes from launch.

Nerves are beginning to get the better of Jonas: his fit, muscle-ridden body breaks out in goose bumps and the hairs on the back of his neck are raised erect within the cooling environment of his glass bubble. A handful of the sixty on-duty technicians are glancing over at him as they walk past the glass structure whilst working through their final preparations with a military precision; instinctively, Jonas sticks out his chest, clasps his hands behind his back and a small sigh escapes from his lungs as he concentrates upon the airlock door which is situated directly in front of him.

Captain Jonas Dean attempts to control the onset of his agitation: ten minutes have passed since his medical team took a blood sample, a urine sample, an X-ray and a full MRI body scan. The medical team are presently measuring the results against the baselines they've taken over the course of the previous twelve months, making sure he's in the right physical shape to take command of the Starship Zx12.

Twenty-three dry runs have been simulated in preparation for Jonas's impending mission. On each and every occasion, he has been assured that it will take approximately seven minutes from the time his samples are taken to being given the all-clear for his spaceflight; eleven minutes have now elapsed and Captain Jonas Dean is beginning to worry that the first space mission for forty years will be aborted at the eleventh hour.

The airlock door to his Glasshouse slides open and his three-strong medical team step inside the sterile room. The Chief Medical Officer, Doctor Grace James, wears a tight smile as she speaks to Jonas. "Sorry we're late, Captain. We've checked and double-checked all of your test results and I'm very pleased to say that you're in excellent physical shape."

A broad grin extends across Jonas's clean-shaven face; four years training of his mind and body have prepared him for the mission at hand and the all-clear from his medical team is another step towards him achieving his ultimate goal of Spaceprime astronaut.

Beyond Doctor Grace James and his Europa Spaceprime medical team, Jonas views the wide-open expanse of the thriving hangar environment. Suddenly, he becomes aware of the hangar technicians gathering around his glass cubicle sanctum and he lifts up his eyes to his medical operatives who are by now bearing down upon him.

Doctor Grace James has taken up her pre-assigned position directly behind the spaceman-to-be, from where she vehemently commands: "Captain Dean. Bend over."

He leans forwards and winces even before the good doctor has picked up the single syringe containing seven razor sharp needles which is carried on a tray by Doctor Aileen Grey.

The pain hits his brain before the syringe has been fully inserted into his backside. Captain Jonas Dean of the First Order of the Spaceprime has been trained to be impervious to pain, however on this occasion he falters and his face screws up momentarily, although he doesn't cry out. The technicians who've gathered around his inner sanctum cheer and applaud enthusiastically; the ground crew give Jonas the thumbs-up sign and slap each other upon the shoulder before wandering off to finish their final checks before lift-off.

Captain Dean feels winded, yet the jab is a necessity as the synthetic fluids will have a number of effects on his body: the medicinal cocktail will firstly strengthen his immune system and make him less susceptible to contracting any off-world virus that he may come into contact with on his three-month mission. A liquid booster will allow his body to function normally even though he'll be rationed to one dry pack meal and one crystallised drink per day. There's also a drug in the vials which will enhance his brain activity, thus giving him greater in-flight focus, and inhibitors to keep his heart beating at a steady rate, especially during the take-off and when his hyperdrive comes online.

Doctor Aileen Grey and her assistant Doctor Rob Jamieson open up a compartment at the rear of the glass cubicle which houses Jonas's spacesuit; the spacesuit is standing upright and looks as if it's currently being worn by an invisible man. The traditional white garment is linked via two umbilical cables to the Europa Spaceprime Mission Control's mainframe computer.

The spacesuit has five visible markings upon its specially designed cloth. Over the heart area is the British flag, Jonas's chosen flag: the historic Union Jack. Underneath this, his name and title are stitched: 'Captain Jonas W Dean'; below this hand-embroidered name tag is his badge of rank, a badge of honour. On the opposite breast, the Spaceprime logo is stitched: four vertical wavy S shapes sewn in black, and on the left sleeve of his suit are the markings of the Earthprime: four horizontal wavy S shapes, also sewn in black.

With her electronic pad to hand, Doctor Grace James peers over her rimless glasses. "Captain Dean, you know the drill, turn your back to the suit and take one step backwards," she commands.

"One giant leap for mankind," Jonas mutters.

Jonas Dean complies with the direct order and places his arms into the spacesuit, careful not to make any sudden movements, remembering having been told on many occasions that his specifically made-to-fit spacesuit is irreplaceable, whereas astronauts can be replaced at the stroke of a pen.

Once Jonas's five-foot, eleven inch frame is fitted into the suit, Doctor Jamieson speaks with a voice lacking concern as he leans forwards and attaches three electronic sensors directly onto his chest area. "As you're aware Captain Dean, you have three heart monitor sensors attached to your body and there are also various sensors built into your suit which will monitor your pulse, your temperature, your respiration; there are also sensors fitted inside your space helmet to allow us to monitor your brain activity in-flight. These are all linked to the mainframe computer at the Europa Spaceprime Mission Control, so that when you're in deep space we can monitor your life signs from the signal sent back to Earth which is boosted by the state-of-the-art communications system onboard the Starship Zx12," he says as he regurgitates the operations manual in a monotone.

Jonas hasn't heard a word of Jamieson's deadpan brief as the inhibitors in the shot he was given earlier have just kicked in and he is momentarily feeling very mellow and extremely chilled out.

Doctor Rob Jamieson unhooks the umbilical cables from the spacesuit and Jonas takes a tentative step forwards.

Doctor Aileen Grey will soon begin the process of attaching

Jonas's space helmet; however, his space helmet will not be sufficient in the cold isolation of deep space and so Grey unfolds a clear membrane which she attaches to the rear neck rim of his suit, before pulling the clear film up and over the back of Jonas's head and then down over his face, sealing the membrane airtight over his head.

Whilst Captain Dean begins to breathe his suit's regulated oxygen supply, Grey places the space helmet over the membrane which is loosely covering the suited astronaut's head and flicks two external catches to fix his helmet into position.

The helmet's technologically advanced visor is of special importance to Jonas as on either side of his main view he'll be able to obtain up-to-the-second readouts of his heart rate, respiration, body temperature and external temperature as well as being able to check oxygen levels within his suit's regulated supply and obtain any alerts from the Starship Zx12's onboard computer.

Grey's final task is to make Jonas's suit fully operational. The membrane inside the space helmet expands away from his face as she pressurises his spacesuit. The clear film is inflated to follow the contours of his cranium leaving a four-centimetre gap between his head and any part of the membrane. The clear membrane is a last line of defence against the unnatural elements of space – if Jonas's suit should ever fail him, he'll still have at the very least a chance of survival.

Doctor Grace James stands before a suited and booted Captain Jonas Dean and, like a proud parent, states authoritatively, "Good luck, Captain Dean. Come home safe. You're now at T-minus one hour and nine minutes to launch and I've already informed mission control that you're a provisional go-flight from the medical team. As you well know, your life signs are all patched into the main computer at the Europa Spaceprime Mission Control, so if you do stop breathing then we'll know about it."

Jonas gives out an edgy laugh. "I do believe Doctor James that you've finally developed a sense of humour," he says.

Yet etched graveness falls upon James's features as she speaks with a controlled concern, "You must be careful – many of us here at the academy harbour the belief that the hyperdrive has not yet been fully tested. In short, you'll have a huge firework strapped to your backside and very little control over it."

"I'm aware of all the dangers. I'm trained and ready and I know what the Starship Zx12's capable of, and if we do not meet again, Doctor James," Jonas hesitates, "Grace, it's been a great pleasure working with you," he says with an austere attitude.

Jonas holds out a suited hand and James takes a firm grip of the offered glove. "Captain Jonas Dean of the Starship Zx12, you're either brave and bold or just plain stupid," the Doctor states with a mischievous smile, before she motions with her eyes outside of the cubicle. "Captain Dean, it looks like you have a visitor."

The King of Europa stands proudly in front of the Glasshouse with two of his loyal generals at attention behind. He's unaccustomed to looking up at anyone, but in this particular case he's willing to make an exception. Behind the King, the hangar technicians are standing in a single line; all of them have taken off their work caps and are holding them across their chests in rigid formality.

Jonas Dean feels immense pride that His Majesty the second King of Europa is here to greet him; it is something he'll be sure to tell his father about upon his safe return.

His parents aren't attending the lift-off event as his father thought that the strain of the launch would be too much for his wife; instead, his parents are staying at their retirement home, just off the beach at Atlantis Strand, and watching the ascent of the Starship Zx12 on their streaming digital vision feed.

Whilst he's on-mission, Jonas has asked his father to look after his beach house retreat which is located two miles along the Atlantis coastline and his father has readily agreed.

His parents had visited him two days earlier and they'd all ventured out for a family farewell meal, during which his mother, Evie, had constantly worried over her only son and tried her best to hide her growing trepidation, while Jonas had done his best to reassure her and let her know that there was nothing to be afraid of and that he was in the best possible shape and in the best possible hands.

His father of course knows the truth; Josiah Dean, a veteran of the Europa Spaceprime, knows that this is a dangerous mission, that only one other manned mission has been sent out into deep space, some forty years previously, and that all hands had been lost.

Against all Europa Spaceprime rocket regulations, Jonas has spoken privately to his father about the full status of his mission to the stars and his father has listened intently: his mission is to search for a lost starship, a Stargazer class vessel called the HMS Neon-Lit City, at its last known set of co-ordinates in the vicinity of a large cluster of asteroids which orbit Jupiter.

According to the old story, the Stargazer class vessel had been built using private funds by four men who wanted to live out the rest of their lives in space, mapping the stars. The four men were all civilians who, over many years, had collected as much historic documentation as they could find: from old NASA records to Russian and Chinese space program reports and old European Space Agency mission logs. All of the information was collated and, from the historic spacecraft specifications which they'd had at their disposal, the four ageing men designed and built the HMS Neon-Lit City. The old King had thought that the venture was far too risky as there was still so much pioneering work to be done on the Earth and the Moon. However, when it looked likely that the craft would be built, and although it was to be a purely civilian flight, the old King finally gave his blessing and hence the ship was granted His Majesty's Starship status.

The four men, all of whom were alleged to be in their late seventies, had travelled with their four young wives and blasted out towards Jupiter in the year 2108. Their homing signal had been transmitted back to Earth over the course of the next seven years until the beacon's signal had abruptly ceased: Captain Jonas Dean had been charged with trying to find the wreckage of the HMS Neon-Lit City and ascertaining a reason for the ship's demise.

The King presses the intercom button to the sealed Glasshouse and looks directly at spaceman Dean. "Captain Jonas William Dean," he barks, "By the First Order of the Spaceprime, I command you – blah, blah, blah." The King smiles and the hangar technicians laugh at the Sovereign Prime putting everyone at ease with his acidic humour.

"Jonas, my boy, I'm so proud of you. The peoples of this planet are proud of you and they'll watch in their millions this evening as you set out on your great adventure. For the next three months, they'll look to the heavens and they'll think only of you. The peoples of the Kingdoms of the Earthprime will see a star that shines brighter than any other star in the night sky and they'll know that you and only you are our representative in the known system. I know how dangerous this mission will be as you'll be pushing back the frontiers of space and I'll be praying for your safe return," the King of Europa says, heralding his Starship Captain.

In a more thoughtful mood, the Europan regent continues. "Captain Dean, you are of course aware of your mission and, with due respect to you, I must explain why I'm asking you to undertake the mission at hand. When we lost contact with the HMS Neon-Lit City back in the year 2115, my father, the late King of Europa, made a vow to the families of the crew that he'd find out what happened to the Stargazer class vessel. I am duty-bound to honour his vow, so that the families of the men and women who journeyed onboard that vessel can live out the rest of their lives knowing what happened to their loved ones. I hope that you understand this, Captain Dean, because if the Europa Spaceprime were to lose you, I'll make personally sure that a mission is sent out in search of you," the King says with a royal gusto.

The King of Europa wheels away from the Glasshouse in a theatrical sweeping motion, before ceasing, turning and facing a suited and booted Captain Jonas Dean. With a warm smile glowing across his regal face, he stands up to his full height and salutes majestically. "Good Luck Captain and Godspeed," he says with heartfelt honour.

Captain Jonas Dean returns his King's salutation by offering him the best salute that he can from within the confines of his spacesuit. "Thank you sire," Dean replies.

Within two minutes of His Majesty's departure, the hangar is deserted — the King has withdrawn to witness the launch of the Starship Zx12 from the Europa Spaceprime Mission Control and all of the hangar technicians have departed to witness the lift-off event on the various streaming digital vision feeds which are located around the Spaceprime Central complex.

The Glasshouse digital clock strikes 2300 hours exactly.

T-minus one hour to launch and searing alarms ring out throughout the hangar bay whilst red strobes bounce their light off the cubic glass shell as the wide expanse of the steel hangar doors start to slowly slide open.

The radio crackles within Jonas's space helmet. "Captain Dean, this is Spacecraft Capsule Communicator Cap-com Officer Hubert Snow. You're T-minus fifty-nine minutes and thirty seconds to launch and you're now under the supervision of mission control," Snow says formally.

The glass cubicle with astronaut Dean inside lifts up on a cushion of air and starts to gradually move towards the hangar doors; the journey to the Starship Zx12 is short as the final preparation hangar has been purposely built close to the launch site.

The glass chariot moves out through the wide expanse of the hangar doors and into the balmy summer night, and Captain Jonas Dean catches his first glimpse of the magnificent structure of the Starship Zx12, the very first manned spacecraft to be built with a fully functioning hyperdrive that'll allow the Starship to travel at interstellar speed.

There'd been a twenty-year struggle to develop the hyperdrive engine: the first three unmanned Zx class Starships exploded upon the launch pad whilst the next four failed to fire after leaving the Earth's orbit and were intentionally crashed into Mars.

The following two test rockets had both been hailed a major success: one had crashed into an asteroid field after coming out of hyperdrive, while the second was lost amongst the stars and is still floating around the deepest regions of the galaxy.

The final two test rockets which had been launched had each carried a pair of monkeys, and both missions had been successful – both sets of monkeys had lasted for fourteen days before their limited oxygen supplies had run out and their life signs were extinguished.

The Starship Zx12 was the twelfth incarnation of the Zx class space vehicle and its sleek structure's gantry was clamped and ominously lit-up by the fixed white lighting situated at intervals around the boundary of the launch site; all of the white lights were pointing inwards at the new-age rocket ship, creating an otherworldly effect and a sense of foreboding.

*

"Here comes Captain Jonas Dean, isolated within his glass chamber as he makes his way towards the Starship Zx12," announces the streaming digital vision feed commentator over the live picture feed, unable to keep the excitement out of his voice.

Kira Yu takes a firm hold of her remote and presses the mute button; normally on a Saturday evening she'd have been studying for her master's degree in Biochemistry, but for the first time in six months she's decided to take the evening off to watch the historic lift-off event.

Having spent three years in the Europa Spaceprime Academy with Jonas Dean, Kira Yu is acutely aware that this is to be his big day. Jonas had been a source of immense frustration – the minute she'd laid eyes upon him, Kira could tell he was trouble: cocky, intelligent, charming and handsome, and he knew it.

Kira was born and raised in the Kingdom of Americas. Her parents had died when she was very young and she'd been raised by a rich aunt who, although giving her everything she'd wished for in life, had never really attempted to form a parental attachment with her.

Kira had withdrawn into herself and shut the world out, taking solace in her books and her study. Consequently, Kira Yu was to become the top student in her school and in the top one per cent of the Kingdom, and when she'd graduated it was the Europa Spaceprime that had offered her a place with its training academy, where she could major in her favourite subjects: Biology and Biochemistry.

The majority of the world's population would be tuned into the milestone launch. The events of the twenty-first century were by now a distant history as peace had descended upon the planet and a new world order had been created. Central to this was the formation of the five Kingdoms of the world: the Kingdom of Europa, the Kingdom of Americas, the Kingdom of Asia, the Kingdom of the North and the Kingdom of the South. This, Kira thought, was a commonsense approach to looking after the interests of the planet as the five Kings would meet regularly, make policy and discuss issues involving all of the peoples of the world and, in true democratic fashion, the majority vote would rule.

With her long flowing jet-black hair cascading towards her shoulders, Kira sits alone within her sparsely furnished apartment in her plastic restive chair which hugs the contours of her slim body. Her tumbling dark locks cover the porcelain features of the left-hand side of her face whilst she sits and intently watches the digital vision feed of Jonas's personalised Glasshouse slowly making its way to the base of the Starship Zx12. The see-through structure rises upwards to the hatch entry point of the new-age rocket ship, passing orange-coloured fuel tanks on its ascent, before locking onto its designated position adjacent to the interstellar craft's entry point.

The Glasshouse transporting Dean attaches itself by suction to the hatch on the hull of the Starship Zx12, whereupon a suited Captain Jonas Dean disembarks from his transparent confinement to make his way to the forward-end of his spacecraft.

"Get a move on, Jonas as you're T-minus forty minutes and you still have to do all of the on-board preparation," Kira says out loud to the wall-mounted streaming digital image. "If I'm going to watch the rest of this feed, I'll need crisps, chocolate and alcohol," she says, mocking the screen fitted to her apartment wall.

Kira Yu scurries off to her kitchen to raid her fridge.

*

"Cap-com to Captain Dean, we've confirmed that you're in flight position and are now sealing the hatch. Confirm, over," Snow says languidly.

"Confirmed, Cap-com," Jonas acknowledges.

Jonas takes a look around his confined cockpit. If he'd been in pre-flight simulation then he'd have been getting butterflies, but he figures that the serums which have been administered to him pre-launch have begun to work their way through his system and have taken the edge of his nerves. He has some nagging doubts about his mission, but he thinks that this is only natural.

During the take-off phase of his mission, Jonas is just along for the ride: all initial operations will be monitored and initiated by his ground control team at the Europa Spaceprime Mission Control because the Captain of the Starship Zx12 is viewed by the hierarchy as an appendix within the body of the Europa Spaceprime.

Through his closed communications link, Jonas will only be able to speak with his two communications operatives when on-mission: Cap-com Officer Hubert Snow and his Supervisor, Chief Communications Officer Katherine Jenkins. Although Jenkins is the more senior, it is Snow who is Dean's lifeline and he will happily place his complete trust in this man.

Jonas knows every inch of his Starship and his body and soul have been a slave to his mission for the last four years; he has sacrificed everything for his great adventure and has conditioned himself to be his master's willing servant.

There's only one item onboard the Starship Zx12 which appears to be out of place as Jonas has been allowed to take only one personal possession with him and he's arranged for it to be placed in a sealed glass unit above the main console of his cockpit array.

*

Hubert Snow is a picture of concentration as he stands over his desk at the Europa Spaceprime Mission Control with his hands upon his hips, looking across at the adjacent workstation to where Katherine Jenkins is seated. "Confirm hatch is sealed and Zx12 is airtight. Confirm communications are in full working order," Snow says in a confident and thorough manner.

Jenkins does not acknowledge Snow's assessment but instead she stands, turns and faces General Thalt, one of the King's three generals and also the Flight Director for the mission to the stars.

"General, we're a provisional go-flight from the communications team at T-minus twenty-five minutes and ten seconds," she confirms.

The General nods an acknowledgement before he takes his leave to the royal viewing gallery.

*

The King of Europa arrives at the Europa Spaceprime Mission Control and surveys his centre for off-world operations: protocol has been waived and he doesn't expect anyone of his operatives to stop and acknowledge the fact that he's entered the arena.

"I almost envy you, Jonas Dean," the Europan Monarch whispers as he stares intently at the main monitors which are situated at the front of the operations centre.

The largest monitor in the centre of the bank displays a map of the solar system with an oversized red flashing dot blinking upon the surface of the Earth: a beacon signal which is being sent back from the Starship Zx12's state-of-the-art communications tower.

There are banks of monitors positioned at either side of the main screen; one of them displays the weather conditions within the vicinity of the launch site and others display real-time Zx12 telemetry and operations data.

A bank of four monitors show the status of the astronaut: Jonas's heartbeat steadily beats across one large monitor and his vital signs are being monitored on the other three.

The King of Europa has grown up with the stories of the historic Moon landings, space stations and Moonbases, the failed Mars missions and the ill-fated mission of the HMS Neon-Lit City. He'd once wished that he could have gone to the stars himself, but he had too many responsibilities and the peoples of the Europa Earthprime wouldn't take too kindly if he neglected his duties to fulfil his own personal ambitions.

Protocol permits that the King should take a wife and he's under immense political pressure to do so, yet as a lonely man his mind would often wander to the exploration of the vast wilderness of space.

The Europan Monarch glances at the mission clock as he makes his way to his private viewing gallery with the launch countdown at T-minus fifteen minutes and fifteen seconds.

Greeting their King on his arrival at the royal viewing gallery are his three generals and a representative from Nanosec (Nanotech Space Engineering Corporation). With a pensive smile, the King of Europa nods to his generals. "Gentlemen: what is our current situation?" he asks whilst looking directly at General Thalt.

"Sire, we're all systems go and we don't have any reason at all to abort the mission; weather's clear, Captain Dean's undertaking final checks and we've a provisional go-flight order from all my team at mission control," Thalt states factually.

Sensing their unease, the King looks across at all three of his generals whilst ignoring the Nanosec representative from the Kingdom of Asia.

"And yet?" the King of Europa states bluntly.

"Sire, if I may speak freely," General Thalt says whilst almost choking on his words.

"Yes General, carry on," the King replies reasonably.

"We've planned this mission for eight years and trained Dean for the last four and we still don't know if the hyperdrive engine will work on more than one occasion on a single mission. It'll be dangerous enough as it is to engage the hyperdrive as you cannot predict exactly where your exit point in space will be. Captain Dean will have to use the hyperdrive on at least two occasions: once to get him to his destination and once to get him home. I'd like it noted that I'm still deeply uncomfortable about the effectiveness and reliability of the hyperdrive engine onboard the Starship Zx12," Thalt says, speaking his mind.

The King's two silent generals both look directly at their regent as he surveys them one by one, before nodding in agreement.

The Europan King turns to the Nanosec representative, the Asian attaché Tashi Chi, who amongst her many other titles is also the Chief Science Officer for the Kingdom of Asia; the King of Asia has helped to resource the Europa Spaceprime's mission to the stars and, in return, his Kingdom has been given the green light to trial some of the latest Nanosec Nanodrone technologies on the maiden flight into the void.

"And what would the King of Asia say, Miss Chi?" the King says directly to the Asian attaché.

Tashi Chi pauses momentarily. "No spaceflight is without risk, sire. I guess it's an occupational hazard," she replies in an ice-cold tone.

"Exactly," the King interjects and turns to his three generals. "Every spaceflight undertaken by mankind has carried some form of risk; an adventure into the unknown. We shall take this step together and if we should fail, then I'll forever carry Captain Jonas Dean's fate on my conscience," he says boldly.

The King of Europa pulls back his shoulders and salutes his three attending generals with his eyes nailing hard onto General Thalt. "Flight Director, we're a go-flight from command at T-minus nine minutes and fifteen seconds," he decrees.

*

Having filled up her glass, Kira Yu sits back down upon her plastic restive chair, places an open bottle of wine on her imitation stone flooring and turns up the volume of her streaming digital vision feed which is centrally positioned upon her apartment wall.

The digital feed production breaks away from live pictures and begins to broadcast library footage of the inside of the Starship Zx12: a virtual guided tour.

"As the viewers can see, the cockpit of the Starship Zx12 is of a futuristic design, apart from the powder blue stone which is encased in a small glass unit and situated above the main cockpit console array. If all the rumours are to be believed, it's an item that has been washed ashore at Captain Dean's beach house residence; the Starship Captain obviously wanted to take a piece of home with him," the streaming digital vision commentator announces as he reaches for the truth.

Kira sits bolt upright and spills apple wine onto her stone flooring with her mind racing. "It's a stone; it's my stone!" The words come tumbling out of her mouth as she stares intently at the enhanced pictures from her streaming digital vision feed.

Kira stands and paces her floor as she checks her solid silver watch at T-minus eight minutes and eleven seconds to the launch window.

"Men," Kira shouts out loud as her mind churns over the events of the previous four years. She thinks momentarily about switching off her digital vision screen-feed and going to her bed.

Kira Yu had hardly spoken to Jonas Dean throughout their early years together at the Spaceprime Central Academy, yet during the last few months of their training they'd formed a close bond and she'd once spent a solitary revision weekend out at Jonas's beach house when they'd both helped each other out with their final examinations.

Kira sits upon the body hugging plastic chair once more and takes hold of her glass of wine which she gulps down in one hit, before she reaches for the open bottle that resides upon her floor and refills her glass to the brim. She's made her decision to stay put and watch the ascent of the Zx12. "It's my stone," she whispers as she stares at the streaming digital vision feed.

*

Jonas Dean is fully into his last-minute pre-flight checks. He's walking himself through the rocket regulations manual in his head and his routine will be done at least four more times, just to be sure, checking all of his dials and making sure that all of his gauges are showing the standard data or the relevant setting. He listens intently to the chatter over his communications link; his mission to the stars appears to be on schedule.

Captain Jonas Dean really should be focusing on the mission at hand, yet all he can do is fix his gaze upon the encased stone within his line of sight and think of Kira Yu.

*

Jonas Dean had met Kira Yu on the first day of the first semester at the Europa Spaceprime Academy, where they, along with seven other candidates, had been singled out as outstanding world students and were to be given advanced training in Aeronautics, Astro-Physics, Advanced Technologies, Biology and Biochemistry.

It had been a foul weathered first day which had been unusual for the planet still escaping the grip of the previous century's global warming.

The rain was lashing down and Jonas had to watch his speed

whilst riding his vintage motorcycle to the academy at Spaceprime Central because the visibility was so poor.

As he pulled up to the tall grey angular structure of the Europa Spaceprime Academy, he noticed a young woman standing outside the training centre in full Europa Spaceprime Academy student uniform and getting absolutely drenched.

An act of chivalry was necessary, so Jonas jumped off his bike, pulled out his brolly and jogged up to the main entrance to where the young woman was standing in the rain's lash. He was about 20 metres away when the doors to the academy swung open and the young woman bolted inside; as Jonas leapt through the doors after her, they both ended up facing each other in the academy foyer.

The young woman standing before Jonas Dean was about six foot tall, of Oriental appearance and had light blue eyes, although Jonas could only see her right eye as a long mass of curling shoulder-length hair which had been dampened by the rainstorm was obscuring the left-hand side of her face. This raven-haired Asian beauty was shivering cold, wet through and looking somewhat dishevelled.

"Hi, Jonas Dean," Jonas said, plying her with his best smile.

Kira Yu looked straight through him.

"Is it raining?" Jonas asked in an attempt at humour and immediately regretted it as the words escaped his mouth whilst the look that Kira gave him was answer enough.

"I really think that you need to get out of those clothes," Jonas stated, meaning this as a statement of fact, yet it really didn't come out that way and caused Kira to just walk off.

"I didn't catch your name," Jonas shouted after her.

"I didn't give it," Kira said without looking back.

And although they were on the same three-year training course at the academy together, and with only nine students in the classroom, it would still be another two and a half years before their next real conversation.

*

Jonas is smiling to himself in the cockpit of the Starship Zx12 as he recalls the past when his radio crackles into life.

"Cap-com to Zx12, you're T-Minus four minutes and fifty seconds to launch. What is your status, over?" Snow says whilst trying to keep the nervous anxiety out of his voice.

"Zx12 to Cap-com: all systems are functioning within required parameters. We're a go-flight from Zx12. I repeat we're a go-flight from Zx12," Jonas replies almost jovially as Kira Yu is still preying on his mind.

Snow is about to turn to Katherine Jenkins and relay the go-flight order from Captain Dean when his radio crackles into life unexpectantly: "Zx12 to Cap-com," Captain Dean quietly urges.

Hubert Snow bites down hard on his lip as Captain Dean's unauthorised transmission is definitely not in the rocket regulations manual.

"Cap-com receiving Zx12," a deeply concerned Snow replies.

Katherine Jenkins's head bolts up from her console and she immediately picks up her headset to listen in on the conversation.

"Hubert," Jonas says quietly.

Hubert Snow is completely thrown by the unofficial broadcast as it's unusual for Captain Dean to be informal with him; Jonas and he had met on a few occasions during mission training and flight operations simulation and they both had a mutual respect for one another, but this was against all of the written Europa Spaceprime rocket regulations and not part of the strict laid down lift-off procedure.

Katherine Jenkins stands up from her console with a serious frown spreading evenly across her brow and Snow is fully aware that she has the authority to abort the mission.

"Yes, Captain Dean," Snow says worriedly.

"Hubert, if anything should happen to me, tell my parents that I love them, and tell Kira," Dean pauses, "tell Kira: it was always Delta."

A troubled Hubert Snow replies, "Roger that Captain Dean and good luck," he continues as he conveys an informal shrug to his Chief Communications Officer.

Valuable seconds have been lost by the unexpected conversation and Snow immediately turns to his Chief Communications Officer. "We're a go-flight from Zx12 at T-minus three minutes and five seconds," he says hurriedly.

Chief Communications Officer Katherine Jenkins eyes Snow, but instead of relaying the necessary information to her Flight Director she bluntly asks the able Cap-com for further clarification: "Who is Kira?"

Snow shrugs. "I don't know," he replies.

Jenkins snaps back into her real world of lapsing mission time and turns on her heel to face her Flight Director General who's awaiting an update. "General, we're a go-flight from the Starship Zx12 at T-minus two minutes and thirty-five seconds," she conveys with authority.

"OK people," General Thalt barks. "We're now in final phase countdown."

There are two operatives in attendance at each workstation, where all of the supervisors are standing as one to face Thalt whilst their seconds continue to monitor their field of operations.

The countdown clock on the main screen shows the time to the launch window as T-minus two minutes and ten seconds.

"Weather report?" Thalt demands as he moves swiftly through the motions of procedure.

"Weather is clear: go-flight."

"Medical report?" Thalt orders.

"Astronaut has a clean bill of health: go-flight," Doctor Grace James sternly advises.

"Operations?"

"All systems operational: go-flight."

"Communications?"

"Communications are online and crystal: go-flight," Jenkins relays efficiently whilst throwing Cap-com Snow a nervous glance. She hadn't expected Captain Jonas Dean's last message; it has unnerved her and she's now having serious doubts about Dean's state of mind.

Flight Director General Thalt ends his final mission control assessment and proudly surveys the mission control arena with the Europa Spaceprime deep within the shadow of its historic launch. "Good luck people; let's put our man in the game," he says impressively.

Thalt's head tilts towards the private viewing gallery to a King who's flanked by his two fellow generals and Tashi Chi, an Asian attaché who occupies a seat at the back of the gallery and who's currently talking on her mobile phone; no doubt the King of Asia is on the other end of the line, Thalt thinks.

The King of Europa looks directly at his Flight Director General and exaggerates a nod.

"No going back now," Thalt says quietly under his breath.

"T-minus one minute and counting," the Operations Assistant announces as he confirms the countdown and continues it in a monotone:

"Fifty-seven, fifty-six, fifty-five…"

Kira Yu stares blankly at the events unfolding upon her digital vision feed. Never has she had such overwhelming conflicting emotions and she doesn't know whether it's love, loss, anger or hurt pride. She looks on helplessly and is unable to intervene.

"Forty-one, forty, thirty-nine..."

Jonas Dean's inner circle of friends had often told him how brave and how bold he was, although there were a few who thought his maiden voyage to be a suicide mission. In the dark hours when he thought about his mission to the stars, he'd even admitted to himself that they were the ones who were probably right. Yet for Captain Jonas Dean of the First Order of the Spaceprime, this was the crowning glory of his life's endeavour and it was too late to have any self-doubt, it was too late to change the past; the day that he'd spent upon the beach at Atlantis Strand with Kira Yu could have changed the direction of his life forever. Jonas Dean had made what he'd thought was the right choice: to follow his dreams; it was ambition's choice and he'd readily accepted it.

"Thirty-four, thirty-three, thirty-two..."

Cap-com Snow glances nervously across to Katherine Jenkins as the precious seconds fall away to the culmination of a Kingdom's progression.

"Twenty-six, twenty-five, twenty-four..."

Captain Jonas Dean exhales steadily and glances around his cockpit for one final time to check that there are no warning lights which would dare to halt his pathway to the stars.

"Do I have the right stuff or do I have the wrong stuff?" Jonas whispers.

"Nineteen, eighteen, gantry away, fifteen, fourteen, switch to onboard computer, eleven…"

A Mission to the Stars

Ten,
Nine,
Eight,
Seven,
Six,
Five,
Four,
Three,
Two,
One.

I've fled away,
Hope I'll be back one day,
I'm lifting off into the sky,
A brave new day,
A new horizon dawning,
I'm speeding on into the night.

I'm on a mission to the stars,
I've just flown past the moon and on my way through Mars,
I'm on a mission beyond the sun,
A new frontier has just begun,
I'm on a mission to the stars.

I've sped away,
I will be back one day,
I'm light-speed on hyperdrive,
I'll chart new worlds,
I'll see black holes imploding,
A space pioneer in full flight.

I'm on a mission to the stars,
I've just flown past the moon and on my way through Mars,
I'm on a mission beyond the sun,
A new frontier has just begun,
I'm on a mission to the stars.

Now I'm floating here, high inside the void,
I've set a course, out to an asteroid,
Darkness all around me, infinity out beyond,
Moving out amongst the stars, my Starship hurtling on.

I'm on a mission to the stars,
I'm on a mission to the stars,
I'm on a mission to the stars,
I'm on a mission to the stars.

I'm on a mission to the stars,
I've just flown past the moon and on my way through Mars,
I'm on a mission beyond the sun,
A new frontier has just begun,
I'm on a mission to the stars.

I've sailed away,
I'll be back to you one day,
I'm burning out the hyperdrive,
I'll name new worlds,
I'll see event horizons storming,
I'm speeding on into the night.

I'm on a mission to the stars,
I've just flown past the moon and on my way through Mars,
I'm on a mission beyond the sun,
A new frontier has just begun,
I'm on a mission to the stars.

I'm on a mission to the stars,
I'm on a mission to the stars,
I'm on a mission to the stars,
I'm on a mission to the stars.

CHAPTER TWO

I'm Falling

Kira Yu wakes early from her fitful slumber, before her alarm raises her; the events of the previous evening come flooding back into her waking memory.

The Starship Zx12 blasted off from the Anglian desert at ten seconds past midnight, local time; the main booster fell away four minutes and ten seconds later, and Captain Jonas Dean had reached the Earth's orbit within nine minutes of his historic launch.

Kira watches bleary-eyed until four in the morning to make sure that there are no hitches from the launch event, but after the initial excitement, her streaming digital vision feed has slipped into showing archive footage of the lift-off and the ascent of the Starship Zx12.

Kira checks her solid silver timepiece; time check: seven-fifteen precisely. She has only had three hours sleep and today is Sunday which is traditionally her day off. Usually, she would have spent the day in her apartment, but today will be different as Kira has decided that she's going to travel to the Europa Spaceprime Mission Control at Spaceprime Central because the most vital part of Jonas's mission will take place within the next ten hours: he will be initiating the Starship Zx12 hyperdrive at approximately 1700 hours.

*

Katherine Jenkins leans across to her able Cap-com. "Snow, go and get your head down as I need you back here at 1400 hours for hyperdrive mission preparation," she orders.

Hubert Snow nods listlessly; it has been a long day and an even longer night – the Starship's launch has been a major success and everything has gone like clockwork.

Snow stands up behind his console and grabs hold of his regulation issue jacket and a half-drunk coffee.

"Oh, and Snow," Jenkins says with a half-smile. "Good job, today."

Cap-com Hubert Snow wearily departs the Europa Spaceprime Mission Control to find a bed in one of the many rooms within Spaceprime Central's main building; after bolting the door shut, he'll attempt to catch up on his sleep.

Katherine Jenkins puts her headset on. "This is Cap-com to Zx12, over," she drawls in her Southern American accent.

"Zx12 to Cap-com. Snow, you do sound a little rough this morning? Over," Jonas says as he tries to keep a straight face.

"Knock it off, Captain Dean. Cap-com Snow will be back later. What is your status, Captain?" Jenkins asks.

Jonas scans his cockpit console array. "My status is within operational requirements and Zx12 appears to be in good working order," he replies formally.

Katherine Jenkins double-checks her onboard computer read-outs to confirm Jonas's assessment. "Copy that Zx12. Captain Dean, your course has been plotted and your onboard computer will fly you out beyond the Moon in readiness for hyperdrive initiation. Captain Dean, it's now time for you to get some sleep, over and out."

Katherine Jenkins is about to remove her headset when Jonas suddenly begins to talk through his comms once more. "Jenkins, can you tell me something?" he asks.

The Chief Communications Officer fleetingly scans the Europa

Spaceprime Mission Control arena to make sure that no-one else has inadvertently patched into the Zx12's closed communications; Jenkins is willing to give Jonas the benefit of the doubt over his state of mind but wants to keep it under wraps. "Make it quick, Captain Dean; I've a feeling that what you're about to say to me is not mission critical," she surmises over the airwave.

"Is anyone present in the viewing gallery?" Jonas asks.

Jenkins turns to the royal viewing gallery which is situated directly behind her console. "Captain Dean, the King has been in attendance for the launch with all three of his generals and some blonde from Nanosec, but they all left a couple of hours ago. I think they'll be back for the big game," she confirms to Dean.

"I actually meant the public viewing gallery," Jonas replies.

"I thought that your parents were staying away from all of this?" Jenkins says.

"I just thought that someone else might have turned up," Jonas attempts to remark in an off-hand manner.

"Kira?" Jenkins offers as she remembers the pre-launch conversation between Captain Dean and Cap-com Snow.

"The public viewing gallery is empty and has been all night. I'm sorry, Captain Dean," the Chief Communications Officer confirms as she tries to sound sympathetic.

"Thanks, I'd better get some shut-eye; Zx12, over and out," is Jonas's final reply.

The Captain of the Starship Zx12 is feeling tired and hopes that sleep will revive him; he doesn't need much, just a couple of hours. Jonas decides that he'll try to sleep in the seat of his cockpit which is by no means comfortable, but he doesn't want to use his bunk until after the hyperdrive mode of his mission is complete.

At midday, a refreshed Kira Yu pulls out of her driveway at the New Buildings estate and makes for the coastal road which will take her to Spaceprime City.

The New Buildings estate is a sprawl of recently developed apartment blocks which are situated to the south-west side of Spaceprime City. The abodes are all sleek, sparse and spacious and are one of a number of developments that have been built for the specific use of Europa Spaceprime students.

Kira is painfully aware that once her studies have finished and she's been assigned her commission she'll have to vacate her premises, something she's not looking forward to.

It's an eighty-mile drive to Spaceprime City, a journey which will take a little short of three hours in her solar-powered, battery-enhanced car.

With her eyes hidden behind dark sunglasses, Kira hits the coastal road that will take her most of the way to the city.

Whilst en-route, she allows the cool onshore winds to breeze freely through her hair – the few cars in existence in the twenty-second century are all factory built and open-topped, wide open to the elements due to the fact that it only rains inland for an average seven days a year because of the global-warming of the early twenty-first century. It has become a standing joke for the city residents to stand out in the warm monsoon rains when they come and watch the motorists who haven't bothered to check the local weather forecast dart for cover as their precious cars become sodden inside.

At the wheel of her open-topped vehicle, Kira looks across momentarily at the forests and the moors that run adjacent to the coastal road; the scarred landscape reminds her of the dark history of a previous century.

It was so nearly the end of the human race, Kira thought.

*

In the early part of the twenty-first century, technology and illegal file sharing had become so advanced that any form of digital information gathered in one part of the world could be securely accessed and sent to another part of the world, where it could be immediately assessed and acted upon in the blink of an eye.

All governments had known everything about each other which had led to a new arms race, and not just between two superpowers, but between every developed country in the world; all of the developed nations had obtained nuclear capability and all had developed weapons of mass destruction to stand alongside their own conventional weaponry.

Unease had grown amongst the old nations of the planet and back-door diplomacy had become a nostalgic politic of the past; old alliances disappeared overnight and no-one dared forge new relations as trust had become a used currency.

All of the old nations had stood isolated, watching and waiting, knowing that the day would finally arrive when another nation would set about them and steal their resources – oil, gas, minerals – and strip the annexed lands of their riches and use the ravaged lands laid bare as a dumping ground for any excess population they wanted rid of.

This was the long and drawn out affair of the world cold war. Nobody could pinpoint the day when these events had actually started, but all of the Earthprime population knew the date that the war of the mind had ended and that day was the day that World War Three had begun. The Armageddon event had lasted only seven hours and yet, over one hundred years later, the Kingdoms were still rebuilding under the leadership of the five visionary Kings of the planet.

Every Earthprime subject had sworn an oath never to allow the events of the twenty-first century to be repeated.

"We must learn our lessons from the past," the old King had always said.

World War Three had been the biggest mistake in humanity's history and it had not manifested itself because of one man's delusional paranoid vendetta or due to the insane decision making of a single rogue state.

On 1st of July in the year 2038, at 0729 hours Greenwich Mean Time, solar radiation had ripped through the ozone layer along the equatorial line. Millions had died in the initial wave of the unseen killer; the deadly solar activity had lasted for exactly four minutes and caused radiation levels within one thousand miles of the equator to peak beyond known scales.

Due to the global tensions of the world cold war, all of the isolated developed nations thought that they'd been simultaneously attacked. At 0735 hours Greenwich Mean Time on 1st of July in the year 2038, every nuclear warhead and conventional weapon that was armed and aimed at an alpha target was fired.

History couldn't tell the population of the new fledgling society who'd pushed the button first.

Too many millions had died in the first few hours, too many millions more in the first few weeks and months after; yet many had survived. Only 10 per cent of the nuclear warheads fired reached their designated targets as some missiles didn't get off their launch pads due to technical failure, some fell short of their respective targets and many more had been shot down by the developed nations' various missile defence systems.

There was immediate governmental and economic breakdown across the globe, yet people being people tried to carry on and live out their lives the best way that they could.

Dark days had dawned upon planet Earth, but eventually new

communities arose from the holocaust's ashes; new leaders emerged and society was slowly hauled back onto its knees.

The new leaders managed the main issues of the day: lack of clean water, hunger and starvation, plague and grief. They gave the new world hope and moved purposefully onto the rebuilding of infrastructure; housing and education became a priority and the power grid was brought back online.

Technology had been used everywhere to help society move off its knees and onto its feet, and it had soon been recognised that there was a lack of trained workers to do even the most basic of projects and so the Spaceprime was spawned; its task was to use technology to improve the lives of the peoples of the rising Kingdoms of the world.

The Spaceprime's motto was, "When the lives of the peoples of the Earthprime whom we serve are complete, we shall look to the stars."

The Spaceprime was made up of one per cent of the entire population of the new Kingdoms and its members were not given any preferential treatment with one exception.

All of the members of the Spaceprime are also members of the Earthprime and all of the peoples of the planet are members of the Earthprime without any exceptions.

The new leaders of the new Kingdom of Europa had appointed one of their own as head and crowned him as King. The King of Europa had been ordained Commander in Chief of the First Order of the Europa Spaceprime and his chosen Queen would be crowned the first lady of the Europa Earthprime.

The old King had ruled for fifty years before his death in 2138 when his only son and heir had ascended his father's throne to carry through his visionary work.

The new King had surveyed his predecessor's reign, consulted his inner circle and conversed with his fellow Kings and, with their astute backing, he had looked to the stars.

The old King of Europa and his young heir apparent had once stood side by side and watched the glorious ascent of the HMS Neon-Lit City, and the old King had often spoken to the young King-to-be of his vision of humanity's progression into the vast wilderness of the void. His father's insight, coupled with his boyhood memory of the launch of the ill-fated Stargazer class vessel, had fuelled the new King's desire to find out the reason for the demise of the great ship and also why the HMS Neon-Lit City had been sent on its mission to the stars in the first instance.

*

It's a shame the King of Europa has not taken a bride as it's surely got to happen someday, Kira thinks as she checks her solid silver watch; time check: 1400 hours, and she is only an hour's drive away from Spaceprime Central.

*

Jonas is still awake; he had thought that he'd be able to sleep if he tried, but the seven-needle syringe which had been embedded into him pre-launch has wired his brain, so for the time being sleep is not a viable option.

During the previous hour, Jonas has watched as the Moon slipped by – a truly awe-inspiring event as none of the colours of the Moon would have made it onto the spectrum of light; a mesmerising sight of black, grey and white all embroiled together in differing shades and defined over a barren landscape of rock.

The Moon falls away behind as Jonas checks his rear view monitor upon the Starship Zx12's cockpit console, where he watches Earth's oldest satellite change from a hypnotic ancient rock portrait to a particle of dust on a black screen canvas; very soon it'll be just another infinitesimal spec upon the black barren landscape.

Jonas averts his gaze and stares longingly at the stone which is encased securely out of his reach and thinks only of Kira Yu.

*

Jonas Dean had made it to class on time on his rainswept first day of training and Commander Marks had welcomed him as he walked through the classroom door. He took a seat in the second row of the training room, where seven other candidates were already sitting; they were all male and they all looked the same to Jonas Dean – short cropped hair, chins stuck out, sitting to attention, all believing they were invincible. Jonas grinned as he sat down and gave the guy next to him a cheeky wink which went unacknowledged.

Jonas privately hoped that he was nothing like the rest of the students in his classroom, but deep down he knew he was not too dissimilar to his fellow attendees: he had thick short-cropped black hair, thought that both mentally and physically no-one could possibly hurt him and he had sacrificed everything for the Spaceprime cause to further his career; Jonas Dean could be as ruthless and as heartless as the next guy to get the required job done: ambition's path.

Taking a good look at the other students, he realised that these clones were his opposition – everyone in this training room was aware that this course was a fast-track to Europa Spaceprime Special Projects, where just maybe someone within this gathered group of the elite core would get the ultimate reward of Spaceprime astronaut training. This wasn't so much a training course, but an endurance and mental agility beauty contest.

Commander Marks had been speaking for the last five minutes and pandering to his students' egos, telling them all that they were the elite and the future for all of mankind, using phrases such as "best of the best", "cream of the crop" and telling them that the peoples of the Kingdoms of the Earthprime would not be able to survive without the honest endeavours of the men and the women of the Europa Spaceprime.

Who said we don't live in a classless society, Jonas thought as he sat upright and started to listen intently to his Commander as it's time for him to step into line with the Spaceprime.

Suddenly, the door to the academy classroom was thrown open and in strode Kira Yu.

"Ah. Miss Yu, I'm so glad you could join us. Please, take a seat," said the Academy Commander.

Jonas leaned forwards in his chair and watched Kira intently as she walked into the student-filled room; he didn't know how she'd managed to do it, but within 15 minutes of taking such a drenching she was as dry as a bone.

Kira wore dark sunglasses which concealed her eyes, her hair had been combed through and some of her flowing locks had been brushed forwards over the right-hand side of her face. Jonas watched as her head tilted slightly as she surveyed where to sit. The two desks situated directly behind Jonas were both vacant, and yet Kira chose instead to sit at a second-row desk on the other side of the classroom.

Cool, classy and she hadn't whined to the Commander about being drenched by the rain which she could have offered as an excuse for being late, Jonas thought idly.

"Right, listen up," Marks shouted. "I have two items for the day. Firstly, I'll be giving you your one single item that sets you apart from the rest of the Europa Earthprime and then I'll be setting out the single task that each of you will have to undertake for a full twelve months over the course of the next two years," Commander Marks smiled menacingly and his voice rose a couple of decibels to reinforce the point he was making.

Jonas noticed the shoulders of one or two of his fellow students lowering slightly and a few of his fellow students began to look around nervously. He glanced at Kira Yu who hadn't flinched: her head was unmoved behind her darkened shades.

A ceremony began and one by one all of the students were individually called up to face their Commander. Marks saluted, to which his students individually reciprocated, before one by one they shook his firm hand and he gave each and every one of them a small black velvet case.

Jonas Dean was the last student to receive his grey rocket insignia box and he placed his case upon the desk in front of him. He already knew what resided inside as his father had an exact replica and it had saved his life on two occasions.

"You may open your cases," Commander Marks ordered.

Dean opened his velvet case to reveal its contents – a solid silver watch and a small needle. He picked up the timepiece and held it proudly in his hands – it was a precision-engineered piece of great beauty. He turned the watch over in his hand to view his name engraved upon the back.

Memories played through Jonas's mind of what his father had always said to him whenever he'd taken his watch out: "On good days son, this thing can actually tell the time."

Marks began to elaborate: "Now listen carefully class, you must decide which wrist you prefer to wear your watch on and then pick up your needle and push it into the back of your favoured wrist. The needle contains a small microchip which monitors your life signs. You'll have your watch identifications entered into the main computer at Spaceprime Central. If your life signs fall outside of the required parameters, then your Europa Spaceprime watch will send out a signal to the main computer at the academy and Spaceprime medical units will be at your location within ten minutes. This is our guarantee to you as Spaceprime operatives."

Jonas plunged the small needle into the back of his right wrist, his favoured watch-wearing hand. He placed his timepiece on, did up the strap and admired its simple elegance.

He had officially made it: Jonas Dean was a Europa Spaceprime.

The Commander continued in a similar vein: "Europa Spaceprime employees are valuable commodities, so we take you, we train you, we shape you and we make you. You're the Kingdom's most vital assets, and we cannot afford to lose any of you. This is why we give you the watch as it may save your life one day."

The Commander took two steps forwards and stood to immediate attention. "Law, Kite, Jacobs, Walt and Dean: stand up." Marks's voice left no doubt in any of his students' minds.

Jonas snapped up onto his feet at the command.

Commander Marks ran an eye over his upright students. "You'll take the rest of the day off to put all of your home affairs in order. It's imperative that you make the necessary arrangements with your families and report back to the classroom at 0800 hours tomorrow. Do not expect to be going back to your own homes for the next twelve months and if any of you are claustrophobic or have a history of any illness, however small, then I need to know and I need to know now," Marks paused. "The rest of you, twelve months in the classroom."

Commander Marks had finished talking and yet nobody had moved. Jonas Dean had been expecting to be officially dismissed.

"Well, what are you waiting for?" Marks boomed as he managed to pull off the remarkable feat of shouting at everybody at the same time.

Jonas bolted for the classroom door.

The following day, Jonas Dean arrived back at the Europa Spaceprime Academy at Spaceprime Central. Putting his affairs in order had been a relatively easy matter – he'd visited his father and shown him his watch, before asking him to look after his beach house for twelve months. His father had agreed far too easily and Jonas had suspected he'd already known what was about to unfold in his training: Josiah Dean, a veteran of the Europa Spaceprime, still had his connections at the academy.

As for the few friends Jonas associated with, he only met up with them on occasions and his father had agreed that if anyone asked about his son's whereabouts then he'd tell them that Jonas had gone away on a long-overdue vacation.

Jonas Dean was somewhat perplexed by proceedings and by what may follow in the next twelve months. Upon his arrival back at the academy he was escorted by two Europa Spaceprime twin operatives to a warehouse on the edge of the Spaceprime Central complex; the two operatives, who wouldn't speak to him directly, led him inside.

In awe, tinged with uncertainty, he took in his new surroundings. Jonas's jaw dropped as the extremity of his situation dawned upon him.

As he stood there in the middle of the warehouse, he saw what could only be described as a human fishbowl: a rectangular glass cell with a bed, a small living area and a kitchen unit, but no sign of a bathroom.

What have I let myself in for? No wonder the Commander had found this amusing, Jonas thought.

"Dean!" Commander Marks called out in a raised voice, having appeared behind him.

Jonas Dean immediately snapped to attention upon hearing his Commander's call.

"At ease son," Marks ordered calmly. He wanted Jonas to be as relaxed as possible, because he knew it would be a difficult day for those students entering their respective tanks.

"Cadet Dean, if you've heard the rumours doing the rounds within the Europa Spaceprime Academy, then we're apparently looking to send one of our own to the stars. The rumours are all true and nine good men and women have been shortlisted and I'm sure that you've guessed by now that you're one of them," Marks briefed.

"Yes sir," Jonas replied enthusiastically.

Commander Marks continued: "There's been a special project under way for a number of years now to build a rocket ship which can carry an astronaut back to the stars. Building the Starship's not an issue and we should be ready by the launch date we've set ourselves. The problem we have is to find the right person to take her up and to make sure that our handpicked astronaut can survive in space for the three-month mission," Marks paused. "Hence the tank! You'll live here for the next twelve months and you'll have two operatives who'll observe and oversee you. They'll not give you their names and you'll not talk directly to them for the duration, any communication will be done via the local computer. They've been assigned the task of carrying out a number of tests on you during the next twelve months and these tasks will include," Commander Marks consulted his notes, "starvation, placing limitations on your oxygen supply and sleep deprivation. You'll also be asked to undertake further tasks, some simultaneously. You'll undergo a series of medical tests during your time in the tank and will also be asked to take newly developed pills and to self-inject prototype serums. There may be other tasks which we haven't thought of yet," he concluded.

Lab rat, Jonas thought.

Marks's stare pierced Jonas Dean as he continued to speak: "This is the only way we can be sure, Dean. I know you've just been awarded your Spaceprime watch, but you'll need to give it up. If you want out, type: 'Extract me now' on the keypad and you'll be free to leave your confinement assignment."

Failure was not a viable option for Jonas Dean and he was afraid he would be thrown out of the Europa Spaceprime if he desisted: the termination of his life's ambitions.

His pride got the better of him and Jonas handed over his watch and, without a word, stood by his tank. One of the glass partitions slid aside thus allowing him to step inside.

Shortly after he entered the tank, he turned to face Commander Marks who had been consulting his two operatives. Jonas gave them all his best salute as the sliding glass sealed his confinement.

Commander Marks reciprocated, before having a quiet word with one of the twin operatives and then marching off to attend to his next student.

For the first few days, the tank was bearable. Plenty of reading material was available, most of it Europa Spaceprime Academy literature linked to the official course. The bed was surprisingly comfortable, but there was no bath or shower and also no mirrors. And no privacy from his operatives in his washroom area, where he had only a toilet and a basin with one tap: cold water only and no shaving materials.

For the first few days, Jonas Dean found his routine. He ate two dry-pack meals a day and sucked on crystallised water. On the fifth day, he was asked to take two green pills. Jonas wasn't sure what they were for and they made him ill for the next four months. Which was the catalyst for his operatives to start some of their more intensive testing.

They denied him food and drink, and only occasionally posted him dry-pack meals and crystallised water when they thought he was becoming too weak and incoherent.

His operatives woke him at all hours of the night and asked him to do tasks for food; some of these tasks he would realise later could not be accomplished as his operatives were testing his reaction to hunger and failure whilst in a weak and sickened state. Jonas had no alternative but to keep a lid on his frustration during these desperate times.

Prolonged sleep had become almost impossible for Jonas and on the odd occasion when he did drop off, his operatives would quickly wake him with yet another task to undertake. That was the worst time for Jonas as he became gaunt and terminally tired from the endless induced sickness and sleep deprivation.

The low point finally arrived when his operatives asked him to take another pill which did nothing more than give him severe stomach cramps and rampaging diarrhoea.

His voyeuristic operatives stood close to the partitioned glass and watched Jonas writhe in agony on the cell floor for hours on end, laughing at him and antagonising him as they controlled his environment.

It was a living hell: the mind games and the starvation he could handle, it was the perpetual illness he was finding hardest to cope with. Then, after four months, his operatives sent him through a blue pill which made him feel much healthier.

His operatives stabilised his diet, so that he was now on one dry-pack meal and one crystallised drink per day. Jonas had learnt the importance of food and how to live at length in a confined environment under severe physical and mental stress.

His operatives went easy on him for a couple of weeks and Jonas took to sitting upon the end of his bed in a beard-ridden dishevelled state, staring at his keepers and wondering what they had planned for him next.

Was he six months in? Jonas wasn't sure; he had tried keeping a mental calendar for the first few weeks, but he couldn't tell whether it was day or night as his operatives controlled the warehouse lighting. There was never any lighting on in the warehouse, only in his prison cell, where his lights were switched on and off at random intervals.

Jonas woke one day after a rare full night's sleep to find a parcel of food in the middle of his floor.

There was a note.

It read:

CONGRATULATIONS DEAN. WORST IS OVER. WE STILL WANT YOU TO UNDERTAKE FURTHER TESTS, BUT WE WILL GIVE YOU MORE INFORMATION ABOUT YOUR PILLS AND INJECTIONS.

Jonas looked up and nodded at his two assigned watchers – his mind had become razor sharp and focused, yet he still couldn't bring himself to trust his two keepers.

His treatment improved dramatically during the remainder of his stay and he was allowed to build up a routine. His operatives sent in more coursework for him to do which consisted mostly of mathematical equations; he was also given books to read at his leisure.

His operatives, however, would not provide him with any hot water or shaving materials, although Jonas requested these luxuries on every possible occasion.

Jonas continued to test pills and serums, which seemed to arrive every other week, and only on one other occasion did he become violently ill, whereupon his operatives soon became concerned and he quickly realised his illness was not part of their master plan. He managed to recover his strength within two days.

His operatives began to send in top-secret files from Spaceprime

Central in which he saw, for the first time, historic schematics of various spacecraft including the HMS Neon-Lit City blueprints. He was also given access to star charts, samples of Moon rock and files of ex-NASA and ex-European Space Agency data stretching right back from the first Moon landings up until the old nations had built the last pre-Third World War Moonbase. There were also files on Nanotech engineering and the new DNA healing methods.

Jonas was getting close to the end of his year-long assignment; he was able to sense it as it had been a lot easier for him to track time for the final six months with his operatives seemingly operating a sixteen-hour lights-on, eight-hour lights-off policy. He had counted lights-off on 183 occasions.

His watchers stopped sending him anything new to help him pass the time; his medication also ceased and he found himself rereading old literature. Jonas started to become increasingly edgy as he felt sure he had now gone well past the twelve months of his assignment.

His operatives sent him another typed message:

WOULD YOU LIKE TO GET OUT NOW?

To which Jonas replied on his keypad:

NO, I'VE STARTED ENJOYING MYSELF.

The Europa Spaceprime student had got wise to his operative's game and was determined not to give his keepers good reason to prolong his tenure. He began to question whether Commander Marks or the Europa Spaceprime would ever set him free, but kept this opinion to himself.

Then, after weeks of boredom, his operatives woke him early one morning. For fifteen hours, they sent him test after test, equation after equation and exam after exam. By the end of this intensive period, Jonas was both mentally and physically exhausted.

His operatives finally switched out the lights and Jonas went to his bed, but within ten minutes of him falling asleep, the lights were back on and more and more questions and calculations were sent for him to answer in a set time, a situation that reoccurred over the course of the next six hours: when the lights went down, Jonas would go to his bed and when the lights were switched on, he would wake and work through whatever test or examination his operatives asked him to undertake: a slave to their warped reasoning.

Eventually, Jonas was allowed to sleep and he dreamt as he always dreamt: of the beach at Atlantis Strand, the sea, the waves, the sunset and the alarms ringing.

Jonas woke with a start and was immediately fully alert to the loud alarm ringing throughout his glass holding capsule. This is new, he thought; he'd never heard this sound before. He sat himself upright and started to cough: the lights weren't on in the warehouse, yet he could see shadows flickering and falling around his cell. He coughed once more, spluttered and realised he was gasping for air. His first thought was that this was his oxygen deficiency test, yet the smoke filling his nostrils told him differently. He leapt off his bed and saw flames licking up the sides of his imprisoning glass, whilst in the dark flickering light, he thought he could see four people watching over him: his two operatives and two women, both of whom were wearing white gowns and surgical masks.

Fear coursed through Jonas's veins as he perceived that the gathered operatives were here to witness his death and then perform an autopsy: he had dutifully played the lab rat and was now an expendable Spaceprime asset.

All of his accrued paperwork which had been sent into his cell, his books, his files and his coursework, had been piled up high underneath the spartan sink unit and then set alight.

Frantically, Jonas grabbed the blanket off his bed and started beating at the burning books as the flames roared off them. He lunged for the cold water tap but was beaten back by the heat. He kept on thrashing at the wild flames and lunging for the tap, yet on each and every occasion he was defeated by the intense heat. Finally, the smoke thickened and turned the conditioned air acrid which ultimately sent Jonas stumbling back from the uncontrollable blaze.

Jonas slumped down at the end of his bed and passed out. "This is not how it's meant to end," was his last rational thought, before his consciousness drifted away: ambition's death.

It was the brightness which initially threw him as he retched violently and gasped for air. Jonas hoped he had gone to a better place, far away from the psychological hell of the previous twelve months. The realisation that he was still in his warehouse environment only came to him when an oxygen mask was placed over his mouth and he was given an injection. He lay exhausted upon a steel table outside his glass cell whilst a doctor attached a drip to him via a needle which she had already inserted into the back of his hand.

His shadowing operatives had disappeared and the two female doctors who had been present for the combustion act were poking and probing his body and writing their notes. For over an hour, they went over every inch of his naked flesh, taking skin samples, a blood sample and also wiring him up to a medical unit so as to monitor his heart rate and respiration.

Jonas's strength finally returned and he sat up without being asked.

One of the masked doctors stepped out from behind the regular pinging monitor and approached Jonas whilst holding a white surgical gown in her right hand. "Cadet Dean, put this on," she bluntly commanded as she thrust forward the garment.

Jonas complied with the cold order.

"I'm Doctor Grace James, the Senior Medical Officer for Spaceprime Special Projects. My colleague and I are here to monitor your situation for the short term. Your course project in the tank is now complete. We're undertaking some tests at present and when we're satisfied that you're fit enough to leave then we'll allow you to do so," she said without feeling.

Jonas flinched as James pulled out a blade which she'd concealed within her tunic.

"Calm down, Cadet Dean. I need to shave you," the Doctor said.

Jonas smiled for the first time in over a year.

"I wouldn't get too excited, Dean. I just need the hair from your beard as a DNA baseline," James said sternly.

"Cold," Jonas managed to say out loud, which Doctor James ignored.

After an hour, and in the dead of night, the initiated Spaceprime Cadet was allowed to leave the warehouse environment, accompanied on either side by his two doctors. Jonas tried to keep in step as he shuffled towards the main building, where he was walked up two flights of steps to a non-descript room, which he realised was his old student classroom.

"Take a seat and you'll be debriefed shortly," James said icily.

The two doctors left Jonas in the classroom, which at first sight appeared to be empty. Jonas made his way to the familiarity of his desk in the second row.

The disorientated Spaceprime student sat down and faced forwards before realising that, although he hadn't initially noticed, Commander Marks was already in the classroom.

Jonas should have snapped to attention and given Marks a salute, but he remained seated.

Marks marched up to Jonas, saluted and then casually went at ease with his hands rigid behind his back as he stood over his prize pupil.

"No more formalities tonight, Dean. We sent you to the tank, punished you, used you and abused you; hell, we damn well nearly killed you, and yet you passed the assignment and we now know what you're capable of under a severe amount of pressure. As you can see, only one candidate out of your group has passed the tank assignment and that's you, Cadet Dean." Marks pointed at Dean with a look of respect which resonated over the Commander's face.

"I'll debrief you again in six weeks, but until then you're on leave. A rest will do you good and we still need to allow time for some of the toxins to wash through your system. Do you have any questions?" Commander Marks asked as he sat himself upon the desk directly in front of Jonas.

"I have three questions, sir," Jonas slurred as he hadn't had a full conversation with anyone for over a year.

"How long was I in for?"

Marks bowed his head before thinking better of it, and instead he looked Jonas Dean straight in the eye. "Fourteen months exactly; the extra two months, as you probably will already have guessed, were part of the test," he replied.

Jonas snorted in recognition of the fact, before asking, "Have the other four students gone in yet?"

Marks nodded in the affirmative and replied, "I sent them in a month ago as the other four tanks were all free by then."

Jonas's only thoughts were of Kira Yu and how long she would last.

With his strength continuing to return, Dean uneasily took to his feet and began to walk towards the classroom door, where he stopped and, with a sudden change of mind, redirected himself to Commander Marks's desk and sat upon it.

The Commander turned fully round to face Dean.

"I'm curious: when did the oxygen starvation test occur?" Jonas asked.

Marks was beaming as he spoke: "It happened in the first three months and you were so ill that you never even noticed." His voice dropped to a more serious tone. "I was really proud of you for sticking it out as that's the time when the students usually walk."

Tank-tested, Dean jumped off Marks's desk and his cockiness returned to the fore. "Well Commander, you'd better get someone to give me a lift home as it appears that I'm on leave," he said.

"I'll take you myself," Marks replied as he jumped off the desk which his bulky frame had occupied and headed for the classroom door.

"Oh and Dean, don't forget your watch," Marks said proudly as he handed back his prize pupil's personalised solid silver engraved timepiece.

*

"Cap-com to Zx12, come in Captain Dean, over," a refreshed Snow says.

The able Cap-com has managed to get over six hours sleep and has also eaten a decent hot meal in the canteen. Katherine Jenkins had been relieved from duty four hours previously and Snow is fully aware that she'll not be able to get much sleep before the hyperdrive mode of the mission commences.

Jonas has been reliving some of the past events which have got him to the verge of outer space and the Zx12 is at a dead stop as his radio crackles into life in his earpiece.

Snow views the large monitor showing the solar system at the front of the mission control arena: the red winking dot of the Starship Zx12 is flashing away on the far side of the Moon while Jonas's heartbeat steadily pulses on an adjacent screen. Cap-com Hubert Snow is unconcerned at present that Captain Jonas Dean is ignoring him.

"Cap-com to Zx12, come in, over," Snow says, sounding more purposeful.

"This is Zx12. I'm reading you Cap-com, loud and clear," Jonas replies.

"Captain Dean: what's your current status?" Snow asks.

"Cap-com, we've come to a dead stop in the middle of nowhere," Jonas replies.

Hubert Snow ignores Captain Dean's barbed comment as he already has all of the information he requires. Snow double-checks his console monitor for a confirmation before he turns to an upright General Thalt. "Flight Director, I can confirm Zx12 is at a full stop at target area," he says to the general in charge of the mission.

"Acknowledged Cap-com. Hyperdrive mission is T-minus fifty-five minutes." Thalt offers no more before he turns on his heel and strides to the private viewing gallery, where he'll brief the King of Europa and his fellow generals.

*

Wearing her trademark dark sunglasses, Kira Yu pulls into the carpark at Spaceprime Central and rushes through the academy doors; Kira is on her own mission as she needs to gain clearance for the public viewing gallery and there's only one person who'll be able to get her the access pass she requires.

Kira checks her solid silver watch to confirm that she has only fifty minutes until the Zx12 hyperdrive is due for activation.

"Cadet Yu," Marks booms, almost appearing happy to see her.

Kira and Jonas had always laughed about how the Academy Commander had a happy knack of always being in the right place at the right time, and they both suspected that the chips which they had self-inserted into their wrists were more than just medical emergency devices.

"Commander, I need access to the public viewing gallery as I'd like to witness Captain Dean's hyperdrive mission," Kira blurts.

Commander Marks rubs his chin in paused thought as he'd given Yu and Dean a hard time during their tenure at the academy. "Alright, you'll be my guest. I'll be going over there in about twenty minutes, so follow me and I'll get you your clearance," he says.

Kira visibly sighs and Commander Marks, who's known her for well over four years, thinks it's unusual for her to display any form of outward emotion.

*

The King is seated in his private viewing gallery with two of his generals sitting at either side of him; to the rear of the gallery, the Asian attaché Tashi Chi has a phone pressed to her ear. Two other guests are also present: Lady Anne, the King's aunt and, since the death of the King's mother, the overseer of Earthprime affairs; and Lady Guinevere, a distant cousin of the King and an aide to the King's aunt.

General Thalt enters the gallery and follows the laid-down royal protocol by saluting his ruling regent. "Zx12 is at designated target position sire. We're at T-minus forty-four minutes until hyperdrive activation," he briefs.

"Well done, General Thalt. How's our astronaut holding up?" the Europan Monarch asks.

"He seems in good spirits sire and I think he's enjoying the ride," Thalt replies with an almost smile.

"Good. I'd like to speak to Captain Dean before he fires up the hyperdrive engine onboard the Zx12," the King states whilst leaving no doubt in the Flight Director's mind that this will happen.

Thalt nods in agreement.

"Thank you, General," says the Europan King as he returns to the comfort of his seat. He's become fearful of the hour to come and needs time to think of what he'll say to Captain Jonas Dean of the First Order of the Spaceprime in advance of his unprecedented mission.

*

Katherine Jenkins arrives back at her post. "Snow, situation report," she demands immediately.

It's good to see her back to her formal self, Hubert Snow thinks.

"Zx12 is at a full stop at target position and hyperdrive will be activated in T-minus thirty-five minutes," Snow says, giving his supervisor the update without glancing at her as he's busy readying himself for the unprecedented mission by double-checking Zx12 telemetry.

"Cap-com to Zx12, come in Captain Dean, over," says Snow to the Starship Captain, knowing how important this spaceflight is to the Europa Spaceprime and, more importantly, that Captain Dean's life is at stake on this mission.

"Hubert: what's the weather like down there?" Jonas replies as he's getting bored.

"Captain, it's time to get serious as you're T-minus thirty minutes to hyperdrive initiation. I want you to leave the cockpit and go into the ship and make sure everything is locked down and then I want you to run through your final mission preparation at least twice," the able Cap Com directs: Hubert Snow is in the zone.

"Roger that Cap-com," Jonas replies. He's already walked through the ship twice and done his final checks a dozen times, but he'll do them again because Snow has asked him to and his respect for the diligent Cap-com is growing by the hour.

Jonas leaves his cockpit once more and surveys the mid-section of the Starship Zx12. His Starship has been split into four sections and his cockpit is classified as the forward section. The discarded section's booster rockets had fallen away shortly after take-off. The in-flight rear section houses his hyperdrive engine which is cut off from the main body of the ship, whilst the mid-section, which he's now standing in, is completely empty – all of his Nanosec utilities have been sealed away on the port-side of the mid-section, while his bunk, general utilities and rations have been sealed away on the starboard-side. Jonas checks that everything is locked down securely and, when he's satisfied everything is safely in order, he checks once more, just to be sure, before returning to his cockpit seat.

Captain Jonas Dean of the First Order of the Spaceprime surveys the deep void of space from out of his small cockpit window, through which he can clearly see the nose of his vessel with its long communications antennae pointing in the direction he'll be travelling in.

"An arrow waiting for the bow to be pulled back and released," he says into his communications channel which is always open.

"Roger that Captain Dean," Hubert Snow notes and smirks at the Spaceprime Captain's insight.

"Confirm final checks, Captain Dean."

"Final checks confirmed, Cap-com."

"Good luck, Captain Dean. You're T-minus nine minutes and thirty seconds to hyperdrive initiation." Hubert Snow falls silent.

"Thank you Hubert and remind me to buy you a drink sometime, Zx12 out."

Katherine Jenkins, who's been listening in on the transmission, faces her Flight Director General. "We're a go for hyperdrive activation General at T-minus nine minutes and fifteen seconds," she says authoritatively.

Flight Director Thalt nods in recognition, before he purposefully strides down the row of workstations to speak directly to the Operations Supervisor. "Plot and fix hyperdrive course and then send the co-ordinates to the computer onboard the Zx12. Lock the countdown at T-minus eight minutes and make sure Captain Dean can see this on a monitor," Thalt orders.

General Thalt strides back to his command point position. The unstoppable chain of events have been set in motion and all he and the rest of his Europa Spaceprime Mission Control operatives can do is watch the mission clock recede.

*

Commander Marks uses his swipe card to gain access to the public viewing gallery. Kira Yu follows her Commander into the glass-lined room and they both take a seat at the front of the soundproof booth. Kira quickly casts a glance around her surroundings; her view is a little restricted, but she can see most of the main monitors. A small sigh of relief escapes her as she mentally registers all of the monitors displaying Jonas Dean's life signs, as well as the periodically flashing red dot upon the main screen that signifies the Starship Zx12's position beyond the Moon.

Marks and Yu do not speak; the tension within the mission control arena is already beginning to seep into the glass-lined gallery.

The King of Europa, who doesn't miss anything that happens within his theatre of operations, leans over to one of his loyal generals. "Who's that with Commander Marks?" the King quietly asks, intrigued.

"I do not know sire, perhaps it's one of his many students," the general offers. "I could find out for you?"

"That won't be necessary – we've more important issues to attend to," the King of Europa says as he brushes his general's offer aside.

The Europan Monarch, flanked by his two generals, rises as General Thalt enters the private viewing gallery.

"My lord, Zx12 is on the main speaker and now would be a good time to speak to Captain Dean," General Thalt says uncomfortably.

The King smiles as he steps forwards as Captain Jonas Dean can be heard whistling an incomprehensible tune.

"Command to Zx12, come in Captain Dean," Europa's sovereign says clearly.

Jonas hears his regent's voice as he's watching time fall away on the countdown clock upon one of his cockpit console monitors. "It's good to hear your voice, sire," he says enthusiastically.

"Jonas, the Kingdoms await and the peoples of the land have a new hero and his name is Captain Jonas Dean. Your name will shine brightly within the new history of the twenty-second century. Good luck Captain," the King says, feeling rather pleased with himself – it has often been remarked that he is a great motivator of men.

The words of the King resonate within Jonas Dean, but they do not stop the cold shiver of doubt from running down his spine and the realisation that the odds are stacked against him ever completing his mission. But for Captain Jonas Dean, there's no backing down – the countdown to hyperdrive activation is at T-minus three minutes and ten seconds.

Jonas quickly recovers his composure, before he states, "Thank you sire, and remind me to buy you a drink sometime." He's decided to play the cocky astronaut to the end.

The King of Europa laughs jovially out loud. "Carry on General Thalt, let us see what the Starship Zx12 can do," the King says with a nod to his Flight Director.

General Thalt can do no more: the mission is set and the clock is ticking at T-minus two minutes and thirty seconds.

The main speaker is to be left on during hyperdrive initiation and the interstellar release of the Starship Zx12, meaning all of the Europa Spaceprime Mission Control and the peoples of the Kingdoms of the Earthprime will be able to listen in on the historic event.

*

Kira Yu sits in her gallery chair, taking in the unfolding events. Behind the dark tint of her sunglasses, she smiles as she hears Jonas's voice and nearly laughs when he offers to buy the King a drink.

Typical Jonas; life and soul, Kira thought.

*

Hubert Snow stares at the public viewing gallery – he hadn't witnessed the arrival of Commander Marks and the young woman who is accompanying him.

"The woman in the public viewing gallery, is that who Dean has been waiting for?" Snow hesitantly asks his supervisor.

Katherine Jenkins turns her head towards the gallery. "Maybe, but if it is, you can't tell Dean now as he must concentrate on the mission at hand. Hyperdrive initiation is in T-minus one minute and forty seconds. Hubert, you're not going to announce this to Captain Dean on an open mike with the King sitting ten feet away and millions listening in to this transmission."

Hubert Snow sits back in his chair and runs his hand through what's left of his hair; Katherine Jenkins is right and Snow accepts this immediately. The final minute is fast approaching and the culmination of a Kingdom's progress is at hand.

*

Captain Jonas Dean cannot take his eyes off the countdown clock upon the Zx12 cockpit console as the last seconds begin to die away.

Thirty-five, thirty-four, thirty-three…

The First Order of the Spaceprime Captain leans back into his metallic seat and places his arms onto the hard rests as the countdown clock ticks down to thirty seconds; his figure-hugging made-to-fit Captain's chair adjusts around him and Captain Dean sinks into his seat as it tilts to a forty-five degree angle.

Heavy-duty metals which are built into the structure of his cockpit seat snap around his shoulders, head, arms, legs and midriff; Captain Jonas Dean is strapped, trapped and tethered tightly into position.

Nineteen, eighteen, seventeen…

"Cap-com, my position is fixed, over," Dean confirms.

"Copy that Zx12. I've acknowledged your position is fixed and we've a clear route through the void and hope to bring you to a full stop one thousand miles short of the asteroid belt, over," Snow says calmly.

Twelve, eleven, ten…

Jonas isn't amused by Snow's use of the word hope.

Seven, six…

The King stands up on impulse, unable to contain his enthusiasm, and holds on tightly to the cold steel rail that runs underneath his soundproof glass window view which is situated at the front of his private viewing gallery.

"Fly, Jonas, fly," His Majesty whispers.

Three, two, one…

"Hyperdrive initiated, Zx12," Snow shouts to Jonas over the open communications channel with the world listening in.

*

There's a three-second delay as several thousand high-density laser beams shoot out from the forward section of Jonas's Starship; the beams are sent to the final exit point of the Zx12, the calculation of which has been made by the Europa Spaceprime Mission Control mainframe computer and uploaded to the Starship's onboard computer: if any of the beams are broken then the ship's computer will make a micro-millimetre adjustment and send out another set of laser beams. When none of the beams come back as broken, then the hyperdrive will immediately initiate as the path to the target exit point will be clear.

Jonas hears a low rumbling growl and the Zx12 begins to violently shake as the roar from the hyperdrive engine grows to a crescendo.

"Here we go," Jonas screams from his confined position, adrenalin coursing through his veins.

If Captain Jonas Dean could have described the sensation at that particular moment in time, he would have said it was like being shot from the barrel of a gun or like the fastest rollercoaster ride in the history of mankind.

The special dampeners fitted inside the Starship's hull negate the g-forces: Jonas will probably not pass out, but even he can't be sure of the effects that the hyperdrive will have on his body.

The hyperdrive engine works in a simple manner: the superior drive system grabs one hundred thousand miles of space at a time, then the exit point is bent into the entry point and the Starship is forced through. The exit point then becomes the new entry point which causes a concertina effect. So if you wish to travel twelve hundred thousand miles, then the hyperdrive would be configured to do ten hops which will allow for one hundred thousand miles of space as braking distance and leave you one hundred thousand miles short of your destination.

The Zx12 races forwards; this certainly beats riding my bike, Jonas thinks as the cataclysmic forces drive into his immobilised body. The g-forces are incredibly powerful, and although Jonas is fixed into his cockpit position, he can still feel the heavy load slamming into his imprisoned frame.

*

There's a deathly quiet within the mission control arena and all that can be heard is a steady stream of static as the communications are down when the Starship's hyperdrive is initiated.

Hubert Snow checks his solid silver watch at one minute and ten seconds into the mission mode; he'll know within the next ninety seconds if the mission mode has been a success. He glances over to Kira Yu in the public viewing gallery. Although he can't tell what expression she wears on her face, which is masked behind her shades, he can clearly see that she is digging her nails into the armrests of her seat.

*

Jonas figures out that the best way to handle the g-forces is to stay as still as possible and allow the force to pin him and wash over him. Upon hearing the hyperdrive engine cut out, Jonas assumes the Zx12 must have hit its final exit point; the Starship brakes hard as its full reverse thrusters deploy.

Jonas is still fixed and bound to his solid cockpit seat. He has limited vision from his confined and angled position – all he can see is the blur of space as his Starship decelerates. There will be a few more seconds of reverse thrust before he is released and able to get to his cockpit console and get his ship back on manual override and take back control of his situation.

Hubert Snow is becoming agitated as his solid silver Spaceprime watch is telling him that the mission mode elapsed time is at three minutes. He double-checks the mission clock on the main screen and it concurs, yet all that can be heard over the open communications channel is a constant static drone.

*

The Starship Zx12 is still braking hard and if his Captain's chair malfunctions, then Jonas will be trapped in his cockpit position for the rest of his short life. This worrying thought is quickly disregarded as his cockpit seat slides silently back into its pre-drive position, his restrictive supports are released and Captain Jonas Dean is back in command of his Starship once more.

Without any hesitation, he switches the Starship Zx12 over to manual steer before he gasps at the vision from his cockpit window. "Five planets: where in hell am I?" he shouts.

*

Hubert Snow witnesses the Zx12 switching back to manual drive; although the automatic hyperdrive shutdown hasn't flashed up on the main screen, it comes over as a command message on his computer screen at the Europa Spaceprime Mission Control.

Snow is up on his feet with his hands on his hips. "Cap-com to Zx12, come in, over. Cap-com to Zx12, can you read me, over."

All eyes are on Snow and Thalt instinctively knows that his faithful Cap-com is probably onto something, although all that can be heard throughout the Europa Spaceprime Mission Control is progressive static.

*

The Starship Zx12 is still braking out of hyperdrive and Jonas is confused by the five spherical objects which fill his panoramic landscape.

Alarms ring out, two of them blaring in tandem while three lights are flashing upon his cockpit console screen: all Proximity alerts. Jonas's next move is to find out how close the unidentified masses are to his Starship, so he interrogates the onboard radar upon his cockpit console array to find that two obtrusive objects are on a direct collision course with his ship and how big they are is irrelevant as they're virtually on top of him.

Jonas's instincts take over and he steers the Starship Zx12 into the two unidentified objects whilst his ship is still braking out of hyperdrive, causing two more proximity alert lights to flash immediately upon his cockpit console display.

Immediate action is required: he has seconds left before an impact and there is only one more decisive course of action that Jonas can take. "Zx12 to Cap-com, hyperdrive mission was successful: Mayday, Mayday," he maniacally shouts through his open comms.

Jonas breaks off from his emergency update as an oblique asteroid tumbles into his cockpit view and moves through his field of vision at an alarming rate of knots.

With his eyes fixed on the space berg, Dean is totally unprepared as his Starship lurches violently to one side from a strike to its stern by a smaller lump of travelling space rock.

"I'M HIT! I'M HIT!" Jonas yells into his communications.

A split-second later, as he's instinctively checking for a breach, and under flickering power, the mountainous asteroid which he has already witnessed tumbling through his cockpit view shears off his ship's state-of-the-art communications tower.

Captain Jonas Dean, the new hero of the First Order of the Spaceprime, is thrown out of his metallic cockpit seat by the heavy impact.

I'm Falling

My whole life implodes around me,
And I think of faces that I may never yet see again,
My ship is breached and now I'm all at sea,
This would not be for me a fitting end.

I hear a calling in the distance,
It's a sound my heart it makes before it breaks,
I never thought that I could fly 'til I met you,
And yet I didn't seem to have just what it takes.

It was just my way to never give us time,
And I know that you would have asked yourself, as to why?
But what we had they can never take away,
And I'm sure you don't believe it was all a lie.

I've no fear of my impending fate,
If only I'd have trusted my heart to be true,
And as I fall off the narrow and the straight,
My final thoughts will always turn to you.

I'm falling, I'm falling off my horizontal plane,
I'm falling, I'm falling from out the sky,
I'm falling far from your warm embrace,
And I don't even know the reason as to why.
I'm falling, I'm falling on the vertical descent,
I'm falling, I'm falling from out of view,
I fall away from the light into the dark,
As I fall far, far, far away from you.

CHAPTER 3

This Desolate Land

Silence is the master within the Europa Spaceprime Mission Control arena. The ground team have been shocked rigid and are all still trying to come to terms with what they've just heard and what they've just witnessed over the airwaves.

Hubert Snow's jaw drops and beads of sweat begin to break out upon his brow as Jonas Dean's last communication has finally registered with the able Cap-com. The Starship's communications had vented a static signal for three minutes and twelve seconds during the hyperdrive mission before a static-filled mayday message had then been received; moments later, Jonas's cry of 'I'm hit! I'm hit!' had enveloped the mission control arena, before the heavy discharge of static immediately returned.

However, it isn't the final communication which has ripped out Snow's gut, nor the sudden disappearance of the bright red dot from the star map upon the main screen: it's the sight of the Europa Spaceprime elite medical team.

Doctor Grace James and Doctor Aileen Grey are frantically typing in data, checking and double-checking systems, trying everything in their known comprehension to change the state of the medical monitors.

Snow reaches up and pulls off his headset as he can no longer draw his eyes away from the medical monitors. Every single one of them is displaying the same read-out – a single flatline runs steadily across the entire bank of visual display units that monitor Captain Dean's life signs. It's of no comfort to anyone within the Europa Spaceprime Mission Control arena that the hyperdrive mission has been a success as Captain Jonas Dean is dead and the Starship Zx12 is lost.

*

General Thalt has been stunned into silence as his worst fears have been realised and, even though the hyperdrive engine has been proven to work, it's of little consolation.

Europa's King reacts first, stepping ashen-faced into the mission control arena from his private viewing gallery to decree his orders: "General Thalt, we need an immediate news blackout. I want the Operations team to go over the calculations for the hyperdrive mission, I want Captain Dean's last-known set of co-ordinates and I want the Communications team to signal the Starship Zx12 for the next twenty-four hours. Get on to the new Moonbase and see if any of their listening devices are operational and I'll speak to the Kings of the Kingdoms of the Earthprime and ask them to point the high-specification telescopes within their Kingdoms' observatories to the last-known position of the Starship Zx12."

His final two royal demands are already doomed to failure as the new Moonbase is still under construction and no long-range listening devices or high-spec telescopes are as yet installed upon the Moon, because their blueprints are still upon the drawing board and won't be operational for a further five years.

There is only one long-range telescope in existence upon the planet: at the ancient Greenwich Observatory, an archaic relic of the past's vision that fell into disrepair after being badly damaged during the Third World War of the previous century. To the King's knowledge, it is no longer operational: he is selling false hope.

Thalt inhales deeply. "OK people, you heard the man, let's get on it," he commands.

General Thalt looks up at the main monitors and visibly slumps. "Dean is lost," he quietly utters to himself.

*

Tashi Chi, the Asian attaché, appears beside the beleaguered King of Europa. "My deepest regrets sire, we are all terribly sorry for the loss of your mission," she says coldly, incisively and efficiently as she shakes her host King's hand, before turning on a high heel and departing.

The Europan Monarch looks on as Tashi Chi leaves the Europa Spaceprime Mission Control behind. She is due to take a late evening flight back to the Kingdom of Asia whose King will be fully briefed by morning and who won't be too pleased at having lost his Kingdom's sourced technology.

*

Kira Yu sits stunned as events unfold around her. There's no outward emotion, just a cold blank response as the events of the previous minutes churn over in her mind. Jonas Dean is indestructible, Kira knows that – the Europan hierarchy had tried to break him in the tank, but they'd failed.

Kira sits in her chair in the public viewing gallery, listening to the heavy discharge of static whilst intensely watching the medical monitors as she waits for Jonas to spring back to life.

*

The shock has spread throughout the mission control arena. All of the operatives are busying themselves with what they have to do, but only one voice can be heard above all: "Cap-com to Zx12, come in, over. Cap-com to Zx12, do you read me, over." Hubert Snow has rolled up his sleeves and he isn't about to give up that easily.

*

Captain Jonas Dean is sprawled barely conscious upon his Starship's metallic mid-section. "How the hell am I still alive?" he asks whilst shrugging off shock and realising he's going to have to make do with talking to himself as the communications system onboard the Starship Zx12 is irretrievably damaged.

It has certainly been a rollercoaster ride, Jonas thinks to himself, recalling how he had taken manual control of the Zx12 for a few seconds in which time he'd managed to initiate one manual manoeuvre by turning his Starship into the oncoming bogeys, before realising too late that he'd veered his ship into a meteorite shower.

All he could do was watch as a mountainous space berg had tumbled into his view; the Starship Zx12 had pitched violently as it caught a glancing blow from a smaller meteorite, before the much larger berg he had initially sighted sheared off his state-of-the-art communications tower at the forward-end of his Starship. The collision had thrown him out of his cockpit seat and into the mid-section of his ship, where Jonas is now gathering himself up as his Starship continues to pitch wildly and fall at a terrifying speed.

A fire breaks out in the hold and Jonas rushes back to his cockpit console array to activate his ship's mid-section fire extinguishers; a sudden rush of halon spray contains the outbreak.

Jonas watches from his cockpit window as hundreds of small shards of rock race in and out of his view.

The Zx12 is hit for a third time and jackknifes in the uncharted void, causing threatening alarms to ring out throughout the vessel, before his ship loses all power.

With his ship having been breached by the third strike, Jonas straps himself securely into his cockpit seat as he feels the air within the Zx12 rushing away through the damaged section of his Starship's hull.

The meteor storm passes, yet new danger is looming as his ship is caught within the gravitational pull of one of the five planets he identified on exiting hyperdrive.

A sudden realisation overwhelms him as he exclaims aloud: "Oh no, we screwed up the calculation," he says in frustration as he realises that somehow, on hyperdrive initiation, his plotted course has been miscalculated by the Europa Spaceprime Mission Control and wrongly programmed into the ship's onboard computer. His Starship's exit-point has been fixed beyond the asteroid belt, and Captain Jonas Dean has flown the Starship Zx12 right through the asteroid belt and has come up short of one of Jupiter's Moons. He can see three Moons from out of his cockpit window and a fourth lies to his rear whilst beyond the Moons he gazes upon the tarnished red, orange and white hue of Jupiter with its rampant world storms betraying the planet as it fills the backdrop of his view.

The Zx12 is falling into a Moon of Jupiter without air and without power. Get a grip, Captain Dean thinks, I don't need air as I can survive in my suit for another forty-eight hours. What I need is power.

Jonas prioritises as he needs to replace the damaged circuits which have blown and caused his Zx12 cockpit console systems to go offline; he has specially made replacements and he knows how to fix his problem. His year in the tank has honed his survival instincts and the four years he spent training for his mission to the stars have given him all of the tools deemed necessary to complete his task. If he fails, then he'll just slam into a large lump of rock doing a couple of thousand miles an hour: there are worse ways to die; you could die of a broken heart.

Captain Jonas Dean of the First Order of the Spaceprime pauses.

*

Jonas lay upon the beach at the coastal home which he's often called his own personal sanctuary; the sun burned high in a deep blue sky and the sounds of the waves were filling his head. Commander Marks had given him another day off as he was so far ahead in his coursework.

The last twelve months had been an easy ride for Jonas compared to the time he'd spent inside the tank and he'd grown to respect the Academy Commander.

On his return to the Europa Spaceprime Academy, Marks had gone into minute detail about every test, every pill, every injection and every act that his operatives had instigated during his tank assignment: the whole damn thing had been pre-planned down to the smallest detail as the Europa Spaceprime needed to run scenarios, they wanted to know how his mind and body would react under severe amounts of pressure, they needed to know if certain drugs or cocktails of drugs would work on his body; the Spaceprime had to know how his mind and body would cope within a stressful claustrophobic environment.

Jonas had asked question after question about his confinement assignment and, after Commander Marks had finished answering all of them in full, he'd felt purged of the tank.

Marks had asked Dean to attend the academy at 2200 hours that evening and Jonas was curious as to why: he'd worked late before now, but he'd never been asked to start that late whilst he'd been back in the classroom environment.

Deep down, Jonas had a gut feeling that the last four students were to be released from the confinement of their respective tanks as it had been fifteen months since they'd been placed into the horrific isolation chambers as part of their training.

Jonas thought of Kira Yu almost daily. He had seen Doctor Grace James on campus on a number of occasions, and was tutored by Commander Marks on a regular basis, yet they'd never offered any news on the tank-testing students' wellbeing and Jonas wouldn't ask.

They're due, Jonas opined.

He slept during the afternoon, covered up under a burning sun at his beach house retreat. He then awoke, ate and showered and, at 2100 hours, walked his vintage bike down to the main road and set off for the half-hour ride to the academy at Spaceprime Central.

Jonas rode through the Anglian desert. There had been large-scale flooding during the late twenty-first century and for many decades the sea had reclaimed the land, but in the early part of the twenty-second century, the seas had receded and, having washed all of the nutrients out of the soil, the sun had then roasted the land and the desert had been formed.

Jonas rode the desert trail to Spaceprime City and arrived early at the Europa Spaceprime Academy.

*

Still falling towards the Moon's surface, the Starship Zx12 begins to rotate in freefall as its speed increases within the grip of the Moon's gravitational pull.

Jonas has changed his circuit boards for a second time and is attempting to reboot his cockpit systems; after his first attempt, he bangs his fist upon one of the console panels. "Come on you piece of space junk," Jonas shouts, increasingly frustrated as he's certain he's connected the circuit boards correctly.

Captain Jonas Dean leans forwards and touches the glass panel which houses Kira's stone and attempts to reboot his cockpit console systems once more.

The system lights upon his cockpit console array flicker twice and come back online. "Now come on baby, get me out of this mess," Jonas shouts as he switches to manual drive and triggers all of the reverse thrust he can get out of his ailing Starship.

His ship's freefall rotation ceases immediately and although his craft is still falling towards the Moon's surface, the Starship Zx12's speed decreases measurably.

About five hundred metres from the solid Moon surface, Jonas regains full control of his ship. He uses his radar and the view from his cockpit window to look for a level landing site within the rocky terrain, guides his craft to his emergency designated landing spot and sets his Starship down.

After his soft landing, Jonas sits wearily back in his cockpit seat; if he could have taken off his space helmet and the impenetrable membrane covering his head, then he would have kissed his front panel display.

He begins the arduous task of post-flight procedure as his Starship's systems and structural integrity will need to be checked and double-checked and then checked again, because Jonas requires the Zx12 to be prepped and flight worthy: if his Starship cannot break orbit, then he will eventually die on this lump of dead rock.

But Captain Jonas Dean is alive for now.

*

"Dead," Thalt says bluntly, and two generals nod in agreement at General Thalt's remark.

Having lost the Starship Zx12 ninety minutes earlier, the King of Europa and his three generals have locked themselves away in conference within the private viewing gallery with the Europan Sovereign having already dismissed the two first ladies of the Europa Earthprime, both of whom have been sent back to the royal palace apartments.

It doesn't bother the Europan Monarch that the Europa Spaceprime's credibility is in tatters, and he doesn't have a care for the amount of time, resources and effort that have gone into the mission; he doesn't even flinch at having to brief the press about the loss of the mission to the stars – but as a true King who won't shirk his responsibilities, it is his duty, and his duty alone, to tell Captain Jonas Dean's parents that their son is missing in action, and it is this duty alone which affects him deeply.

The King of Europa walks away from his silent generals and looks out through the soundproof glass into the mission control arena, whereupon he sighs heavily with his head slightly bowed and rubs his thumb and forefinger upon his temple.

The constant drone of the communications static is no longer audible within the private viewing gallery, yet His Majesty the second King of Europa can clearly see the flatlines running across Captain Dean's medical screens, and he watches from afar as Hubert Snow, the able Cap-com, helplessly attempts to raise the lost Starship.

The finality of Dean's last message has hit the Europan King hardest of all. The data returned by his Operations team has confirmed that the hyperdrive calculations uploaded to the Starship Zx12 had been incorrect, causing the Starship's hyperdrive systems to grab more space on each of its hops, which in turn had sent the new-age Starship hurtling headlong at interstellar speed into the asteroid field. His Operations team has been unable to provide the King with a fixed set of final exit-point co-ordinates, and therefore the King and his generals have surmised that the Starship Zx12 has exited hyperdrive within the asteroid belt itself with the Laws of Probability stating that the Europan Captain's Starship would have ultimately crashed into an asteroid upon braking, hence Dean's panic: a certain death for a new-age hero of the Spaceprime.

The crowned Sovereign of Europa surveys the mission control arena, but is unable to bring himself to look directly at his three loyal senior men. "My generals, you will all stay at your posts and oversee operations for the next twenty-four hours and we'll deal with the press in the morning. I'll now visit Captain Dean's parents," the King says, winded by events that are out of his control.

He doesn't wait for a reply and the King in mourning departs the Europa Spaceprime Mission Control to visit the father of a Captain who has been lost on his royal watch.

*

Kira Yu is in a catatonic state. For well over ninety minutes, there's been no emotional response from her as she's been expecting Jonas to send a communications signal to let everyone know he's still very much alive.

Commander Marks has also remained silent throughout the hyperdrive mission mode, only leaving Kira temporarily to get coffee. Kira's cup is still full and resides at the foot of her chair, where it's been left untouched and is by now stone cold.

Looking directly at Kira, Marks leans forwards and touches her right arm. After a moment, she turns with eyes hidden behind tinted shades to face her Commander who's holding out a swipe card for the public viewing gallery. "It's no use me telling you to go home and promising that I'll keep you informed of events here. I'll make arrangements for you to have this access pass for the public viewing gallery for the foreseeable future. I'll also make sure that you're granted clearance to this restricted area and that a bed is made up for you across the hall. I have things I need to attend to, Cadet Yu, and only you will know when it's time for you to let go and return to your studies," Marks informs Kira. Kira senses the inevitable end for Captain Jonas Dean in Commander Marks's voice.

"Thank you, sir," says a subdued Kira without turning to watch her Commander as he exits the soundproof glass surround of the public viewing gallery without another word and walks to the glass security door, where he stops only briefly en-route to check the ongoing situation within the mission control arena.

*

Jonas Dean consults his star charts and finds he's done a pretty good job with the landing of his craft. His full systems check of the Starship Zx12 has established that his ship's hyperdrive is fully operational, which is his best news as he now has a chance of getting home. His cargo had been stashed before hyperdrive initiation and all other systems are online and functioning whilst the only commodity of any value which he lost out of his Starship when it had been breached was his air.

His only problem is the tear in his Starship's hull and he smiles to himself as he inspects the area of damage from within the confinement of his spacesuit as Captain Jonas Dean has a visionary built Starship with a hole in it and he also knows how he's going to fix it.

His star charts have confirmed to him what he'd already suspected: that he has emergency landed upon one of the four Galilean satellites of Jupiter. The surface is predominantly rock-based and he can see some dark patches from out of his cockpit window which he assumes are ice formations, but Jonas cannot be totally sure.

His best guess is Ganymede, as Io's and Europa's surfaces are a different composition, although he could be on Callisto which is also rock-based, but also the furthest Galilean moon from Jupiter and Jonas is sure that this Moon was towards his rear when he'd entered Ganymede's gravitational pull.

Captain Jonas Dean has made up his mind: he's going for a walk.

*

Upon a cold autumn night, Cadet Jonas Dean arrived at the Europa Spaceprime Academy; the warm clammy days always led into colder nights at this particular time of year.

He stood momentarily outside the bleak unlit angular building which looked more like a mausoleum than the vibrant heart of the Europa Spaceprime.

Jonas pushed at the supposedly locked academy door to find it already open which took him slightly by surprise; Commander Marks had probably unlocked it minutes earlier, he thought.

Without bothering to search for any light switches, Jonas meandered his way through the dimly lit hallway and up the two flights of stairs which would take him to his classroom, where he found the door he was searching for and strolled inside.

The classroom was brightly lit and he quickly scanned the room to find that there was no-one else around. Jonas checked his solid silver watch; time check: 2152 hours. It was still early and so he decided to sit at his desk and wait.

At 2200 hours, on the button, Commander Marks entered the classroom looking somewhat perturbed. "Cadet Dean, I'm glad you've arrived as I'll need your help this evening. I'm sure that you already know why you're here," he said uneasily.

Commander Marks was evidently agitated and Jonas Dean reached for a reason. "My best guess sir is that the tank training students are due to make an appearance," Dean guessed.

"One student Jonas," the Commander stated forthrightly.

"Cadet Kira Yu," Dean replied with a certainty.

Commander Marks locked his intelligent eyes onto Cadet Dean. "How could you know that it'd be Cadet Kira Yu who would withstand the tank assignment?" he asked.

Jonas smirked and pronounced one clear word: "Gut."

Marks began to pace the classroom floor, an unusual act for the Academy Commander, as he continued with his brief. "Cadet Dean, as you well remember, we gave you a rough time in the tank for fourteen months. Cadet Kira Yu has been assigned to the tank for almost fifteen months whilst the three other students didn't make it past the first few weeks. Cadet Kira Yu has had a hard time with her assignment – she handled the managed illness very badly and was then violently ill on three more separate occasions. I've done something very stupid. I should have let her out a month ago, but because we got behind in her tank schedule after all of the imposed sickness, because of the serums we were giving her, it was agreed that as she'd come this far she should see out the full training programme," Marks said wearily.

Jonas stood up from his desk as he needed to be on his feet. "Is she alive?" he asked, concerned.

"Yes, Cadet Kira Yu's alive," a repenting Marks replied. "The tank operatives instigated the fire two and a half hours ago. We had to get her out of there pretty damn quickly as she made no attempt to put out the blaze. The Medical Officers have examined her fully and she's malnourished, drawn and hasn't slept properly for over three months. We've taken the decision to sedate her and I just pray to god we haven't broken her."

Jonas let Commander Marks's words wash over him, before he asked, "Can I see her?"

"Follow me," Marks said and immediately marched to the classroom doorway, where Cadet Jonas Dean fell into line behind his Commanding Officer.

*

Kira Yu lay in an allocated bed within the medical block which was one floor down from Jonas's classroom and located inside the

Spaceprime Academy buildings; she was still wearing her regulation surgical gown whilst her hair was matted and there were blackening indentations under her closed eyes due to her lack of sleep over the course of her confinement assignment.

Doctor Grace James and Doctor Aileen Grey were tending to Kira and Doctor James looked up from the side of her bed as Commander Marks and Europa Spaceprime Cadet Dean walked into the medical bay. "Commander, we've sedated her and her prognosis looks good as she's a tough cookie. Cadet Kira Yu is now breathing unaided and we'll have a drip on her for the next couple of days. Physically, all she needs is a long rest whilst mentally, well, that'll be down to her," James offered as her diagnosis.

Jonas stood over Kira's comatose body and asked, intrigued, "Why am I here, Commander?"

Commander Marks sat on the end of Kira's bed. "When Cadet Kira Yu wakes up, I want it to be in familiar surroundings and I want you to accompany Doctor Grey and take Kira to her home and tend to her for the next few days until she's strong enough to take care of herself," Marks stated.

Jonas looked down at the sleeping form of Kira. "Yes Sir," Dean replied in full agreement with his Commander's assessment.

*

The King of Europa's car draws up the driveway at Josiah and Evie Dean's residence on the coast of Atlantis, where it's a sultry, close evening as the sun begins to subside behind the distant hills.

His Majesty's driver parks the solar-powered, battery-enhanced royal limousine, and the Monarch's chauffeur steps out of the vehicle and opens the rear door for his regent. Yet the crowned head of Europa remains seated, having already placed his mobile phone to his ear. "General Thalt. What is the latest situation?" he says into his handset.

Thalt's news is as expected – the situation is the same as it was an hour previously and the same as the hour before, and Captain Jonas Dean is lost to the Europa Spaceprime.

The Europan King steps from his limousine and walks solemnly up the driveway whilst gathering his thoughts in solitude.

*

Josiah Dean had watched the transmission of the hyperdrive mode of his son's mission in silence alongside his wife. And he'd heard, along with every other person on the planet who'd tuned in, the final words of Captain Jonas Dean, his only son: "I'm hit! I'm hit!" followed by a minute's static and then silence.

His wife had walked out of their beach house without saying a word whilst Josiah had continued to watch the streaming digital vision feed for a further three hours, waiting for the live transmission to restart, until he'd finally accepted that any further news on Jonas's situation would not be forthcoming.

Josiah is now sitting on his favourite chair on his veranda with his thoughts always drifting to his only son and refusing to accept the worst, whilst at the water's edge, Evie Dean stands with her arms folded and stares out to sea in the cool evening onshore winds that blow into Atlantis Strand.

The King of Europa walks silently down the side of Josiah and Evie Dean's beach house and watches Josiah for a short while before stepping out onto the veranda where the old wooden decking gives his royal presence away, whereupon he can only cease his step and hold Josiah Dean's gaze whilst still not knowing what to say to a father who's just lost his only son.

Josiah Dean spies his King, rises from the false comfort of his chair and moves silently towards the Europan Prime – the old man of the Europa Spaceprime can already read the situation and he doesn't need to be officially told.

Jonas's father has aged considerably over the previous twenty-four hours and he leans into his realm's Sovereign and holds onto the King tightly whilst the tears begin to well in his eyes.

"I'm sorry," the Europan Monarch offers quietly into Josiah Dean's ear.

Josiah Dean lets go of his King. "Thank you for coming, sire," Jonas's father says with a voice which is cracking and sombre.

No further words are exchanged between the two old men of the Europan Kingdom as Josiah Dean walks off his veranda and onto the beach at Atlantis Strand and down towards the seafront in an effort to join his wife who stands upon the wet sands as spent waves lap around her ankles.

Old man Dean doesn't even get halfway before he collapses onto his backside, lost upon the early evening sands with his head bowed between both of his legs, his ageing hands grasping at greying hairs on the top of his head and his tears flowing readily.

Evie Dean turns to see her husband's predicament and races up the beach to comfort him as the King of Europa stares on helplessly before returning to his waiting vehicle, choked and with regal head bowed.

*

Jonas Dean busies himself within the mid-section of his Starship, wherein he opens up several compartments on the port-side of the Zx12. He is in no rush to complete his procedures as he has enough air in his spacesuit to last for two days and if he connects his suit to his spare oxygen supplies onboard his Starship then he'll be able to survive for at least another ten years.

Jonas extracts a small metallic box from his port-side

compartment hold and places it upon the floor within the mid-section of the Zx12; he kneels down before the box and types a four-digit command code into a small numbered keyboard embedded into the top of the unit.

The top of the box slides open to reveal a data point which is strategically placed in the bottom left-hand corner of the unit. He then reaches up into the open compartment and takes hold of a loose length of dormant cable; he pulls the cable out until he has enough spare length to plug the loose cable end into the box's vacant data point.

The box glows red and Jonas retreats to his Starship's cockpit console array, where one of his monitors is flashing a warning message:

NANOSEC TECHNOLOGIES
Warning – Nanodrone activation imminent.

Jonas brings up a schematic of the Starship Zx12 on one of his secondary monitors and from this image he pinpoints the precise position of the breach within his ship's hull. He then pinpoints an unaffected part of the ship's hull within twenty centimetres of the damaged area.

Jonas is now ready and on his keyboard he types:

NANOSEC ACTIVATION UTILITY

After typing in his security code for a second time, Jonas follows the programming protocol which he learnt as part of his mission training. Effectively, he gives the metallic box that contains billions of microscopic Nanodrones a schematic of the Starship Zx12, the pinpointed position of the damaged area of the hull and a part of the ship's hull which, although in a similar position, is completely undamaged.

Jonas runs a simple programme that will action his Nanosec Nanodrones to make the breached area of the hull conform to the unaffected area of the hull at the pinpointed position identified on the schematic, and thus Captain Jonas Dean will have billions of microscopic Nanodrones doing his repair work for him.

The programme is written, yet he still has a couple of issues he needs to take care of and Jonas hurries back to his mid-section's open compartments, where he requisitions a piece of scrap metal which has the same metallic composition as the hull of his Starship. He places the scrap material within the vicinity of the glowing box, so when the Nanodrones are released it will be this piece of metal they will break down and use as raw material to fill the gap in the ship's hull as the Nanodrones are programmed to use the nearest available relevant material to fulfil their programming.

The Nanosec Nanodrones will strip the scrap metal down into microscopic particles and then reassemble the metallic molecules within the breach itself. Upon activation, a few residual Nanodrones will then self-destruct to provide heat as part of the process to reassemble the metal within the damaged area of the hull.

Jonas sets the start time for his programme at one hour; the program will run for a further four hours until his repair work is complete when all of the Nanosec Nanodrones will return to their box chamber and be sealed away.

It's important for Jonas not to be in the Starship Zx12 when his programme activates, because if the Nanodrones were to mistake his spacesuit or his flesh and bone as a suitable component for renewal maintenance then he wouldn't survive the invisible attack.

Jonas has two final tasks to action before he can set foot upon the Moon's surface and he preps his Starship for his Nanosec programme to run.

Jonas is aware that he is alone on this barren land and he doesn't know what he may encounter upon his moonwalk, so he also preps the Starship Zx12 medical evacuation procedure.

Finally, Jonas sets a four-hour timer on the Starship's onboard computer which will then relay a task completion message to his space helmet display. When Jonas is finally satisfied that his preparation is in order, he activates his Starship's hatch door and places a space boot upon the ladder which will take him down to the Moon's surface.

He steps down the short vertical ladder with his heart beating apprehensively and feels the solid rock of a new world greeting him. "By the First Order of the Spaceprime, I name this planet Deansville," says Jonas with a wry smile.

At the foot of his ship's ladder, Captain Jonas Dean peers through the gloom. He cannot see the alien terrain due to the absence of natural light, so he activates the lamps which are attached to his space helmet, walks tentatively away from his spacecraft for about fifty metres, stops walking and switches his space helmet over to night sight scope.

Jonas turns three hundred and sixty degrees in a slow clockwise manner to take in the Moon landscape. On three sides, to the north, to the east and to the west, lie high mountainous peaks and treacherous ridges, and for the first time Jonas can visibly see that he's landed his Starship within a shadowy hollow and he realises he was lucky to find his landing spot.

With his night sight scope activated, he turns south to where the solid ground slopes gently upwards for about four hundred metres; a sloping path that leads towards a dim light which is faintly glowing in the distance.

For a second time, he circles three hundred and sixty degrees and rationally concludes that there's no way he'll get very far by walking north, east or west. He looks once more to the south, where the glow of light emanating from over the brow of the upslope is barely visible through his night scope lens.

"Oh well, I've got four hours to kill; the barely lit path it is," Jonas says out loud and with some trepidation.

He checks his life signs upon his helmet display, noting only that his heart rate has picked up slightly.

Jonas steps out to the brow and walks cautiously whilst watching every single step he takes; he's walking upon solid rock and he can feel the loose stones under his boots as he strains on the slight inclination.

About halfway to the top of the rise, he pauses and turns one hundred and eighty degrees to check his Starship is still in view through his night sight scope.

Having checked that his Starship landmark is still visible, Jonas carries on walking to where the emanating light is beginning to brighten; the light appears to shine from over the brow of the upslope.

Gradually, he walks closer to the top of the incline, towards the glow that is being thrown from over the brow beyond and which is beginning to cast long dark shadows around him, causing Dean's heart rate to dramatically increase and his breathing to become shallower with excitement's manifestation.

Captain Jonas Dean takes his final strides to the top of the rise and the light shines directly onto his space helmet; the illumination is strong enough to affect his field of vision and he realises that he'll no longer require his night sight scope.

Jonas adjusts his helmet for natural light and holds his breath as the intensive light spill has a source which he needs to witness in its full glory. He reaches up with both of his hands and flicks the catches on either side of his helmet which hisses with escaping air before loosening in his gloved hands.

Captain Jonas Dean carefully removes his space helmet and slides it under his arm; the impenetrable membrane which covers his entire head allows him to breathe freely while giving him the panoramic view he so desires.

The light source is the distant sun; Jupiter and two of its Moons are filling the sky, and the sunlight is lighting up the surface of the mysterious planet and reflecting out onto Jupiter's Galilean satellites. The dull light is illuminating the view that Captain Jonas Dean witnesses before him.

This Desolate Land

I'm standing upon a rocky outcrop,
High upon a ridge with the valley below,
Nothing can survive in this barren land,
You can see for miles in this cold dark wasteland.

Beauty can be found in this desolate land,
Wonder can be traced to this desolate place,
All that can be found are the grains of sand,
The final frontier of the human race.

I walk out upon a dried-up seabed,
Arid deserted plain in the valley below,
It's been centuries since the rains fell,
This ancient river would have stories to tell.

Beauty can be found in this desolate land,
Wonder can be traced to this desolate place,
All that can be found are the grains of sand,
The final frontier of the human race.

Looking out upon a distant horizon,
This sight will take your breath away,
The huge moons tower overhead,
The afterglow of pale light it leads my way,
It always seems to be dusk out here,
You must not breathe the atmosphere,
It's so damn cold your breath will freeze,
The shudders on the surface would put you on your knees,
In this vast alien landscape,
Gravity does not weigh me down,
Time's lost pace in this solitary place,
Witnessed only by this human face.

Beauty can be found in this desolate land,
Wonder can be traced to this desolate place,
All that can be found are the grains of sand,
The final frontier of the human race.

CHAPTER 4

Jupiter's Moons

"General Thalt: time of death is 1705 hours, August 17th in the year 2148." The invasive desperation penetrates Doctor Grace James's tone as she struggles to hold back her tears whilst an exhausted and defeated Doctor Aileen Grey slumps down into her chair; the medical team have worked diligently throughout the late evening and the early hours of the day to get any sort of response from Captain Jonas Dean's life sign readings, yet none have been forthcoming.

The medical monitors all remain online, where flatlines run suspended across all of the screens and it's only after a thirteen-hour period that Doctor Grace James has decided to call time of death, after all of the operational data has been sifted over.

Thalt nods and picks up his Europa Spaceprime issue handset, so as to advise the Europan King that Captain Jonas Dean is now officially deceased.

*

Jonas Dean has never felt so alive and the view of the groove valley which is set out beneath his boots holds his gaze for an eternity: an untouched bleak beauty unspoilt by any form of known life.

Jupiter and two of its Moons, Io and Europa, hang like huge globular lanterns in the starlit sky, where they radiate diminished light over huge grooves which penetrate the valley floor below and roll into the distant landscape as far as the human eye can see.

Dean surveys the craggy outcrop of land and refits his space helmet as he sets his mind to finding a way off the ridge. It will have to be as controlled a descent as he can manage within his durable suit, so bending his knees he steps onto the steep decline and clambers down the sloping scree whilst in the places of greater vertical angle he manages to scramble down upon his backside, taking great care not to snag his spacesuit. With a self-imposed patience, Dean makes his way to the base of the ridge to stand at the head of the valley below, where three groove channels merge into one.

Captain Jonas Dean chooses the middle channel and starts walking.

*

A disconsolate King of Europa sits forlornly in his conservatory, a huge glass expanse that also houses his tomato plants, where the heat is oppressive during the middle part of the day, yet bearable in the early morning and late evening.

He has often sat in this heat-ridden environment during quiet moments of his reign to reflect on Europa Spaceprime issues and make decisions on behalf of the peoples of the Europa Earthprime.

The King's mobile phone vibrates and he answers upon its second buzz with his mood darkening as General Thalt relays to him the news that he's already expecting.

"Thank you, General Thalt," he says in acknowledgement of the official news, before ending their short conversation abruptly, his confidence having been further rocked by his loyal general's official confirmation of Captain Dean's death.

Lady Guinevere enters the conservatory and takes a seat next to her forlorn King.

"My lord, you're troubled?" Guinevere asks earnestly.

"Yes, my dear," the King of Europa replies, feeling some comfort in the presence of this beautiful and slender woman, before the overburdened Europan Sovereign sighs. "A great man once said: with great power comes great responsibility. My fellow Kings, my generals and I have all toiled with our consciences to aid us in making the correct decisions, yet fate can often deal you an ugly hand and on this occasion fate has dealt me a horrific hand and it's my responsibility to play it," he says regretfully.

"What will you do, my lord?" Guinevere asks with concern as she reaches out and places a hand upon his arm.

The King of the Europa Spaceprime, whose grey hair has whitened considerably over the previous twenty-four hours, pats her comforting hand gently. "I'll address the Kingdom at noon and tell the peoples of the Europa Earthprime nothing but the truth as that's all that I have left to give," he says.

Lady Guinevere squeezes her King's arm tenderly, before she leaves him alone to plough through the wreckage of his thoughts.

*

Kira Yu awakens alone in the dark within her allocated room at the Spaceprime Central Academy with the events of the previous evening flooding back in waves.

Kira had sat in the public viewing gallery until the small hours of the morning, listening to the constant stream of heavy static as she'd watched the monitors and prayed for a change in the finality of the outcome. She'd finally dropped off to sleep in one of the uncomfortable chairs within the soundproof gallery. Commander Marks had carried Kira to her allocated room within the Europa Spaceprime Mission Control complex where, unbeknown to the training academy Commander, she'd awoken as he laid her down upon the bed. Only after the Commander had switched off the lights, leaving her in mild comfort, had she dispensed with her dark glasses and allowed sleep to overcome her.

Donning her dark shades is also Kira's first action upon waking, and waking to a single thought: Jonas wouldn't have allowed Kira to dwell on his demise. Yet thinking of him only, her hand reaches for her pocket, so that she can touch the swipe card which is still where she placed it the previous evening.

Kira has convinced herself to spend the rest of the morning in the public viewing gallery and in the late afternoon she is resolved to return to the New Buildings estate and throw herself back into her Europa Spaceprime Academy studies.

Kira turns the swipe card over in her hand; at any time, I'm able to visit, she thinks.

The door to her allocated room swings open to reveal Commander Marks standing in the doorway with a full tray. "Breakfast and hot coffee," he offers soberly as he sets the tray down upon the bed, before briefing her: "I have some tough news, Cadet Yu. The medical team pronounced Captain Dean 'Dead' an hour ago. There's also a rumour that the King will confirm this at midday."

"Thank you, Commander," Kira mumbles and averts her dark-glassed gaze from Marks. "I'll be reporting back for duty first thing tomorrow morning, so long as I can keep hold of this," Kira says as she shows her Commander the swipe card that he'd given to her the previous evening.

Commander Marks nods his agreement. "Tomorrow morning it is," he confirms.

Kira eats her breakfast, drinks her coffee, ties back her long black hair and makes her way to the public viewing gallery to view a critical situation which has not changed, although fewer staff are occupying seats within the Europa Spaceprime Mission Control arena and the medical team has already vacated the mission control arena.

However, Chief Communications Officer Katherine Jenkins is still listening into the static signal whilst intermittently trying to raise the Starship Zx12 and Flight Director General Thalt is sitting at attention at his workstation, thumbing through reams of telemetry and data.

Kira wears a tight smile as she surveys the mission control arena, where not everyone has given up on Captain Jonas Dean just yet.

*

Jonas Dean has been walking for three arduous hours and the central groove which he's chosen to hike is only a few metres wide at the head of the valley. As he walks the valley floor, its steep rounded sides have begun to expand away from him, so that he can now no longer see either edge of the groove valley due to the absence of natural light within the basin which is in twilight shadow. He passes by vast dark shadowy areas which he thinks might be pools of frozen ice and that he intentionally steers clear of, as Jonas doesn't wish to walk upon the ice, because if he were to slip and fall then he may do irreparable damage to his suit.

Jonas collects a few rock samples and also takes a small number of digital photographs using the camera that is hidden away within his spacesuit. When he thinks it is nearly time to head back to his Starship, the edges of the groove valley have become visible once more to his naked eye and he can sense that he's walking upon another upslope, so he switches his space helmet to night sight scope and squints into the distance to where the groove valley sides have begun to merge and their steep rounded sides converge onto a high plateau.

If only my family, my King and the peoples of the Kingdoms of the Earthprime could see me now, Jonas muses. And Kira: especially Kira.

Captain Jonas Dean of the First Order of the Spaceprime keeps on walking.

*

Within the Europa Spaceprime Academy block, Jonas held a heavily sedated Kira Yu in his arms whilst Doctor Aileen Grey held onto her attached drip. They both retreated in unison out of the ward within the medical block and into the academy corridor to undertake the short walk to the lift doors, whilst Commander Marks and Doctor James took the stairwell, so as to meet Kira Yu's entourage within the Spaceprime Academy lobby.

Commander Marks left the angular academy building by its front door to commandeer one of the fleet of Europa Spaceprime ambulances which he then backed up to the main entrance, before opening the ambulance's rear doors. Jonas took his Commander's action as his signal to carry Kira to the rear of the ambulance, whereupon he positioned her in a comfortable posture on the stretcher in the back of the requisitioned vehicle and securely strapped her in.

Jonas intended to steadily drive the solar-powered, battery-enhanced ambulance along the unlit coastal highway whilst Doctor Aileen Grey stayed in the rear of the vehicle to monitor the unconscious cadet.

At midnight, Jonas pulled out of the Europa Spaceprime Academy driveway and made for the coastal road that would take him to the New Buildings estate situated eighty miles south-west of the city, a journey that would take a little short of three hours.

Jonas hit the coastal road and wound down his driver's window thus allowing the cool evening air to circulate inside his ride.

The ambulance's full beam lit up the road ahead, where at this time of night he'd be lucky to encounter another vehicle. Jonas felt his muscles relax as he drove the coastal highway which was devoid of road markings, highway lights and traffic; I guess driving wasn't this easy in the twenty-first century, Jonas thought as he recalled what his father had once said to him when he was a child: your grandfather always preached that day-to-day life was so different in the early part of the twenty-first century and then we had the war. A lot of people perished, yet perversely the planet was saved for future generations to come.

Eighty per cent of the world's population had died due to the initial solar radiation strike, the war and its after-effects; disease and famine were rife in the post-apocalyptical world and malnutrition their vile accomplice. Food became a rare commodity and many had starved, whilst others lost all hope and just sat waiting for death to take them. And for fifty years, all that mattered was basic survival.

It had been the environment which had caused the greatest problems for mankind: the nuclear fallout had lasted for a generation and there had been many no-go areas on the planet, as there are still to this day.

Thirty years after the war and radiation was still an issue as unattended nuclear power plants succumbed to meltdown, the resultant fireballs tainting their immediate areas for a further half century. Fuel plants which had lain idle for decades leaked their resources into the rivers and seas, causing widespread pollution, and natural gas plants that had become unstable after many years of neglect exploded into inferno without any prior warning.

The holocaust survivors used their instincts and moved away from the major cities and industrialised areas to populate the countryside and the rugged, previously underpopulated areas of the country.

The internet ceased overnight as large waves of Electro Magnetic Pulse unleashed by the more advanced nations during the last of all wars consigned the World Wide Web to history, rendering all lines of digital communication obsolete and the lights went out on the world for fifty years.

And then, when it looked as if this was how it would always be, messengers had been despatched throughout the lands and a scattered population was duly informed that various historic cities across the nations of old had been re-entered and so the peoples began their drift back into the conurbations. Within the new-age open cities, the clean-up operation had begun. There was plenty of food, an abundance of residences and, more importantly, a promise of a better life: a rekindling of hope.

The newly appointed Kings of the Kingdoms had created order and the peoples of the planet had fallen into line behind them.

Nuclear power plants had already been cleaned up and decommissioned, major oil spills were still being chemically treated and the limited electrical supply which was required for the reduced populace was taken from restored hydro-electric power stations.

Pollution and nuclear fall-out had also wreaked havoc on the weather and, combined with the global warming of the early twenty-first century, extremes of weather had become commonplace until eventually, at the turn of the century, inland rainfall had become extremely scarce within the Europan hemisphere.

Although the initial impact of the short war had sent the planet tumbling close to uninhabitable, man-made pollution had immediately ceased after the conflict. The Earth initially struggled with the long-term environmental cost of the Third World War, but after seventy years, the planet was gradually starting to heal itself.

Inland rainfall had increased from negligible to averaging seven days a year and this was projected to increase to twenty-eight days a year within a decade; it had also become noticeable that the seasons had returned – nature's trees and plant life found their cycle once more and bird migratory flights began to return to the familiar patterns which had not been seen since the early part of the twenty-first century.

The King of Europa had recently announced to the peoples of the

Europa Earthprime that tests from the Kingdom of Americas had proven that the ozone layer had begun to heal itself, sea levels had fallen and the ice-caps had begun to reform at the North Pole. This news had been met with rousing jubilation.

Jonas could see with his own eyes that the area where he lived, which had been underwater for decades, was now habitable and, as with the rest of the peoples of the Kingdoms of the Earthprime, he was grateful to the Kings of the Kingdoms for their leadership and direction, because it had allowed him to fulfil his life's ambitions; the Spaceprime's motto having left an indelible mark upon him.

Jonas looked out of the side window of the ambulance and across the bay into the clear skies of the black night to where the starlight was shining proudly within the heavens above. "When the lives of the peoples of the Earthprime whom we serve are complete, we shall look to the stars," he said boldly to himself.

*

Jonas halts his walk within the valley with his night sight scope activated so he can view the high plateau summit's base. He can clearly see the valley's grooves converging on either side of him and he focuses upon plotting a path to the top of the plateau's rise.

The information screen within his helmet flashes with new data and he's informed by the main computer onboard the Zx12 that the Nanosec programme he instigated has run its course and the Starship Zx12 can be re-entered.

"Let's hope the hole's been plugged," he says out loud.

Jonas has been walking for four hours and he isn't about to turn back until he's stood upon the raised plateau situated above the merging grooves at the foot of the valley.

Captain Jonas Dean, with no thought of returning to his Starship, walks on.

*

The ambulance pulled to a halt outside the New Buildings estate and Jonas jumped out, strode to the vehicle's rear and pulled open the ambulance's rear doors to find Doctor Aileen Grey holding Kira's hand. "She'll be out of it for a couple of days, but her life signs are stable. If you can carry her up to apartment sixteen on the third floor, I'll follow you with the monitoring equipment," the Doctor said efficiently to Jonas.

Jonas stepped forward and undid the holding straps which had fastened Kira securely for her journey home, before taking her in his arms whilst Doctor Grey lay the attached drip on top of Kira's torso.

Grey took out her mobile and phoned the House Manager for the New Buildings estate. "Open all the doors for access to apartment sixteen," she said formally.

Jonas heard a barely audible reply from the doctor's handset. "Confirmed," Grey stated through her Europa Spaceprime issue mobile phone.

Jonas held Kira close as he walked towards the apartment block and pushed through the entrance doorway. Once inside the general lobby area he was confronted by a single lift with an "Out of order" sign posted upon its steel door.

Typical, Jonas thought as he made for the dark stairwell instead: the House Manager had opened all of the access points to the building but hadn't bothered to give him any light to guide him. He began the slow and careful climb up the stairs until he reached the summit of the second flight, where he felt Kira move within his arms which caused Jonas to slow his pace and look down upon her silhouetted form.

Kira pushed her head up to Jonas's shoulder, ran her left hand through his short cropped hair to caress his scalp and then pulled him down towards her, whereupon she kissed him tenderly upon the lips.

The affectionate kiss rooted Jonas to the spot. Kira was a dark shadow in his arms and he could just about make out the contours of her face as she slumped down into his arms once more and, without uttering a single word, promptly fell asleep.

*

Midday has arrived and the King of Europa is standing before three microphones within the well-kept gardens of his royal apartments.

On either side of the King of Europa are the two first ladies of the Europa Earthprime, Lady Anne and Lady Guinevere, whilst his three generals are standing directly behind the two first ladies to form a regal hierarchical arrowhead.

The Europan Monarch is dressed in full Europa Spaceprime uniform: black shoes, black trousers and a matching black tunic. Two emblems stand out upon his tunic: the three embroidered vertical white S shapes which are stitched to his left breast, the signature of the Spaceprime, and a grey rocket crest emblem which is stitched upon his opposite breast.

Stepping forward to the microphones, a desperate King of Europa looks bleakly into the intrusive camera and briefs a watching world: "Peoples of the Kingdom of Europa, peoples of the Earthprime, peoples of the Spaceprime, my people. It's with a heavy heart that I come before you today. We, the Kingdom of Europa, have suffered a terrible tragedy. The greatest wish of my father, the late King, was to push back the boundaries of our known comprehension. With the launch of the HMS Neon-Lit City we took our first tentative steps out into the unknown; the Stargazer class vessel was a symbol of the new Kingdoms endeavours. It was my decision and my decision alone to develop the Zx class Starship to search for the lost icon of the twenty-second century. The Starship Zx12 commanded by Captain Jonas William Dean blasted off from the New Anglian desert at midnight on August 16th. At 1700 hours on August 17th the hyperdrive engine onboard the Zx12 was initiated and at 1704 hours the hyperdrive mission had been confirmed as a major success, but at 1705 hours, Captain Dean, along with the Starship Zx12, was lost to us all and it's my belief that Captain Jonas Dean has perished within the asteroid belt. All of our thoughts at this time lie with his family and I will personally make sure that they are given the necessary time and space to grieve for their only son. The Europa Spaceprime Mission Control for the Starship Zx12's mission to the stars will remain manned for the next twelve months."

The King of Europa, deep in his darkest hours, steps back from the three microphones, turns and walks off the lawns and into his outhouse, closely attended to by the first ladies of the Earthprime and his three generals. The Monarch makes his way through the rear of his outhouse to his beloved tomato plants. The Sovereign Prime stands over a silver tap and fills up a silver watering can, and then, without speaking or making any direct eye contact with his attending generals or the two first ladies of the Earthprime, begins to water his beloved plants.

Lady Guinevere and Lady Anne usher the generals into the main apartment building whilst they watch the King work through his grief. Eventually, Lady Anne decides that the best course of action would be to give the King of Europa some time alone, although Lady Guinevere will not be coerced into leaving her Monarch's side.

For fifteen minutes, the Europan King makes several trips to the silver tap and yet Guinevere doesn't move as she watches him intently.

A quietly solemn King waters all of his tomato plants before placing the watering can beside the last plant he's tended to and he turns, heavy shouldered, tired and withdrawn, to face the lady who's waited whilst he's tended to his plants.

Guinevere gracefully moves towards her Monarch, flings her arms around the back of his neck and holds him close.

The King of Europa rests his regal head upon Guinevere's shoulder as the words come gagging out of him: "I sent a man to his death and I deeply regret it."

Lady Guinevere attempts to soothe a King who is sickened by his conscience: "Don't worry my love, Jonas Dean was a brave man and he knew the risks involved as much as you did. The peoples of the Kingdoms of the Earthprime must always remember him as brave and bold and it's your responsibility to make sure that they'll never forget him."

The King pulls away from Lady Guinevere and smiles gently. "I'm sorry, you're right of course. I always forget you are wise beyond your years. I'll make sure that there is a fitting memorial service. Whilst I draw breath, Captain Jonas Dean's memory will live on in the hearts and minds of the peoples of the Kingdoms of the Earthprime," he says.

And the head of the Europan royal line takes Lady Guinevere's hand and leads her into the main apartment block to brief his generals on his memorial plans.

*

Frozen rigid on the dark stairwell, Jonas waited a moment for any further movement within his arms: Kira Yu had kissed him and that must mean something; it meant something to him.

Kira was not heavy in his arms and Jonas, with a pumping heart, climbed the final flight of stairs before making his way through the shadowy third floor corridor to apartment number sixteen.

The door to Kira's apartment opened easily enough as he leaned his back into it, and Jonas guessed correctly which of the three shut doors that fed off the large sparse living room area was the main bedroom. He carried Kira to her bed, which was positioned under a window, pulled back the bed's linen and lay her down carefully with the drip still positioned centrally upon her lithe body.

Jonas retreated to Kira's bedroom doorway to flick on the bedroom's light and took a moment to allow his eyes to adjust to the newfound light.

Kira was still wearing the surgical gown that the medical team had placed on her after she exited the tank and Jonas decided to rid her of the gown, purge her of the tank. He nervously undid the straps tied around the back of her neck and manoeuvred Kira onto her side to undo the knot tied close to the small of her back and holding her gown in place; the surgical garment slipped easily away.

He repositioned Kira on her back and pulled the bed covers up and around her shoulders, trying hard not to stare intently at her naked form.

There was still no sign of Doctor Aileen Grey, so Jonas retreated to Kira's kitchen and filled up a glass of water which he placed upon her bedside table, before sitting upon her bed and waiting for Grey to arrive as he watched over Kira.

*

If it wasn't for his night sight scope, Captain Jonas Dean wouldn't be able to see his hand in front of his face, but with his enhanced sight he can clearly see that the groove valley sides have converged at the base of the plateau; the plateau surface is about twenty metres above his head and it's steeply inclined, but there are several good footholds of rock that he'll be able to make good use of to aid his climb to the summit.

There is risk involved in the short climb, because if he snags his spacesuit at any point then it will almost certainly mean a breathless death: the cold elements of Ganymede's atmosphere will rush in to invade his lungs and he will suffocate in agony.

But Jonas Dean is not for turning back – this is his great adventure; so he leans forward and takes his first handhold, steadies himself and takes his first foothold then hauls himself upwards.

*

Doctor Aileen Grey strode through Kira's bedroom doorway, holding a long metal pole which she positioned next to Kira's bed; Jonas carefully picked up the drip that lay upon Kira's torso and handed it to the doctor.

Grey hung the drip from the top of the pole and checked it was filtering fluids correctly and then moved quickly out of the apartment to fetch the rest of her monitoring equipment.

Jonas took hold of Kira's hand, the one which the drip was attached to, and spoke softly to her sleeping form: "Kira, I have to apologise as our first meeting didn't go as well as I would've hoped and I was a little brash which unfortunately is not unusual for me," he said.

*

Jonas leans the whole of his body into the sharp incline to maintain his balance and he has one good foothold and two good handholds. With his stability ensured, he raises his head towards the plateau's surface which is only three metres above him. When he's closer to the top than he is to the bottom, his father's words tear into him: "Remember son, when it comes to heights then don't whatever you do look down."

Jonas spies another good handhold, reaches out and takes a firm grip with his glove and hauls himself upwards.

*

As Jonas held Kira's warm and petite hand, he bowed his head.

"Kira, I'm going to make you a promise. You and I, we were the only two students to make it through the tank assignment and from here on in, I'll have your back as I truly respect you for making it out of that god-awful training hole in one piece," he said.

*

Precariously balanced on the ledge of the plateau, Jonas loses his foothold; the upper part of his body lies face down on the plateau's surface whilst his right foot flails and wavers over the drop as he desperately tries to find some leverage.

After what seems an age, he finds a foothold and uses the purchase to push himself forwards which is enough to take him those final few centimetres, so that he's able to roll onto his back and look upwards from the summit of the high plateau's flat terrain.

Jonas blinks several times as the rays of the reflected sun are stronger here than within the valley below; his night sight scope is still enabled and it's too bright for him to fully comprehend the view.

He takes a short moment to catch his breath, before he scrambles up onto his booted feet. He doesn't bother to switch off his night sight scope but instead the Europa Spaceprime Captain flicks the catches that seal his space helmet to his spacesuit, so that he can turn his helmet slightly and lift it off his head, before placing it under his arm.

Through the clear membrane, Jonas looks skywards at the stunning skyline portrayed before him which affects him deeply. His knees weaken and he drops forwards onto them, cautiously placing his space helmet down in front of him; Jonas shakes his head in disbelief as the tears begin to well in his eyes.

*

Kira Yu's eyelids fluttered and Jonas felt some pressure upon his hand as Kira gently squeezed it, and Jonas watched as she opened her eyes and looked up at a watching Jonas Dean at whom she smiled serenely.

Almost immediately, Kira fell back into a deep sleep with her hand entwined within his.

Jonas held his breath as his mind raced in its search for an explanation – he knew there was a name for her condition and he frowned as he searched deep inside his memory, reaching out for the relevant medical terminology. Her eyes, Kira's eyes, were different, not in size or shape, but in colour. Kira Yu had beautiful sparkling eyes; deep, wide hypnotic pools, yet her right iris was a light blue in colour and her left was a pale brown; he'd never noticed before.

"Heterochromia iridium," Jonas whispered in his disbelief.

*

Jonas kneels and stares longingly up towards the heavens, holding his hands up to the stars above.

Jupiter fills his breathtaking background and the planet appears to be a golden globe as sunlight bounces off its vaporous cloak; the Jovian planet's peel is tinged with orange and brown colouration whilst vast red explosions can be seen expanding and contracting upon the outer planet's periphery: the violent storms of a dead world.

Jupiter is the beacon of light, yet it's the view that Jonas witnesses in his foreground which has sent him onto his knees; a sight he thought he'd never again be able to witness within his lifetime of ambitious pursuits: Io and Europa shine gloriously in the heavens, huge imposing Moons looking down upon Ganymede; the dominant powder blue Moon of Europa fills his vision with the slightly eclipsed subtle ochre colouration of Io behind.

Jonas Dean can see Kira's eyes and knows that Kira Yu is watching over him.

Jupiter's Moons

You know what I see in your eyes, I see,
Jupiter's Moons,
You know what I see in your smile, I see,
Some attitude,
You know what I see in your heart, I see,
Love meant for two,
You know what I see in your soul, I see,
The essence of you.

I remember the first time that I saw you; you were standing in the
rain,
I remember the first time that I met you; you nearly drove me half
insane,
I remember the first time that I kissed you; my soul it slipped away,
I remember the last time I was with you; I thought you were here to
stay.

All I'm left with now,
Is a memory of you,
And I know what I see.

You know what I see in your eyes, I see,
Jupiter's Moons,
You know what I see in your smile, I see,
Some attitude,
You know what I see in your heart, I see,
Love meant for two,
You know what I see in your soul, I see,
The essence of you.

I remember the first time that I saw you; you were standing in the
rain,
I remember the first time that I met you; you nearly drove me half
insane,
I remember the first time that I held you; I felt a burning inside my
heart,
I remember the last time that I missed you; it tore my soul apart.

All I'm left with now,
Is a memory of you,
And I know what I see.

You know what I see in your eyes, I see,
Jupiter's Moons,
You know what I see in your smile, I see,
Some attitude,
You know what I see in your heart, I see,
Love meant for two,
You know what I see in your soul, I see,
The essence of you.

CHAPTER 5

The History of My Life

Although he's become the first member of the human race to stand upon one of Jupiter's Moons, a deep sense of loss tarnishes Jonas's euphoria; Captain Jonas Dean understands fully the reasons why he feels like an empty shell of a man.

He kneels for a while, looking up occasionally at the pockmarked lemony-brown colourations of Io and the shimmering soft blue of Europa; Jonas cannot stare for too long as waves of guilt sweep through his being as Kira's eyes burn into his very core.

Jonas bows his head and scolds himself for allowing his ambitions to supersede any hope which he may have had of long-term happiness, but he keeps telling himself that this is his willing sacrifice which he's made unconditionally and that his decision is the correct one. Still though, doubts creep over his soul and penetrate his mind.

Jonas would have dwelt on his own emotional state for far longer, but a deep rumbling sound becomes audible. He unsteadily takes to his feet before instinctively looking down towards his space boots, under which small shards of rock are jumping up from the surface of the high plateau and settling back down momentarily, then leaping upwards again before dropping back to the Moon's surface.

Jonas frowns: "How can this be?" he thinks. His answer comes almost instantaneously as he feels an immense amount of pressure exerting itself onto his knees and the grains of rock begin to leap higher into the thin atmosphere; he swiftly swivels his head towards his space helmet which is being thrown up and down off the plateau's surface.

He quietly swears under his breath – if he'd been wearing his space helmet then the sensors in his suit would have established the seismic event and flashed him a warning message.

Jonas immediately crouches down upon his knees, leans forwards and places both of his gloved hands onto the Moon plateau's flat surface as there is nothing else that he can do and no place for him to take shelter.

The ground beneath his feet begins to shake violently; his exposed body convulses uncontrollably upon the moonquake and he grits his teeth to stop them chattering through the tremor's shockwave.

"If my suit fails me then I'm a dead man and no loss to anyone," he thinks morbidly, before a huge tremor hits directly beneath him and Jonas is lifted up into the thin atmosphere: how high he went, he'd never know.

Jonas closes his eyes as he hangs in the void above Ganymede's rocky terrain.

"This is it: the end," he thinks.

Behind his eyelids he can see the faces of his parents etched before him, and he can see the empty stretch of coastline at Atlantis Strand, feel the coolness of the breeze and hear the waves crashing into the shore. One other soul is upon the beach within his sight's view, and Jonas Dean can only watch as Kira Yu walks away from him, down the long stretch of coastline as the broken waters wash gently over her ankles.

"Kira," Jonas whispers passionately.

Captain Jonas Dean of the First Order of the Spaceprime is

knocked unconscious as he hits the hard ground upon the high plateau. It's an ugly landing, his right shoulder taking the full weight of his fall to Ganymede Moon's terrain, his legs impacting upon alien ground very shortly after; however, the membrane which is protecting his head remains intact, having taken much of the blow when the right side of his safeguard had slammed into the plateau's surface. Dean's prone form rolls over onto his front with his inert guarded head looking down at the plateau's terrain, the membrane shield keeping his mouth and nose hovering just above the flat rock surface of the high plateau.

Jonas's eyes flicker as the whole of his body succumbs to an invasive cold and he can no longer feel his legs or his feet.

"Is this the onset of my own death?" he thinks, his subconscious mind meandering through the different ways in which he might finally submit to the inevitable. He could freeze to death, frozen for all time on the cold isolated Moon of Ganymede, undiscovered for centuries and millennia. He begins to wish that he'd kept a more detailed log of his journey as his story would then have been told in the distant future, but it's too late now. With his eyes still flickering wildly, he thinks that he'll probably die of oxygen starvation and subconsciously starts to breathe more deeply, yet he isn't choking upon the withdrawal of his oxygen supply; another quake would finish him off though as he lies silently in stillness.

"Anytime soon," Jonas thinks, as he's bitten by a cold which begins to penetrate his lifeless form; cold's teeth are chewing at his face, his torso, his arms and his fingers, as well as his unfelt legs and feet; he can no longer feel the right side of his face as it presses down onto an unseen frozen floor.

"Let's hope death will be swift," thinks Jonas, his desire for life fading.

With his eyelids flickering uncontrollably, he becomes desperate for consciousness and begins to move the tips of his fingers down onto the place where he lies; the tips of his fingers freeze and he thinks that Ganymede's cold must have penetrated the inside of his gloves.

His confusion overwhelms him in his lost consciousness and Captain Jonas Dean panics within oblivion's vice; his eyes flicker in retinal spasm and he's desperate for awareness: to be awake. He can feel the side of his head against an ice-cold floor, yet the membrane which is attached to his spacesuit should not allow his head to touch any surface. "Has the membrane failed me?" Jonas thinks. "Is that why I'm so cold? But if this is the case, then why am I still breathing?" Jonas cannot make any sense of his situation as he finally manages to force his eyes open.

Jonas had thought that the harsh elements of Ganymede had penetrated his spacesuit or that maybe he'd gone into shock; however, as his eyes regain their focus and take in his frozen surroundings, he realises that his freezing body can easily be accounted for: he's lying upon a sheet of ice and, to make matters worse, he's naked.

Jonas lifts his head away from the ice-covered floor and sits upright. The onset of his shivering he cannot contain as he wraps his arms around the sides of his body; he rubs slowly at first and then quickens his pace to see if the generated friction will give him any extra warmth and comfort as there's nothing else that he can use as cover against the icy chill, and heat is dissipating out of his body at an accelerated rate.

As his fingers and toes turn blue, Jonas tries to take in his arctic environment, which proves to be painful as his face has become rigid and swollen with cold.

He appears to be trapped within a great ice hall, where a frozen floor blends in with the icy walls and you cannot see where the walls finish and the ceiling begins. Two great ice pillars stand proudly erect before Jonas, casting their shadows behind, whilst between the twin columns of ice, lie four ice steps which lead to a small façade, whereupon a magnificent ice-carved throne is situated equidistant between the two ice pillars: the main feature of the great ice hall.

Pools of freezing melt-water have formed in several locations within the hall which is blighted by frost as icy water drips rapidly from the high ceiling above.

Jonas's vision is becoming impaired and the whites of his eyes are beginning to freeze. He tries in vain to shout for help, but the vocal gets caught deep inside his throat.

Through his blurring vision he can see movement in the shadows behind the tall columns. He attempts to shout once more, yet still no noise can be persuaded to leave his constricted throat: whoever they are, whatever they are, they can take him now; he's not yet ready to die as there's still so much more that he wishes to achieve in his life, but surely it would be better than this cold deterioration.

A tall figure steps out from the shadows and moves in an arc towards Jonas who can barely see the silhouetted thin giant making their way to where he's slowly freezing to death.

Pure white falls before Jonas's eyes as his vision deteriorates to ice-blind, but he senses that the figure which he had indistinctly seen is standing benignly before him and bending over his inferior naked form, and he feels the giant's ice-cold breath upon his own face which has frozen to a prominent shade of blue.

Jonas looks up unseeing and smiles as he figures that events cannot take a turn for the worse and that he's moments away from his own death.

Overcome by a total numbness and with all of his sensations lost, a frozen Jonas Dean can move no more as the palm of a hand is pushed into his forehead and long tentacle fingers grip the top of his head.

Jonas's gasping body arches as the creature's palm and long fingers hold a vice-like grip to his head; a protruding heat rushes through Jonas's body as the heat supply ripples from the top of his head through his neckline, into his torso and down to his fingers and feet.

Craving the palm's touch, Jonas instinctively pushes his head further into the mysterious hand as this is the only source of heat within his icebound world and his body's greed for more has overpowered any other fears and needs.

The hand pulls away sharply and Jonas slumps down onto his back; his body has been reinvigorated by the projected heat supply and Jonas's vision begins to return from ice-blind to blurring.

The heat from his body is no longer escaping and he blinks several times as the fog lifts from his eyes and he slowly builds up his focus on the creature stooping over his naked form.

Jonas lifts himself up, taking the full weight of his body onto the palms of his hands; his skin has turned greyish pink in colour, causing pins and needles to rampage through his legs which makes him feel uncomfortable as the blood supply returns to his extremities.

Captain Jonas Dean stares in wonderment at the human apparition who's looking down upon him. He suspects that this tall woman has nothing to fear from him; that he is the lesser species.

The long gown which she wears covers the line of her shoulders and the uncreased cloth cascades down towards the ice floor, where it flows out for several metres to her sides and stretches back forty metres to the foot of the ice steps; at every point where the deep red braided robe comes into contact with the melt waters, the waters freeze.

Jonas can tell that this is all that she's wearing as he looks deeply into her eyes which are as black as oil; her cold blue lips hold the remnants of a smile, her skin is ice white and unblemished.

Liquid vials of ruby and gold hang as dog-tags around her neckline and she wears a sparkling diamond-studded silver crown which is befitting of her demeanour. The matching silver staff which she holds between her elongated fingers rests easily upon the sheet of ice; if the solid silver staff were to be used in the correct manner, Jonas imagines it would become a lethal weapon; he doesn't wish to find out whether his assessment is a correct one as he's in a severely weakened state.

Jonas's voice returns. "Who are you?" he asks.

The Queen of the ice hall's firmly held silver staff immediately snaps up off the frosted floor as she raises it above her head.

Jonas flinches uncertainly.

Unexpectedly, the tall woman laughs; she hardly seems able to contain herself as she roars with laughter whilst baring her immaculate white teeth.

She ceases as quickly as she started and jabs a finger towards Jonas. "You Earthlings are all the same – you're like ants and I knew that sooner or later one of you would flee the colony," she says.

Jonas's jaw drops open in acknowledgement of the fact that the tall woman can speak and she can speak his language.

A silky long finger is still pointing in his direction. "Yes, you're a rare species indeed with your free will and your free thinking, but all you humans ever do is ask questions and yet you always seem to manage to ignore the answers," she taunts.

The pointed finger drops and she withdraws her staff to her side. "You've fallen upon hallowed ground and stepped into my domain; however, your question, Captain Jonas Dean, will be answered, but first you'll listen to what I have to say," she states.

The tall beautiful black-eyed woman draws a cold breath and holds spaceman Dean's gaze before explaining her existence. "To the Telemonoidians: I am myth. To the Krayloxians: I am legend. And to the Titans: I am a goddess. The Titans call me the Ice Queen: Ashilla. I am older than time itself and a watcher of the known universe; I cannot interfere with the events of providence unless the balance of the known universe is threatened. You, Jonas Dean, are the first humanoid to physically cross my path; it was your destiny. I've watched you for such a long time now and I've often doubted whether you'd fulfil your calling. It still surprises me that a human of all species can travel so far in such a short amount of time. I'd discarded the idea of your race ever breaking free of the world which you inhabit. You're a young species indeed and for centuries never had the technologies to hand to send one of your own into the abyss. I watched as various Earth societies progressed: the Pharaohs, the Incas and the Romans to name but a few, yet conflict, disease and the systemic abuse of power would topple these once proud civilisations and set the development of your species back. I thought this cyclical rise and fall of power-bases would hinder your technological development for an eternity. I've watched closely these past two centuries; the pre-nuclear-war Earth was in a technological position to send a humanoid well beyond its boundaries and I have to admit I became intrigued, yet it was an act of inept incompetence, an abuse of power which set your world back for a further half-century. Your race had come so very close to breaching the beyond and the resilience of your population has always had the power to astound me, however your post-nuclear-war society was better led and regained its focus, and after many years of waiting, you Captain Jonas Dean have arrived." Ashilla pauses to draw breath.

There's only one rational conclusion that Captain Jonas Dean can draw from the existence of an ice maiden upon Ganymede Moon: mind wraith – an imaginary intellect which is just his rambling subconscious and he will let it speak his mind. In response to his subconscious mind's calling, he sits up and folds his arms across his bare knees, where he'll watch and listen intently; still naked but no longer cold.

"Your arrival was foretold and yet your future is less clear and is dependent on the path that you alone choose to take," the Ice Queen says.

The enforced pause is longer this time to allow Jonas to dwell upon the words she's spoken and yet he has no need to engage in conversation with the illusionary watcher myth as he's willing to allow his psyche to have its say.

The Ice Queen remains unbowed as her jet black eyes bore into him. "I have watched you since your birth. Jonas William Dean: born the only son of Josiah and Evie Dean on the 24th of February in the year of 2118. Your parents were kind and loving and in your early years they gave you everything that you desired although they didn't spoil you and they scolded you when you'd done wrong; it was a stable upbringing for a child. You were given direction from a tender age and supported in everything that you did, hence you matured early, learnt quickly and developed a high IQ. Your father, Josiah Dean, a hero of the Europa Spaceprime, was a role model to you and because of him your ambition to join the Spaceprime burned within you. When the Europa Spaceprime accepted you, your father only gave you one piece of advice: always serve your King with honour and pride. So you swore loyalty to the Spaceprime and allegiance to your Sovereign and you accepted their authority without question. You were a willing member and compliant to the values which the Spaceprime upholds and which you believe in and you were faithful to this organisation – if you'd not been a trusted and dependable member of the Europa Spaceprime then you wouldn't be sitting before me today. The King of Europa and his inner circle had noted these attributes in you which set you apart from the rest and the Europa Spaceprime academy was well aware of these traits before you were sent into the training tank, where you needed to be physically and mentally strong to handle the intense rigours of your confinement assignment; a huge abundance of stamina and a backbone of steel were a necessity for you to survive the tank. When you took command of the Starship Zx12 on her maiden voyage, you showed courage, grit and determination. You didn't flinch in the face of crisis and you were aware and resourceful when you turned into an oncoming meteor shower which almost certainly saved your life; you were brave and bold enough to avert your ship from crashing into this world. You've proven yourself, Jonas Dean, as tough and fearless whilst you've always remained focused and have endured," the Ice Queen concludes.

Jonas sticks out his chin, his shoulders rise and his chest lifts up. The Ice Queen, his own mind's apparition, knows more about him than he knows about himself. Jonas becomes thoughtful of the figment Queen's words as he's always acted upon his own instincts and is proud of who and what he is and what he's achieved. On reflection, the Ice Queen's assessment of him has been fair and just, causing Captain Jonas Dean to grin from ear to ear with the heady praise still ringing within them.

As Jonas takes in the Ice Queen's exaltations, she watches his reaction intently; having watched Jonas Dean his whole life, his reaction of pride and immense satisfaction is one that she has expected.

The Queen of Ice draws herself up to her full height and pulls at the sides of her gown, causing her robe to billow out within the cold air environment, before she allows her robe to drop down again to her sides as an icy blast of air expels from beneath her lavish red-robed garment, blowing cold over Jonas's naked body.

Jonas gasps as a cold shiver is sent tumbling down his spine and a defiant Ice Queen pronounces to the fallen ship's Captain, " And yet you're afraid, Jonas Dean."

Jonas truly believes that his near-death psyche is walking him through the final moments of his imperfect life and he replies to the taunting apparition, "You're my life's storytelling subconscious and I'm not afraid of a hallucination." His shouted response echoes throughout the ice hall.

"Oh, but you are, Jonas Dean," the Ice Queen coolly replies.

And doubt arises in Jonas's confused mind as a tentacle finger is once more pointed in his direction, before Queen Ashilla exalts, "Yours is a half-lived life, Jonas Dean."

The cold has returned and Jonas can only stare whilst awaiting her voice.

Her finger drops once more to her side and the Ice Queen has the Starship Captain's full attention. "What's your reason for life? I don't understand; I've never been able to understand. You're driven by one passion alone: ambition. You drink readily from its cup, your thirst never quenched and always the cup grows fuller. You're self-dependent to the point where you shut yourself off from the affections of others, pushing people away and creating distance between yourself and any chance of fulfilment with another. I admit you do have self-motivation, yet this will ebb away with the future regret that you'll feel with all of the missed opportunities that you didn't take. This will then decay your self-confidence which is the very core of your being. Jonas Dean, you've become distant and closed and this will lead to your emotional downfall. If you do not seek passions in other areas of your life then you are nothing and you'll wither and die. It truly saddens me to watch the depreciation of your life; you dare not commit, your feelings are guarded and your emotions are restrained whilst you put up walls around your affections and bury your desires, making no effort to explore these passions, and yet you allow for the status quo to remain. Listen to the calling of your own soul; allow its voice to be heard. If only you channelled your passions into the affairs of the heart instead of your own personal ambitions or other men's ambitions then your rewards would be tenfold," Queen Ashilla becries.

The heat is no longer flowing out of Jonas's body and yet he can still feel the raw chill of cold. Her words have been like sharpened icicles plunged into his heart and his demeanour has changed; he bows his head in deepest regret – he had often thought of Kira Yu during his training for his mission to the stars, but he'd never once taken any action on the spur of the moment to contact her or tell her how he really felt. On that single weekend upon the beach at Atlantis Strand his opportunity had arisen, yet he'd buried his feelings deep inside and distanced his emotions.

Regret flows through Jonas's body: on the launch pad, he'd asked Snow to tell Kira that it was always "Delta" but he now realised this had been a cowardly act and he should have been brave and bold enough to tell her directly. Jonas's head bows lower as he remembers that he's left Kira a gift.

A single tear falls from the base of Jonas's eyelid and runs down his cheek; the droplet freezes halfway and solidifies against his skin. He doesn't try to brush away the ice-tear and leaves it isolated upon his cheek as a reminder of why it's been shed.

The Ice Queen watches the change within Jonas Dean and feels no regret at dissecting the soul of this man. She kneels down next to him, billows out one side of her robe and wraps the deep red garment around his naked body and holds him close.

Jonas can no longer bring himself to speak and her voice is now nothing more than a faint whisper. "To the King of Europa, to the peoples of the Earthprime, to your Spaceprime colleagues and to the woman that you've lost: you're dead to them all. They'll bury you in the next few weeks and within a short passage of time, the memory of your existence will be buried along with it. At some point in the near future, you'll have a choice to make between your own personal ambitions or the discovery of your inner passions. Heed my warning: resolve your destiny at Saturn's gate. If you should choose ambition and if you venture beyond the great ringed planet, you'll be placed in grave danger and I'll not be able to help you. Here you may come into contact with the Arachnids of Kraylox-Duel, the Fighting Hordes of Telemonoid or the Angels of Gelsen who would grant you immense prolonged gratification whilst they feed off your very soul; at least with the Fighting Hordes your death would be swift."

Captain Jonas Dean of the First Order of the Spaceprime will live through another second, the following minute and the next hour, yet his perception of himself and the life which he's led has changed forever.

He leans into the Ice Queen's cold and comforting body; the ice-tear remaining frozen upon his cheek.

The History of My Life

Is this the history of my life?
Is this the story of my wasted years?
It couldn't get any colder than this,
I never thought that it would end in my tears.

Is this the history of my days?
Is mine a tale that'll remain untold?
My life has changed in so many ways,
I never thought that I could feel so cold.

I could've stayed,
You would've shown me the way,
We could've taken it day by day,
I could've stayed,
If the choice had been mine,
If only I'd have had a little more time,
I could've stayed,
I should've listened to you,
I didn't know what else I could do,
I could've stayed at home with you.

Is this the history of my life?
Is this the story of my failure to see?
Have my eyes been blinded of sight?
I never thought I'd end up in this waking dream.

All I ever wanted was to live for the day,
All you ever needed was a sign from me,
I could've given you a reason to wait,
I never thought that I was wrong you see.

I could've stayed,
You would've shown me the way,
We could've taken it day by day,
I could've stayed,
If the choice had been mine,
If only I'd have had a little more time,
I could've stayed,
I should've listened to you,
I didn't know what else I could do,
I could've stayed at home with you.

CHAPTER 6

My Atlantis Home

Jonas Dean pushed forwards on his elbows with his chin an inch from the dirt; his knees and boots worked in tandem as he inched slowly forwards at a bellied crawl through lazy tall grass to the edge of the treeline. A clearing lay ahead of him and his target was some twenty metres beyond.

His preparation had been the key: his face and hands were caked in mud as he gripped tightly onto his rifle; he had covered himself from head to toe in green camouflage; his helmet was criss-crossed with wire mesh and within the wiring he had placed as much green foliage as would reasonably fit.

Jonas reached the overgrown perimeter which led to the clearing and stopped. Too easy, he thought; his target was within touching distance.

Jonas waited; this time he would wait, not like the last time and the time before that when he had given his position away too early; this time he'd stay put.

He lay quiet and still as he watched for movement whilst his hearing strained for any noise: a cracking of a twig or a rustling of a branch.

His mind started to play the game and he allowed the various scenarios to kick around his head: Jonas's perfected game plan meant that he should stay put for an hour or maybe more; there was no time limit therefore what was the rush?

Patience was an esteemed virtue for a Europa Spaceprime Cadet, and yet Jonas Dean didn't allow his rational thought to complete all of the differing scenarios – he was up on his feet and running, covering the gap from the treeline to the target area with his legs pumping hard, his rifle across his chest and his focus always upon the main prize.

Almost there, he thought as he pushed himself towards his target.

Jonas picked up the sound of the two gunshots as he fell forwards onto his midriff, catching his chin on his rifle on the way down, before landing heavily upon his weapon.

The first shot impacted just above the back of his left ankle, the second was a more painful blow upon the back of his right thigh; the double blow sent him off balance and crashing down to the ground, where his chin bled openly onto hard turf and yet only his pride was hurting.

Jonas looked up and grinned from ear to ear – his target was a tantalising five metres away and he knew what was coming next.

His hand snapped back as he reached for his right thigh, so that he could rub at the moist wet liquid, before bringing his hand back up to his eyeline; he had to be sure. The sticky purple substance spread evenly across his palm, causing Jonas to laugh out loud.

The rules of the game were simple: take your opponent's flag and get it to your own target area to win the point. If you were shot in the body: you forfeit. If you were shot in the leg or arm: you couldn't use that part of your body for the duration of the game; the game wasn't over until you were shot in the torso.

Commander Marks walked out from beyond the treeline at the far side of the clearing's perimeter, his face lit up by a bright smile. "She got you again, Dean. Best of seven and she's already three-nothing clear. My God she's good and you have to stay in your prone position until she decides to come out here and finish you off. Hell, she could take off and have a hot shower, a hearty meal and then she may decide to come back and do you. Rules are rules, there's no time limit and you are pinned my boy," he said in a mocking tone.

Jonas shook his head in disbelief at another four-nothing defeat – that was three in a row. "Kira. Get your backside out here, shoot me quick and finish the game," he shouted out in frustration.

Jonas listened intently whilst Marks stood grinning next to the red target flag which the tank-tested Cadet had failed to take.

"Kira, if you don't get out here now, I'm walking off this training ground," an agitated Jonas yelled defiantly.

Marks playfully wagged his finger at the rule-constrained Cadet Dean.

"Where do you want it soldier boy?" Kira drawled from behind Jonas's prone position.

With his eyes staring down at sodden earth, Jonas replied to Kira Yu with a question of his own. "How did you manage to get me this time?" he asked.

Kira stood over Jonas with her rifle pointed at his backside. "I climbed a tree and watched you take the outer path to the field. I sort of guessed which route you'd take through the meadow. I then picked another tree on the treeline, climbed that and waited for you to arrive. If it's any consolation, I had you in my sights from the moment you entered the lazy tall grass. It was so boring to watch you take over an hour to scramble through the field on your belly," she said in jest.

Jonas heard the hint of sarcasm in her voice and realised that he had been a sitting duck for the past hour or so of the game. "Congratulations, you caned me again. So what are you going to do, shoot me or talk me to death?" he said.

"Can I talk you to death?" Kira asked.

"Don't shoot me in the back of the head or in the arse. If you do, then you'd better start running," Jonas said as a playful veiled threat.

Kira Yu laughed out loud and stepped back three paces: Cadet Yu didn't wish to shoot Cadet Dean from point-blank range even if it was only with a paintball rifle, so she retreated three full strides from Jonas's grounded position, before taking careful aim at the back of his right shoulder, and firing.

*

"Arghhh," Jonas screams and fills his lungs with precious oxygen; his head is pounding and he cannot move his right arm.

Captain Jonas Dean is awake and alone on a twilight Moon and sure that the apparitional Ice Queen is just a figment of a mind which had slipped into unconsciousness.

He tries to move his right arm and quickly realises he has much greater worries than his visions of cold as the searing pain within his right shoulder screams into his brain. Jonas stiffens as he feels the recoil of the deep ache which throbs intrusively into his neck and head. He realises that he will have to find a more comfortable position without aggravating the damage to his arm.

Jonas stares through his head-covered membrane at Ganymede's rocky terrain and acts upon his decision to get onto his back by shifting his weight onto his left shoulder, before attempting to roll over; he grits his teeth against the invasive pain emanating from his right arm which is borderline unbearable.

Although Jonas is tender, sore and uncomfortable, he manages to reposition his body upon the flat plateau's surface, whereupon he lies on his back and stares up into the heavens at the twin beacons of Io and Europa; their faded light shining weakly overhead as Kira Yu's eyes watch over him.

Jonas is in deep and serious trouble; he could probably have got to his feet, but walking back to his Starship is out of the question, so he lifts his left hand to the control panel on the sleeve of his spacesuit and types a five-digit coded command message into the panel upon his right arm to initiate his Medevac protocol.

Jonas rolls back over onto his front and crawls the short distance to his space helmet; his space boots do the majority of the work during his enforced crawl, his mind trained to shut out his incessant suffering, his right shoulder is merely a passenger as he shifts slowly and deliberately across the planetary surface at a bellied crawl. At the crawl's end, he lies upon his stomach next to his precious helmet and vows to stay alert.

"I must not pass out as to pass out would ensure the death that everyone believes has already befallen me," he thinks.

To stay alert, Jonas Dean fills his mind with memories from a distant past.

*

Always pushing and driving forwards at every available opportunity was how Jonas Dean handled his daily life and there had always been an objective for everything that he undertook. His main goal upon joining the Europa Spaceprime elite Cadet Core had been to become an astronaut and achievement of anything less he would have classed as failure.

His goals had become clouded the moment that Kira Yu had arrived back at the training academy exactly two months after being extricated from the tank. Commander Marks had debriefed Cadet Yu for a full two days and made sure that she'd undertaken a full medical assessment before he allowed her back into the classroom environment.

Kira strolled back into the training room on her third day back at the academy to find Jonas decamped and deskbound at the front of the room. One other empty desk was situated next to Jonas and Kira headed straight for her relocated position. She walked in sway with her pastel-shaded wide intelligent eyes focused upon Dean, causing him to shift in his seat, and sat at her allocated adjacent desk, whereupon she turned to face Jonas and gave him a mischievous wink.

The following six months were the most memorable of Jonas's life. He soon realised that Kira didn't wish to become an astronaut – the parts of the Cadet training course that she was most interested in were the studies that incorporated the evolution of the human body and the human mind, the futuristic DNA healing methods and the use of Nanotech technologies in the healing of medical conditions: Kira had always wished for a medical assignment.

Initially, this had thrown Jonas off balance as with every target and with every goal there had always been one constant: competition. But Jonas soon realised that Kira was not a threat to him realising his ambitions and, for the first time in his life, he began to relax, the front that he had put up dissipated and he began to open up.

Commander Marks stood before his two prize students, both of whom had passed their respective tank assignments, feeling deeply proud of their achievement and effort.

The long hours that Cadet Dean and Cadet Yu would spend in his classroom would most certainly be unforgettable as they both had one thing in common which set them apart from the best of the rest of the Europa Spaceprime Cadets: the will to succeed; it had soon become apparent that they both hated to lose.

Dean and Yu thrived on competition and Marks indulged them by allowing them to compete against each other at many disciplines: chess, speed climbing, wrestling, hand-to-hand combat, paintball and many other activities.

Jonas was good at the disciplines which required speed and

strength; Kira always tried to use guile to beat him. In anything that required thought and patience, Kira was virtually unbeatable and Jonas soon realised that he was hopeless.

On the day that Jonas had beaten Kira at chess, he'd disappeared out of the classroom door and done a victory lap of the academy. When the day finally arrived and Kira managed to pin Jonas on the wrestling mat, Marks and Jonas watched her complete a twenty-minute victory dance: the Academy Commander laughed all the way through her routine, but it took a couple of minutes before Jonas started to see the funny side of his defeat. However, there was never any competition over their coursework: Biology and Biochemistry had always been Kira's forte, Aeronautics and Astrophysics had always played to Jonas's strengths and they both had a good handle on Advanced Technologies.

Kira would help Jonas out on her specialised subjects and Jonas dutifully reciprocated, and they bonded through their shared experience.

*

An alarm silently flashes on the cockpit console monitor screen, where a red flashing message clearly reads:

MEDEVAC INITIATED

A flat solid steel stretcher jettisons from beneath the Starship Zx12 and sweeps out towards Jonas Dean's signal which emanates from his spacesuit's control panel.

The flat steel stretcher traverses the contours of Ganymede's groove valley terrain before landing next to the injured Captain Jonas Dean exactly four minutes after its departure.

Unfortunately, Jonas has passed out and the stretcher sits idly next to his limp form; the Ice Queen, Ashilla, bends down over Jonas's unconscious body and lifts him onto the cold steel surface, places his space helmet by his side and does up the two straps to secure him to his lifeline.

Ashilla whispers into Captain Dean's membrane-covered ear, "Do not fear the choice that you make, Jonas Dean."

She moves her solid silver staff across the line of her body and Jonas lifts up on his steel gurney and is sent soaring by his perceived mind's apparition through the Moon's thin atmosphere in the direction of his Starship.

*

Final examinations were almost upon the two star students of the Europa Spaceprime Academy; both had refocused their competitive edges away from their ongoing battles on the sports fields, the gymnasium and any other place where they can have a one-on-one struggle and had buried their heads deeply within their books.

Kira and Jonas hardly spoke to each other in the run-up to their final examinations as energy and focus could not be wasted on personal banter; when they did converse at the academy it was always Kira who had led the conversation and Jonas who had been the willing listener.

Jonas couldn't help himself at first – he always tried to weigh people up, establishing their ambitions and goals whilst trying to ascertain if they were a threat to him or to his calling. Yet with Kira, he just enjoyed listening to her talk.

Kira had often spoken of her passion for the written word and her fulfilment at seeking out and learning new knowledge; she could talk for hours on a meaningless subject or an irrelevant topic and Jonas would drink it all in.

Jonas often teased Kira. "You could talk for the Earthprime," was his favourite saying, at which point Kira would always smile and know that their conversation was at an end.

With four days to go before their final exams, it was Jonas who had done something quite unexpected and, for all of his cockiness and single-minded determination, quite out of character.

Kira sat upon the sun-drenched lawns outside the Europa Spaceprime Academy's main building with four books open at various pages in front of her whilst pretending not to notice Jonas Dean approaching along the winding academy pathway.

With a single book lodged under his arm, Jonas diverted his course and meandered over the cut grass until he stood over a relaxing Kira. "I need your help," he said whilst swallowing hard.

"I'm pretty sure that I've heard you right, but could you just say that again for posterity?" Kira replied as she tilted her head playfully and looked up at an uncomfortable Jonas.

Jonas sat upon lush grass in front of Kira. "Please, this is hard for me; you know that, but I really do need your help," he said once more.

"OK hot-shot. What do you need? Remember though, this is going to cost you," Kira replied, eyeing Jonas.

"I'm screwed on the Biology paper and I really do need to crash some revision to get me through the final exam," Jonas said helplessly; he wasn't used to asking for help from anyone.

"So what's your plan?" Kira said.

"Why don't you come out to my beach house over the weekend with all of your books, so that we can crash some revision for the finals?" It was almost a plea from Jonas.

Kira feigned doubt, yet for all of Jonas's faults, and there were many of them, he had been there for her when she'd been at her lowest ebb. "Alright, but strictly business mind. We go out to your beach house tonight and I'll stay two days and two nights. I want my own bed and I want you to sign a piece of paper to say that you personally asked me for my help when you needed it most," Kira said straight-faced.

"What?" exclaimed Jonas – he was desperate, but was he this desperate?

"You sign the paper or I don't show," Kira teased.

"OK, OK, I'll sign," Jonas said with a nervous smile, before momentarily losing himself within Kira's diverse pastel-shaded eyes.

Kira was the first to break the eye contact and began to close her books before picking them up one by one. "I'll meet you here at six and then follow you in my car to your beach house," she said forthrightly as she stood up.

Jonas could only nod as his heart began to race inside his chest. Jonas's head was telling him that Kira Yu had become a distraction and one that he didn't require at this moment in his life of serving ambitions – but his heart was beating a different tune.

With her books in her hand, Kira strolled seductively off the trimmed grass and onto the winding pathway which led to the academy buildings. Jonas remained cross-legged upon the academy lawns, watching her light movement from afar and unable to take his eyes off her swaying form.

Kira could feel Jonas's wanton stare penetrating the space that she was gliding so easily through. The first time they'd met, Kira had thought Jonas was cocky, intelligent, charming and handsome, however, once she'd scratched the surface, she'd realised that he was an intensely conflicted man who was also kind, generous and emotionally tender. Kira knew that Jonas would think that having these attributes would make him emotionally vulnerable, yet when he was with her, as hard as he'd tried to erect a wall around his emotions, they were too easily identifiable and Kira was almost certain that no-one had touched Jonas's heart.

As she strolled along the academy pathway, Kira stole a glimpse behind; her head turn compelled her flowing locks to fall haphazardly around her face, whereupon she flashed a wide smile at Jonas who was still staring in her direction.

Kira kept on walking as she followed the winding pathway to the academy buildings, aware for the first time that Jonas was interested in her as a woman; she sensed that Jonas was allowing her to get close and wanting her to get close.

Jonas had withdrawn back onto his chosen path towards fulfilling his dreams and had shut her out whilst preparing for the final hurdle of exams, and it had not been the same; Kira had missed cracking heads with him and she longed for his conversation and yearned for his attentive nature.

And finally it had happened, totally out of the blue. Jonas Dean had asked her for her help and Kira would be spending the whole of the weekend at his beach house residence; the situation had now arisen for Kira to steer Jonas emotionally towards her. Kira was pleased at how cool she'd played things, not appearing over eager.

Screw exams, Kira thought as she strode ever onwards to the academy buildings.

*

General Thalt sits behind the heavily framed desk within his office quarters at the Europa Spaceprime Academy with paperwork strewn across his oak table. He's started to prepare his final confidential reports regarding the demise of the Starship Zx12 and the loss of Captain Jonas William Dean.

In stiffening silence, Chief Communications Officer Katherine Jenkins and Cap-com Hubert Snow both stand at attention before him. Thalt, having already acknowledged their attendance, gathers his thoughts, although he's not yet inclined to offer either of his communications team a seat. It was Jenkins and Snow who had requested an audience with their General who is still somewhat perturbed at the loss of the Starship Zx12's mission to the stars.

General Thalt eventually glances up from behind his desk and leans back into the leather of his chair to witness the look upon his fellow controllers' faces, whereupon he can clearly see that his communications crew, having worked tirelessly over the previous twenty-four hours, are both mentally and physically exhausted.

"Take a seat," the General says whilst motioning with his hand at the two vacant chairs behind his desk.

"You wanted to see me?" he says as he casts an eye over his control room crew with the question directed at Katherine Jenkins as a courtesy to her seniority.

Jenkins answers the question which has been thrown in her direction: "General, Officer Snow and I would like to request to remain assigned to the ongoing operation for the foreseeable future. We both feel that if the Starship Zx12 is still on mission and if contact is made then the best communications team should be constantly available to take Dean's communiqué, sir."

Thalt nearly gives away a smile of respect. "Officer Jenkins, Captain Jonas Dean is dead and the Starship Zx12 is lost. Do you have any reason to believe that Captain Dean may still be alive?" he asks candidly.

Chief Communications Officer Katherine Jenkins remains unflinching. "No sir. I believe that Captain Dean is gone, but both Officer Snow and I wish to continue to monitor the communications, sir," she replies.

Thalt inhales deeply whilst casting an eye from Katherine Jenkins to Hubert Snow and then back to his Chief Communications Officer.

NEW DAWN, NEW DAY

"The King of Europa has decided to keep the Europa Spaceprime Mission Control for the Starship Zx12's mission to the stars operational for the next twelve months; mission control will remain online twenty-four hours a day and I'll assign another member of the control room staff to assist you both with ongoing operations," General Thalt decrees.

"Thank you, sir," Katherine Jenkins acknowledges.

"If that is all, then you're dismissed," Thalt says, returning to his paperwork.

Jenkins and Snow both stand and salute their Flight Director General before making their way to his office door. Thalt doesn't appear to take any notice of their pending departure and instead he buries his head in an open file.

Hubert Snow opens his General's office door for Jenkins and allows his Supervisor to brush past him; he's about to follow her through the open doorway when he hears Thalt's voice carrying easily through his General's Quarters. "Officer Snow, do you believe that Captain Jonas Dean is dead?" Thalt asks as he sits back in his chair and invites comment from his able Cap-com.

Snow holds his doorway position and turns to face Thalt: it's an easy question for an able Cap-com to answer and he's aware that it should simply be a yes or no answer. "Sir," Snow says, "we're about to bury Captain Jonas Dean on the premise that his communications are down and therefore there's no signal emanating from the Starship Zx12, causing all of the monitors in the Europa Spaceprime Mission Control to indicate that the Captain is deceased. We have no idea where Captain Dean exited out of hyperdrive but we've made an assumption that the Starship Zx12 crashed within the asteroid belt. We're burying Captain Jonas Dean because of a communications failure and that assumption, I just feel a little uneasy about the whole situation, sir," Hubert Snow replies as he's compelled to give an honest assessment to his General.

Thalt leans forwards in his chair whilst Hubert Snow holds his ground, awaiting a lecture on hard facts and the role of the Flight Director General in the decision-making process.

Thalt speaks with clarity and coherence. "That is why, Officer Snow, I wish for you to remain at your post for the next twelve months," he says coolly.

Hubert Snow smiles openly at his General, something that he's never done before, aware that if he had been in any other situation then Thalt would have been standing at his ear, bawling him out.

"Yes Sir, General, Sir." Snow salutes and means it.

*

Kira Yu arrives back at her apartment in the late afternoon after spending three hours listening to the static discharge which is perpetually flowing over the communications channel within the Europa Spaceprime Mission Control.

For Kira, the loneliness has crept over her soul upon the realisation that Jonas Dean will not be returning home from his mission. All of her adult life she has been alone and it's a feeling that she's comfortable with and has accepted on her own terms; Kira Yu trusts only herself, there are no insecurities in her life and she has full confidence in her own judgement and ability.

Resolve she has in abundance and neither does she suffer from bouts of depression; however, there's a downside to her self-imposed, no-risk social isolation. Kira has become socially empty: she has no social network of friends, no active social life and not a single confidant to talk to about her inner feelings.

Jonas Dean, whether he realised it or not, had changed her perceived needs when they'd bonded at the academy. Kira had found that she could talk to Jonas about anything and he'd listen; she had felt comfortable in his presence.

Kira sits alone upon her plastic restive chair within her spartan surrounds, thinking of what might have been; the weekend that they'd spent together at Jonas's beach house could have changed the outcome of their entwined existence, but it was too late now as he was dead.

*

Captain Jonas Dean regains consciousness onboard the Starship Zx12, where the first thought that enters his throbbing head is that he feels half-dead.

His eyes roll around inside the back of his skull before he becomes totally conscious and aware of his surroundings, realising almost immediately that his movement is severely restricted.

Jonas cranes his neck as he looks down the entire length of his body to see that two straps are shoring him to his lifeline stretcher. He manages to wriggle his left hand free and undo the restraints which are tied across his chest and upper thighs; it's a slow and painful process. He cannot remember how he got onto the steel stretcher or how he managed to securely strap himself in, but thankfully his space helmet is beside him and he's relieved that he'll not have to go back to retrieve it from the summit of the high plateau.

Jonas holds his right arm close to his body as he stands and stumbles over to the cockpit of the Zx12, where he checks his latest computer console readouts to make sure that his Starship is airtight, the hole and his hatches are sealed and a regulated air supply is pumping throughout the ship.

He begins the agonising process of taking off his spacesuit; his membrane will be difficult to remove with one hand and his suit will also prove awkward, and Jonas has to use all of his concentration to remove his suit without inflicting any damage to the garment – if his spacesuit becomes unusable then he'll not be able to step outside of his Starship for the remainder of his mission and any further breach in his ship's hull will kill him; it was more than his life was worth.

A constant stinging throb permeates throughout every pore of his skin as he takes an age to remove his spacesuit without the use of his right arm, expelling deep reserves of energy to complete his task; he's well aware that he could pass out again at any moment.

Standing in the mid-section of his Starship, naked and in intrusive discomfort, he opens up the medical compartment which is situated on the starboard-side of his Starship, extracts a plastic container full of superior painkillers that he'd already tested in the tank and swallows three which is one more than the prescribed dose. After two minutes, Captain Jonas Dean feels immense relief at the subsidence of his invasive suffering.

He allows his hand to drop down to the sensors which are still attached to his torso as the words of the apparitional Ice Queen come crashing down upon him: 'To the King of Europa, to the peoples of the Earthprime, to your Spaceprime colleagues and to the woman that you've lost: you're dead to them all.'

Jonas Dean rips off his body sensors. "I'm not dead yet," he vents stubbornly, before leaning forwards to his starboard-side locker and taking out white shorts and a white crewneck T-shirt; the garments are emblazoned with the black-stitched S-shaped emblem of the Spaceprime. The shorts are easy enough to slip on, yet donning his T-shirt means that some movement is required from his right arm and to Jonas's relief, the painkillers negate his suffering.

His next task is to clear away the small metallic box which contains the microscopic Nanodrones that have fulfilled their programming task; Jonas is indebted to the Nanotech Space

Engineering Corporation as the new technologies of the twenty-second century have without doubt saved his life.

Once his urgent duties have been attended to, Captain Jonas Dean is able to sit back within the confines of his cockpit seat and stare out into Ganymede's twilight; he speaks his thoughts aloud: "If I'm dead to the world, then I have options: I have a Starship with a hyperdrive engine that actually works and I can visit any place I wish within the known system or unknown universe. I'll not be missed, but I cannot afford to dwell on the Ice Queen's prophetic speech; the words of my unconscious mind. I am what I am and it's too late for me to change, yet I cannot make a coherent decision until my shoulder is healed and that's my priority."

Jonas Dean falls silent: he was who he was; a man with his ambitions still very much alive.

*

The afternoon heat had deteriorated with the onset of cool freshening winds and the awakening winds massaged Jonas's face and swept through Kira's long black hair as they sat side by side upon the beach at Atlantis Strand.

Jonas raised an eyebrow when Kira Yu stepped out of her solar-powered, battery-enhanced car with a large suitcase in her hand.

"Going on holiday?" he asked nonchalantly.

"You did say that I was to bring my revision books over," Kira replied unapologetically.

Jonas grabbed hold of Kira's suitcase and walked her around the side of his rustic beach house residence, onto the old wooden veranda and in through his double-doors. Inside his beach house were three old chairs and a well-worn sofa which encircled a small knee-high table. On the two timber walls that ran down either side of his sitting room his congested handmade bookshelves played host to many of his books which were shelved in no particular order whilst his overspill was stacked up in small piles in front of the old wooden units.

"Homey," Kira said as she smiled at Jonas.

"I like it," Jonas replied with a feigned hurt pride.

Secretly though Kira had immediately fallen in love with the beach house's warming charm – it was something which she should have said but didn't; Kira bit down hard on her bottom lip as she fought back the urge to sit down and sort out all of Jonas's littered books.

Jonas began to talk and Kira gave him her full attention. "The kitchen's out back and the two bedrooms are off either side of the kitchen area," he said.

Kira frowned. "Strange layout," she replied.

"Yeah, I know – I think the guy who built the beach house liked to eat in the middle of the night and always needed to be close to his fridge," Jonas said, laughing at his own aside.

Kira instinctively smiled, but only because Jonas appeared to be enjoying himself.

"I'll show you the way to your room so that you can dump your bags, before we go and sit out under what's left of the sun. We can eat and revise later," Jonas said, on the move.

"OK," Kira replied and followed Jonas into her weekend room.

*

Under the early evening sun, Jonas and Kira ate and spoke without inhibition, listening to each other's stories and anecdotes until darkness fell over the ocean, whereupon Jonas pointed at the dark starry skies and named the constellations in the clear night sky. As the full Moon usurped the night, Jonas liberated blankets from his beach house and built a fire, before they both fell asleep under the Moon and the stars.

*

Captain Jonas Dean has two beds at his disposal within the Starship Zx12: a simple cot that can be pulled out at any time when he needs to get a few hours of sleep or a second option for critical circumstances.

Jonas chooses the emergency second option: the Nanosec medical bed. It was called the lifeboat by his medical team and he'd been given full instructions on how to use the plastic bath, although Jonas had always hoped that it would never have to be made operational. However, for Captain Jonas Dean, this is a dire medical emergency.

His medical bed pulls easily out from the lower base of his ship's starboard-side compartment and snaps readily into its fixed position. Jonas opens up another compartment above the plastic basin to expose the bath's feeding tubes whilst next to his liquid lifeline is housed a small water tank: the water tank is labelled "Nanosec Medical".

Jonas presses a single fat button at the side of his plastic bath, causing his liquid lifeline to glow in deepest blue, before he retreats back to the cockpit of his Starship and stares at his console monitor.

The console computer monitor flashes a red warning message:

NANOSEC TECHNOLOGIES

Warning – Nanodrone activation imminent

Jonas brings up the detailed X-ray and MRI scan which had been taken prior to lift-off and fed into the Zx12's main computer by his medical team. Sitting awkwardly at his cockpit console, he uses his left hand to feel along the bone-line of his sagging right shoulder which is covered in a ripening reddish-purple bruise; he finds the bump on his fracture site and makes his own assessment: a broken collarbone.

Jonas sits up stiffly on the hard metal of his cockpit seat: he already has his medical bed partially set up and a decision needs to be made. "Time for some sleep," Jonas says rationally as he leans forwards to the keyboard upon his cockpit console array.

*

Kira awoke to the soothing sounds of the waves caressing the shoreline and lifted herself up onto her elbow to watch Jonas who was sleeping deeply under the new dawn; the embers of the previous night's campfire were still vividly aglow as Kira sat up to view the waves rolling in upon the beachfront.

Heaven, she thought.

With Jonas still asleep, Kira decided to take an early morning walk along the long stretch of coastline. She grabbed hold of her sweater, wrapped it around her waist and trudged off through freshly cleansed sands to the sea's edge, where she stepped in and out of the tepid waters breaking gently over the fine sands of Atlantis Strand.

Jonas woke as Kira wandered over the sands of Atlantis beach and watched as she moved gracefully down towards the shoreline, fully understanding the peace and tranquillity of his beachfront haven. He smiled warmly at Kira's every movement as she walked through the new dawn's watery coldness, sensing that she was at peace with herself in this restful place. He continued to gaze upon her as she walked along the coastal reach until she finally became a small figurine on the shoreline landscape.

Jonas decided to prepare breakfast, knowing that Kira would return when she realised she was hungry. He arranged the food and only after he had peered out of his double doors and seen that she was making her way back up the shoreline to his beach house retreat did Jonas amble back into his kitchen to fire up his stove, where bacon and eggs were the order of the day.

Kira entered Jonas's beach house just as breakfast was ready and sat at the old wooden table within the kitchen area.

"Feel better?" Jonas asked as he placed a steaming mug of hot coffee in front of her.

"Yeah, the walk certainly helped me to wake up and also helped me to think," Kira replied, sipping coffee gratefully.

"You shouldn't think too much; it's bad for you," Jonas said as he placed the bacon and eggs which he'd diligently prepared in front of Kira.

"You're being ironic of course," Kira replied as she began to eat.

"What do you mean?" Jonas asked as he sat down opposite her.

Kira played her primed statement over in her mind; it's time to probe a little, she thought. "You think all of the time. I can almost hear you thinking. It's not a criticism, it's what makes you who you are," Kira said, pulling up short of what she really wished to say as she waited for a reaction from Jonas.

"You're right, I do think too much and sometimes about things that are not important. I was brought up in an area where the next family lived ten miles away and until I was old enough to go to school I either spoke to my parents or I spoke to myself," Jonas said openly.

Kira used silence as a cover to conceal her own recognition of his upbringing. Jonas's cold harsh truthful reality had affected all of their lives – eight out of ten people had died during the Third World War and society had become fractured which was one of the many after affects that had been encountered by a fledgling population. Jonas had been lucky; at least he'd had his parents to talk too.

Kira intentionally hid her past from Jonas and resolved to press her point home. "As one of the great thinkers of our time, you're not seriously going to consider taking this astronaut gig are you? Because if all of the rumours are true, then you'll be trapped inside a Starship that can allegedly travel at interstellar speeds. Jonas, to the rational mind, it's a one-way ticket: a suicide mission," she said, before reaching out and holding onto Jonas's hand. "I've known you long enough to know that you're a deeply intelligent and rational man. Do you think your life is so worthless that you'd willingly throw it all away? Have you really thought this through?" she asked.

Kira had stunned him with her clinical assessment and Jonas let go of her hand in haste – he had thought that she would have been the one person on the planet who would have understood him. Jonas chose his next words carefully. "I've geared my whole life towards this moment in time and I cannot and must not throw this opportunity away. The Europa Spaceprime would never send me out into the wilderness of the spatial void unless they thought that I'd have a fighting chance of getting back. I of all people know how dangerous this mission will be. The last spaceflight from Earth was lost with all hands, but just think of the sights that I'll see and the journey that I'll undertake. Surely that is something to risk your life for?"

Kira looked desperately into Jonas's eyes, the windows of his soul, but all she could see was the burden of his all-consuming ambitions. Kira had knocked a few bricks out of his emotional wall and yet his wall remained intact as Jonas had closed himself off from any outside influence and was hurtling towards his goal. Although Kira had the rest of the weekend to try to weaken his resolve, she knew in her heart that she would not be able to change or alter his course.

Sipping at her hot coffee, Kira decided to change tack. From her trouser pocket, she pulled out two stones which she had collected on her coastal walk and placed them upon the old wooden tabletop.

"I found these upon the beach this morning," Kira said.

In wonder, Jonas looked down at the two stones that she had placed upon the kitchen table, before catching Kira's eyes; the two beach stones were roughly the same size and shape and the pigmentation of the smooth weathered rocks clearly matched Kira's irises: one was a powder blue and the other ochre brown.

"Pick one," Kira said amiably.

Jonas took an age trying to decide, before giving up. "I cannot possibly choose between your eyes," he replied.

With a reassuring smile, Kira said, "That's OK. Some days I prefer my left eye and on other days I prefer my right eye, but on days like today I like them both the same; you really don't want to be anywhere near me on the days when I dislike them both."

Jonas chuckled. "Does that day happen very often?" he asked.

"No, only on rare occasions," she offered.

Kira eyed her two stones and pushed the powder blue pebble towards Jonas. "I'm going to give you this one," she said quietly.

"Why the blue stone?" Jonas asked, intrigued by her decision.

"I think it's because it'll match my mood on the day that you travel into the dark recesses of deep space," Kira said with a resigned shrug.

And Jonas Dean fell silent.

*

Captain Jonas Dean sits in his cockpit seat in front of his cockpit console array and types in his security code. He follows the medical programming protocol and brings up the X-ray and MRI scan results. On his X-ray, he highlights the area of bone around his shoulder where his break has occurred as this will be the target area for his healing programme and sets the time for the healing event to commence in one hour; Jonas will have one hour to finish his preparation of his medical bed and put his Starship into sleep mode.

He sits stiffly at his cockpit console array – only one decision remains: a broken collarbone will take six to eight weeks to heal. Jonas's final decision is to set the healing time on his medical programme to last for four months.

"If I'm assumed dead then I might as well play dead," Jonas says coldly to himself.

*

Jonas lounged upon one of the old chairs within his beach house residence. The midday sun lit up his living room and also, Jonas noted, the dust. The blue stone that Kira had given him at breakfast was displayed in full view on top of one of his old wooden bookcases. Still neither one of them had crashed any revision for their impending examinations.

After breakfast, Kira had disappeared into her room. Jonas had left her alone and allowed a full hour to pass before contemplating whether or not he should go and knock on her door; at that moment he heard the creaking of the old wooden doorframe and guessed that she was about to make a reappearance.

Jonas's jaw dropped as he cast his eyes over Kira who marched past him to the open double doorway which led out to the midday heat and the warming sands.

Kira was wearing a canary yellow bikini, her long black hair was tied back and her cool sunglasses rested evenly upon the bridge of her nose; an overly large beach towel was draped over her right shoulder and she carried two biology workbooks in her left hand.

Kira turned before exiting the double-doors onto the old wooden veranda and looked back over her darkened shades. "Are you going to sit there all day J.D. or are we going to catch some sun?" she asked whilst putting on her sexiest lilt.

Jonas realised that he had been gaping at Kira's lithe physique and closed his mouth promptly. "Give me five minutes," he replied whilst jumping off the well-worn chair and rushing to his bedroom to find his beachwear.

They spent the day on the beach and in the sea, soaking up the sun and revising for their impending examinations until the afternoon breeze rescinded the midday heat.

Kira went in search of a handful of assorted beach stones to place on top of her workbooks to stop her papers from disappearing to all corners of the seafront in the freshening winds, before once more sitting beside Jonas in the comforting breeze. She had decided that it was time for her to probe a little more. "Jonas, you kissed me once, do you remember?" she asked.

Jonas hadn't seen the question coming and didn't have his answer prepared; he'd thought that Kira was completely out of it upon the night he'd chaperoned her comatose form back to the familiarity of her apartment, so he threw the question back at her. "I think you'll find that it was you who kissed me," he said playfully.

Kira feigned horror. "You took advantage of me," she mocked.

"You took me by surprise. I wasn't expecting it," Jonas replied.

It was time for Kira to bring matters to a head and her question penetrated: "Why haven't you tried to kiss me again?"

Jonas stalled his answer by looking down at the sands but soon realised that however hard he stared at the eternal grains was an irrelevance as he wouldn't find his answer upon Strand sands. Jonas finally found the words to convey his inner doubts. "It would be unfair on you if the next week or month passes by and I'm chosen as the Europa Spaceprime astronaut elect – it wouldn't be right for me to get too involved with anyone, only to leave and maybe never return," he said.

And there it was: Jonas Dean's ambitious nature had reared its head once more. However, giving in wasn't Kira's style. "OK," she said, "I know you well enough to understand your thought processes and how you arrived at your decision. So why did you invite me out here this weekend? Was it Alpha: your one and only interest is to be named as the Europa Spaceprime astronaut elect and you really did ask me out here to help you revise? Was it Beta: you don't really have any desire to be named as the Europa Spaceprime astronaut elect; you just thought that you'd enrol in the Cadet core because you knew that you'd look good in the uniform? Was it Chimera: you invited me out to your beach house retreat because you wanted to gain another notch on your surfboard? Or was it Delta." Kira stopped short as giving Jonas the final option would leave her emotions fully exposed.

Kira reached up and took off her dark shades, and through eyes of ochre brown and powder blue she held Jonas's gaze.

For the first time in her life, Kira exposed her true felt self. "Delta: you fell in love with me the first time that you saw me and now you can't stop thinking about me," she conveyed to Dean.

Jonas's default reaction would usually have been to walk away from an assault on his guarded interior, his instinctive mechanism being to protect himself from any exposure on an emotional level. Yet not giving Kira an answer would have been unfair as Kira, of all of the people he knew, didn't deserve such an ignorant deceit. The question reverberated around his head and Jonas was aware that he'd have to yield an answer to her poised posed directness, and that there was a right answer, which was also the answer that Kira wished to hear, and a safe response to shield his own burgeoning ambitions within the Europa Spaceprime core.

Jonas would have liked to have brushed off the question which he'd been confronted with and to have offered Beta or Chimera as an answer. Yet the only answer which he'd be able to give would be Alpha although he was aware it was an answer that Kira didn't wish to hear – Jonas realised that Kira wished for his answer to be Delta which was the answer that his very heart and soul screamed for.

Jonas had known the answer to the question as soon as Kira had asked it: the answer was Delta, yet Jonas gave Kira the only answer which he could offer to serve his ambitious desires.

"Alpha," Jonas stuttered as ambition's path defeated self-fulfilment.

Kira turned her head away and looked beyond Strand sands towards the open seas and spoke quietly in response. "Jonas, I crave the simple life and someone to share that life with, and I thought I'd seen something in you which led me to believe you felt the same way; I was wrong. Jonas, be careful that you do not drown within your own solitude."

Coolly, Kira swept away from Jonas and walked over the Strand sands of Atlantis beach towards the ocean's swell, where she immersed herself in cold seas and swam to expel frustration's energies as Kira didn't wish for Jonas Dean to see the tears she was beginning to shed.

Jonas watched as Kira swam in tepid waters off the sands of Atlantis Strand; his emotions should have remained unscathed, but he felt deflated and beaten. He couldn't leave the situation as it was as he had already lived a lifetime containing his feelings in isolation and keeping his emotions in check. Kira Yu was the first woman he'd met with whom he'd wished to share his thoughts, fears and doubts with and Kira would never forgive him if he allowed for the status quo to remain. Her thoughts and feelings towards him mattered.

Jonas's protective emotional wall crumbled, whereupon he slowly rose and walked barefoot down the beached sands until he halted at the sea's edge with his mind crammed full of thoughts of what he would say when Kira emerged from her swim, when he would tell her that she was his only thought when he woke in the morning and his last thought at night, before he's overcome by deep sleep. Jonas Dean would tell Kira Yu that she was the one, the only one, and he would ask her to wait for him.

He stood proudly resolved upon the Strand sands of Atlantis beach, smiling through his renewed aspirations and knowing that his life would be whole with Kira standing resolutely at his side.

Kira had chosen to punish herself by swimming against the tide, and she continued to swim, pumping her legs and flinging her arms forwards until on the hint of tiring she began to tread water with her gaze drifting towards the shoreline, from where Jonas was watching her.

The whirring rotors of the twin-bladed helicopter which had appeared from over the distant hills were gathering to a crescendo as the metal bird swooped in low over Jonas's beachfront retreat.

Following Kira's semi-submerged gaze, Jonas Dean looked skywards in the direction of the invasive sound penetrating his idyllic shoreline home and watched as the swooping helicopter attempted a landing about fifty metres from his beach house residence, the metallic bird's twin rotors shifting sands in all directions.

Kira began to swim urgently towards the shore, having already noticed the uniformed crewman jumping out of the landed craft's rear and rapidly making his way to an unmoving Jonas Dean. The helicopter carried all of the markings of the Europa Spaceprime and was stamped with the King of Europa's own private seal.

Jonas watched as the crewman jogged towards him, before turning back to the open seas. Kira: he needed to speak to her privately before he could even think about why the King's helicopter had landed upon the beach. But events were beginning to move far too quickly.

Kira reached the beach at Atlantis Strand just as the crewman of the helicopter stood at attention and saluted Jonas.

The crewman pulled out a piece of paper from the breast pocket of his uniform and handed it to Jonas. "Your orders, sir," he said formally.

A reeling Jonas Dean read his delivered paperwork. "Immediately?" he said, surprised and taken aback by the sudden orders.

"Yes sir. My orders are to get you immediately," the crewman restated, and he would not be taking no for an answer.

Jonas passed his orders to Kira.

BY HIS MAJESTY'S DECREE
ASSIGNMENT: IMMINENT
REPORT TO THE PALACE APARTMENTS AT 1600 HOURS

And the Europan Monarch had personally signed the order.

"Sir, time is against us," the crewman stated.

"I need one minute," Jonas pleaded.

The crewman glanced at Kira and yielded to Jonas's request. "I'll wait in the helicopter, but be quick mind," he said, before turning to his landed twin-blade whose dual rotors were still spinning at high speed.

Although he hadn't expected to be summoned until some time after his final exams, Jonas should have been elated by his summons as this was it: the culmination of his training; his lifetime's ambition achieved.

What could he say to Kira Yu in one minute? Jonas could only stare into her colour-contrasting eyes, unable to find the words to express his soul's desire; his dammed emotions were withheld within, not only to protect himself but to also distance Kira from any hope that she may have had of them having a future together. His pathway was set; his pathway was clear. His mission was very probably a one-way ticket and he wouldn't allow Kira to wait and suffer – they both had to move on.

Kira could see the helplessness in Jonas's eyes as she moved her wet body into his. She held onto him tightly as she quietly whispered into his ear. "Go, and I'll stay and wait for your return," she lied as she tried to make departure easier for Jonas.

Jonas held Kira, a part of him not wanting to let her go as too much had been left unsaid that needed saying. And yet Jonas still could not find the words to convey his inner passions.

Kira pulled away from the pending Europa Spaceprime spaceman, leaving Jonas at arm's length whilst holding both of his hands within hers. "Go, and don't look back," she asserted.

Jonas turned his head towards the beached helicopter and moved with urgency over the churning sands which were being whipped up by the twin-bladed metallic bird; the helicopter's engines roared their approval at his approach.

Jonas reached the helicopter's back hatch and froze at its entry point, glancing back over his right shoulder to see the waves rolling up the beach and breaking over Kira's legs.

Kira Yu: a victim of his own burgeoning ambitions standing gracefully isolated upon the Strand sands of Atlantis beach in her canary yellow bikini, looking out to sea and vowing to never shed another tear for Jonas Dean, yet unable to bear his departure.

For Jonas Dean, that would be the last time that he would see Kira Yu before the ascent of the Starship Zx12.

*

The deep blue liquid settles at the base of Captain Jonas Dean's medical bed; the Nanodrone-infested mixture is programmed and ready for its patient.

Jonas double-checks that there are no outstanding alarms on his cockpit console array and places the Starship Zx12 into sleep mode so that his air temperature and his oxygen supply can be regulated by his ship's computer as he sleeps, because if there's an emergency once he's asleep then he wouldn't be able to awaken.

He dims the lights onboard his Starship. "This might be it, I may never awaken. Has it all been worth it?" he asks himself aloud. Captain Jonas Dean has seen many awe-inspiring sights which no other human being has ever witnessed at first hand. "Is it still worth the effort, if you've no-one to tell?" he ponders. Jonas leaves his final statement hanging in the dimly lit mid-section of the Starship Zx12 as he takes a hold of his pre-prepared syringe and checks the dose that he'll be self-injecting, so as not to knock himself out for a decade; the dose is equal to four months of deep sleep. He finds a vein in his arm, slips the needle in and depresses the syringe until he can feel its measured liquid coursing through his system.

Captain Dean steps into his medical bath and lies down upon his viscose bed. He reaches up and takes hold of the feeding tube from his starboard-side compartment and pushes the plastic tubing into the back of his throat then bites down hard upon the feeder's mouthguard, so as to fix his lips, teeth and tongue into a set position as he sleeps. He secures the feeder's strap around the back of his head and the plastic tubing extends down his oesophagus and into his stomach; the dose which he has self-administered also contains a sedative and Jonas doesn't feel the feeding tube.

He becomes drowsy and begins to sink into the deep blue gelatinous liquid; his body immerses into the coagulated fluid until only his head protrudes from the surface. His eyelids turn heavy as dancing neon blue lights light up in front of his clouding vision; the Nanodrones have activated and they're on the move. In the final moments before sleep overwhelms him, he watches as the microscopically engineered organisms pack his shoulder and harden, providing Jonas with a cast for the next four months as the break in his collarbone heals. Within his plastic bath are more microscopically engineered organisms that will perpetually clean his thick watery bed and moisturise his body, as well as dormant Nanodrones which will activate after a time-lag of one week and begin to massage his body thus slowing down his muscle wastage, staving off sores and allowing his blood to flow more easily through his sleeping form.

Jonas's last thoughts are of Kira Yu: a final vision of her standing upon the beach at Atlantis Strand, wearing her canary yellow bikini and looking out to sea.

"Kira," Jonas exhales her name as sleep prevails.

*

"Kneel as Jonas Dean," the King of Europa ordered.

Jonas knelt and raised his head towards his Sovereign Prime.

The Europan Monarch cleared his throat. "Your mission, Cadet Dean, is to captain the Starship Zx12 and search for the lost Stargazer class vessel, the ill-fated HMS Neon-Lit City, at its last known co-ordinates. Your assignment will be undertaken after twelve months of intensive training. Do you accept your mission, Jonas Dean?" the King asked.

Jonas kept the smile which had been threatening to burst out on proceedings off his face. "Yes Sire, I accept," he replied.

"Then rise as Captain Jonas Dean," the King said, clearly enjoying the ceremony.

Jonas stood from bended knee and faced his Sovereign Prime with his hands clasped behind his back and his proud chest pushing out.

"Captain Dean, you'll be taken from this place to a secret location where you'll undertake twelve months of intensive training as Europa Spaceprime's astronaut elect. At the successful conclusion of your training you'll then be given the honour of captaining the Starship Zx12 on her maiden voyage," the King said, before stooping down low and blatantly winking at his Europa Spaceprime protege.

"Congratulations, Captain Dean," the Monarch of Europa whispered privately before the proud King stood back up to his full height and stepped back two paces.

General Thalt stepped out from the rank and file of the three attending generals who had been standing at attention behind their Sovereign Prime. "Captain Dean, you'll go to your home and collect any essential items that you may need for your astronaut training. Do not then expect to return to your place of residence for the next twelve months," Thalt ordered.

Déjà vu, Jonas thought as Thalt continued with his short brief. "A helicopter will pick you up at your beach house residence at 0600 hours tomorrow. Do you have any questions?" he asked.

"No sir," Jonas replied.

"Then you're dismissed," Thalt said, saluting the Captain of the First Order of the Spaceprime.

As protocol permitted, Jonas returned the salute and then turned on a booted heel and marched out of his King's apartment hall.

General Thalt watched Jonas's back as he made his way down the wide expanse of the King's long hall whilst the Europan Monarch moved magisterially alongside his faithful General.

"Sire, is he our best hope?" a concerned General Thalt asked of his regent.

"Thalt, he's our only hope," the King of Europa replied, laying a hand on his loyal General's shoulder.

Dusk had fallen upon the evening when Jonas finally arrived back at his empty beach house retreat from the King's calling to court; his shack was shuttered and empty: Kira hadn't waited and Jonas couldn't blame her for not staying.

Jonas walked across the Strand sands of Atlantis beach to the waterfront terminus, where the seas were swelling and the winds were rising to gust.

He stood alone upon the beach at Atlantis Strand, looking out towards the ocean as the salt-spray carried on the swirling winds left a bitter saline taste upon his lips; heavy bleak clouds were gathering and sinking on the darkening distant horizon as a rising storm began to hunt down the ocean's waves which were attempting to flee its growing anger.

*

Captain Jonas Dean lies inert in his treacly liquid-filled medical bed, defeated by injected sleep.

Jonas dreams of his beach house retreat and the tranquillity of his Atlantis home, yet his dreams are turning to storm.

He's standing alone upon the beach at Atlantis Strand with a howling gale whipping in off the ocean, shivering as the sea spray soaks him through to his skin and chilling his heart.

Beyond the ocean, heavy bleak clouds are gathering and sinking on the darkening distant horizon.

A great storm is moving in.

My Atlantis Home

I misread the signals and ignored all the signs; I let it all pass me by,
When I walked away, I'd nothing left to say; you must have asked
yourself why.
We had our special days, you had your special ways; I wish I'd
listened to you more,
Now I'm waiting here in this tranquil place; you can give me a call.

If you want me, I'll be at my Atlantis home,
If you need me, I'll be at my Atlantis home,
If you want me, I'll be at my Atlantis home,
You can call me on the telephone at my Atlantis home.

My Atlantis home, idyllic paradise of this island land,
Ocean green, I walk upon the shore and lie upon the sand,
I watch the white horses roll in off the sea,
Bittersweet memories of you come flooding over me.

If you want me, I'll be at my Atlantis home,
If you need me, I'll be at my Atlantis home,
If you want me, I'll be at my Atlantis home,
You can call me on the telephone at my Atlantis home.

At my Atlantis home, the storm clouds gather within a troubled sky,
The ocean's in turmoil, the swell begins to rise on the high tide,
I watch the white horses crash in from the sea,
I remember the days we had and the way it used to be.

If you want me, I'll be at my Atlantis home,
If you need me, I'll be at my Atlantis home,
If you want me, I'll be at my Atlantis home,
You can call me on the telephone at my Atlantis home.

My Atlantis home, a blood red sky consumes the evening night,
Ocean deep, I walk beneath the Moon in the fading light,
I watch the wild horses roll in off the sea,
A melancholy evening we spent watching the sun's retreat.

If you want me, I'll be at my Atlantis home,
If you need me, I'll be at my Atlantis home,
If you want me, I'll be at my Atlantis home,
You can call me on the telephone at my Atlantis home.

If you want me, I'll be at my Atlantis home,
If you need me, I'll be at my Atlantis home,
If you want me, I'll be at my Atlantis home,
You can call me on the telephone at my Atlantis home.

CHAPTER 7

Satellite City

For five hours, five Kings have sat at the pentagonal table and still the Queen of Asia will not look directly at the King of Europa.

An uncomfortable Europan King waits for the votes to be counted. He already senses that one of his arguments is lost, and his political allies also haven't wavered during their denunciation of his second piece of legislation.

Europa's Sovereign Prime sits stony faced; to his left sits his ally, King Johnson of the Kingdom of Americas, and to his right sits the King of the South; upon the two regal chairs facing opposite sit the King of Asia, for so long a natural ally, and next to him a man whose ideology he opposes, King Bern of the Kingdom of the North. The Queen of Asia, with her regal head bowed, is seated directly behind the Asian King and is unable to acknowledge the Europan King's existence.

The King of Europa turns in his chair to where Lady Guinevere and Lady Anne are sitting directly behind him and in front of the King's three generals, who are seated beyond the two first ladies of the Europa Earthprime: Europa's arrowhead aimed straight and true at the pentagonal star.

Guinevere smiles at her King who has turned her way. "My lord," she says.

The rightful Monarch of Europa, whilst keeping his voice low, says bitterly, "I've a bad feeling about this vote, Guinevere, as events aren't going the way I'd hoped. I sense that the first vote is gone and if the second vote is lost then I'll not be amused."

"My lord, I believe that commonsense will prevail," Guinevere replies earnestly, before an intervening Southern King coughs enthusiastically, causing the King of Europa to return to the political fray and view the Southern Prime who is standing ready to make the voting announcements over the pentagonal star. "My fellow Kings, the voting is in. The first item of legislation put forward by the King of Europa is as follows. I, the King of Europa, would decree an extension to the backing of the Europa Spaceprime Starship Zx class Space Program with a particular emphasis on a mission to seek out the wreckages of the HMS Neon-Lit City and the Starship Zx12: Votes cast: five. Abstentions: none. Votes for: one. Votes against: four," he decrees.

The King of Europa doesn't flinch at the announcement. His cold eyes stare down at the symbolic legislative star, fearing that both of the lost Europa Spaceprime missions will now never be found under his reign, and realising that a King's promise to Captain Jonas Dean lies in ruins.

The Southern King continues, "The second item of legislation that has been put forward by the King of the North is as follows. I, the King of the North, would decree a return to an economy-based system whereby a currency is introduced and all of the peoples of the Kingdoms of the Earthprime are paid for their endeavours and a taxation policy is negotiated between the Kings of the Kingdoms and the peoples of the Earthprime: Votes cast: five."

The King of Europa's crossed fingers rest upon his thighs underneath the Pentagonal table.

"Abstentions: one," the Southern King announces.

The Europan King's head lifts sharply and he stares directly at the Queen of Asia who is sitting adjacent to the Asian attaché, Tashi Chi; the Asian Queen catches the King's eye with a sly wink – the King of Asia has not voted against the King of Europa but has instead abstained, and all is not lost.

"Votes for: two. Votes against: two. I hereby decree that neither motion is carried," the King of the South concludes.

The King of Europa immediately takes to his feet and walks with regal authority to his holding room which is situated beyond the circumference of the circular chamber, where he's joined by his most loyal subjects.

The door is bolted shut behind the Europan Sovereign Prime who begins to pace and talk. "Have these people learnt nothing from our history? A return to an economic model would set off a chain of events that would lead to our inevitable downfall. It's happened before; why should it not happen again? Corporate greed, the emergence of a super-class society and the intense bleeding of our natural resources set off the catastrophic chain of events of the twenty-first century and Bern is trying to kick-start the whole process again. We all know what's behind his ideological drive – I think King Bern has found a fresh supply of untapped oil or natural gas in the Arctic regions and is trying to make everyone else pay for his find, instead of following the laid-down procedure of logging the find and discussing with his fellow Kings where the newfound resource can be best utilised."

A sighing King seats himself next to Lady Guinevere, his annoyance melting away into calm. "I thought that the vote to return to an economy-based system was lost as Bern has been pushing for an endorsement of his ideology for well over five years. Lady

Guinevere was right in her assessment: commonsense did prevail; however, it may only be a matter of time until we lose the ideological battle. Since we lost Captain Jonas Dean and the Starship Zx12 exactly one month ago, I fear that my judgement has been called into question even by the closest of my allies. At present, I am a political pariah and I need to enforce a change of attitudes before our next meeting which will take place in four months and when I will once again push for an extension to the backing of our Starship Zx class Space Program. My father, the late King, made a promise to all of the families of the brave and bold men and women of the HMS Neon-Lit City, and I have made a promise to Captain Jonas Dean to send out a mission to search for him, even though I know that he's lost to us all," the King states with his sharp eyes narrowing. His final words on the matter are as hard as stone: "I intend to keep all of the promises that have been made."

*

The able Cap-com Hubert Snow prefers to have the continuous static discharge on the loudspeaker as background noise; the harsh constant noise infringes nightly upon the Europa Spaceprime Mission Control.

For the first few nights after the loss of the Starship Zx12, Hubert Snow had listened keenly to the crackling static through his earphones, trying to hear a break in sound or a hidden background anomaly in the cacophony of noise, but the static's crackle had remained constant. After a week, Snow has decided to run the static discharge over the loudspeaker as it is far more comfortable for him to listen to as he slips into his nightly routine.

Katherine Jenkins and Hubert Snow have decided upon rotating twelve-hour shifts for their twelve-month assignment. Snow has offered to do a permanent night turn, starting at 1800 hours and finishing at 0600 hours, which leaves Jenkins to work the day shift. They have also been approached by Doctor Grace James and Doctor Aileen Grey, both of whom have offered to cover shifts when they can to allow the members of the communications team to have an occasional day off. Although the two doctors have been reassigned to set up the medical facilities on the new Moonbase, they still wish to be involved with the search for Captain Jonas Dean and the Starship Zx12.

At the Europa Spaceprime Mission Control, Hubert Snow stands up from his desk, where his view is filled by a large map of the solar system which is bereft of the signal that should have originated from the Starship Zx12; the flatlines are running constant across all of Captain Dean's life sign monitors, the telemetry screens remain devoid of data and all of the other monitors have been switched off.

Snow runs his hand through what's left of his hair as he vows not to allow his initial hope dwindle in a situation that's well beyond his scope of control.

The able Cap-com grabs his empty cup from his desk and checks the mission control clock which shows the current mission time elapsed at twenty-eight days; coffee is all that gets Snow through the static-filled backdrop of the night. The time is fast approaching 2200 hours and he knows she'll be here soon; Hubert Snow could set his solid silver Europa Spaceprime watch by her.

*

Kira Yu reaches the glass door entrance to the public viewing gallery, holding onto the loaned swipe card which had been given to her by Marks; she inserts it vertically through the plastic card reader and, when the paned door slides easily aside, Kira steps inside, moving with a purpose towards the front of the public viewing gallery and gazing over a now too familiar scene.

Kira places a workbook and an assignment she's been getting to grips with on one of the adjacent chairs and places a coffee that she's been carrying onto the floor next to the seat she always occupies during her nightly vigil, before marching over to a wall-mounted communications device and switching it to the on position, igniting the heady discharge of static within the soundproof public viewing gallery.

For twenty-eight days her routine has been the same. Commander Marks has seconded Kira to the Moonbase medical facilities project under the watchful eye of Doctor Grace James who is not the ogre that everyone has made her out to be and who has allowed Kira to work a permanent afternoon shift. James has been briefed by Commander Marks that Kira Yu and Jonas Dean had been close at the academy and she is mindful to accommodate her medical colleague until such a time comes to pass when Kira will be willing to let Captain Jonas Dean fade from what might have been to memory.

For two hours every night, Kira sits in the public viewing gallery, listening to the incessant static and watching redundant monitors. On her twenty-eighth night, Kira sips at her coffee in the midst of the continuous blistering rhythmic hum and smiles wryly as Hubert Snow appears back at his desk with his freshly made mug. "Hubert Snow and his ten o'clock coffee, I could set my Europa Spaceprime watch by him," Kira says quietly to herself as she tries desperately to make light of her situation.

*

The ritual service would be without pomp and without ceremony; a solemn occasion for the waiting King of Europa who stands flanked by Lady Anne as the twin representatives of the Europa Earthprime. Having arrived back from the World Conference and after a restless night's sleep, this is a day that the Europan Prime hasn't been looking forward to.

The anteroom is situated within the heart of the Europa Spaceprime Academy complex; its close interior walls are adorned with intricately decorated wooden carvings, thus giving the room its mournful character.

"A fitting place to lay Captain Jonas Dean to rest," proclaims the King to the lady who has waited at his side.

The Monarch at Europa's helm quietens as Josiah and Evie Dean respectfully make their way into the chamber of lost souls; Josiah Dean nods to his King in recognition of his own personal respect for the hand of Europan authority.

The four converge and stand silently over the closed empty coffin, Josiah Dean holding onto his wife as she sobs sorrowfully through her grief.

Grief was a powerful emotion that had befallen the Europan Monarch when his father, the old King, had died and the King of Europa will give Captain Jonas Dean's parents all the time they need to seek out the closure which they will never find.

After a while, Josiah steps forwards to his Monarch who has mourned at his side, and allows the King to place a hand upon his grief-stricken shoulder.

The King of Europa speaks to Josiah Dean with a passion. "I cannot comprehend your loss. All the days of his life and your lives have led to this moment in time and I count myself responsible for your son's death. It was my decision to send Captain Jonas Dean out into the heavens and I'll live with the weight of that burden on my shoulders for the rest of my life, but you must know this, Josiah Dean, and I make this promise to you as the King of Europa. I will send out a mission beyond the Moon to find your boy and I make this promise to you, just as my father made the same promise to all of the families of the civilian astronauts onboard the HMS Neon-Lit City."

Josiah lays a hand onto his King's which still rests upon his shoulder. "Thank you my Lord. I don't blame you for what has happened to my son and you must not blame yourself. He was a headstrong lad who knew his own mind and had taken his own risks and you cannot and must not be burdened by his death," he respectfully replies.

Lady Anne's eyes widen — she has been moved by the conversation which has just taken place. The three generals and Lady Guinevere are not present in the anteroom and no other Europa Spaceprime operative has been allowed into the private funeral hall, a decision that was made by Lady Anne who realises that there was never a more correct decision that she has taken as she witnesses a sight which she has never before witnessed in her fifty years of life: the King of Europa is weeping, the tears flowing freely from him, and it is Josiah Dean who is holding onto his Sovereign Prime.

*

Jonas Dean sleeps partially submerged within the viscose Nanodrone-infested medical bath onboard the Starship Zx12, his eyes twitching sporadically as he dreams.

In all of Jonas's recurring dreams there is always one constant; whether he dreams of his tank assignment, the Europa Spaceprime Academy, his journey onboard the Starship Zx12 or his Atlantis home, he's always alone and not a single living soul penetrates his dreams.

And there he lies for four long months, asleep within the darkness of his Starship whilst the Nanodrones sparkle and dance in blue halo light as they constantly work to heal his shoulder.

*

Kira Yu, the King and his three generals, Josiah and Evie Dean and the operatives at the Europa Spaceprime Mission Control have all found some form of routine to get them through the long hard months after the loss of the mission to the stars; the King's plight has not been made any easier after being absolved by Josiah Dean and for Kira, the thought of what might have been will not go away.

*

Jonas's eyes flicker alarmingly before falling open and he takes a brief moment to get used to breathing naturally through his nose as he becomes aware of the feeding tube that's fixed firmly into place over his mouth.

Jonas studies his medical cot: the brilliant bright blue lights which had been generated by the Nanodrones at work have dimmed and the Nanosec program has run its course. He raises his left hand to the side of his feeding tube, presses a miniature button positioned upon the side of his plastic mouthpiece and his tube retracts.

Jonas takes off his strap and drops his feeding tube onto the metallic floor within the mid-section of his Starship, whereupon it spills out excess fluids. He remains partially submerged, allowing his sapped strength to return as he gets used to breathing through his mouth for the first time in four long months. He then takes two deep breaths and lifts his right arm with extreme force through his Nanosec Nanodrone derived cast which shatters on the exertion that he inflicts upon it.

A reviving Captain Jonas Dean tests his hand movement by flexing his fingers and exercising his right arm, and is pleased to find there's no pain emerging from his right shoulder. He tries to stand, but is unable to get to his feet; Jonas has become disorientated from being in a horizontal position for four long months, but with a hard-bitten endeavour, he lifts himself up and over the side of his medical bed, landing heavily upon the Starship Zx12 mid-section's cold floor. He manages to rise to his knees and is able to do a few light exercises on his arms, shoulders and neck, then stretches out his legs and exercises all of the lower muscles within his body. After half an hour, and having given himself plenty of time to loosen all of the stiffened muscles within his legs, he once again tries to take to his feet and finally he manages to stand.

Jonas spends the hour that follows walking around within the confines of his Starship, where he holds onto anything which will help keep him upright until he's satisfied himself that his legs are working correctly and his orientation has returned.

"That's the second time the Nanotech Space Engineering Corporation has saved my life," Jonas says appreciatively to himself, feeling fully healed and totally revived now that all of the drugs and serums which had been injected into him pre-launch have washed through his system.

Captain Jonas Dean has never felt so alive.

*

Within the royal apartments, the Europan King sits in his study, alone at his desk; mounds of his personal paperwork are scattered and piled over the large conference table which resides as the centrepiece of his room.

General Thalt has completed his report which has taken four months to compile: a comprehensive and detailed analysis of the mission undertaken by the Starship Zx12.

The King of Europa turns to the back page of his confidential report, where he finds three words written in capitals before a comprehensive explanation.

The words lie heavy upon the final page.

CONCLUSION – TECHNICAL ERROR

The King of Europa reads the whole of the report whilst his mind plays through the series of events that led to Captain Dean's demise; he tries to find something hidden within the text which will give everything a different meaning. He will have to bury the report as he can't allow the Kings of the Kingdoms of the Earthprime yet another reason to exile him from their decision-making.

Thalt's report is thorough and without contradiction and however many times the King reads the report, he always comes to the same inevitable conclusion.

A miniscule miscalculation had been made by the cockpit console computer onboard the Starship Zx12 resulting in the hyperdrive grabbing more space than was necessary through each of its concertina hops. Although the ship's projected exit point cannot be confirmed, the miscalculation had clearly plotted the course of the Starship Zx12 into the asteroid belt and a certain death for the Europa Spaceprime Captain.

The King shuts Thalt's report on the maiden voyage catastrophe and slumps back into his seat, whereupon he places two fingers upon the bridge of his nose as he tries to clear his head and decide on his next action.

After a few moments he stands up from his desk and walks over to his bookcase so as to thumb through his old book collection; he finds what he's looking for – a thickly bound book entitled 'The Ancient Book of Life'.

The King of Europa places the book unopened upon his conference table when there's a knock at his study door.

"Enter," says a King still in mourning and without glancing up.

Lady Guinevere gracefully enters the study and has positioned herself next to her King long before he realises that it's she who has entered the room, but as soon as he sees her slender frame he stands out of courtesy. "My dear, sit with me for a while as it helps me to think," the King urges.

Lady Guinevere seats herself opposite her King upon his royal invitation as a tired-eyed Europan Sovereign begins to open the historic pages of 'The Ancient Book of Life'.

Upon seeing her King's withdrawn features, Guinevere chides, "It's late my lord and you need to rest."

On occasions, His Majesty the second King of Europa tolerates the first ladies of the Europa Earthprime telling him what to do, but on this occasion he rebuffs her. "I'm not tired and I'll sleep when I'm finished," he says whilst turning the first few pages of the old book; upon reaching the first chapter, he speaks once more to Guinevere as he scans the page. "My father and his fellow Kings founded 'The Ancient Book of Life' back in the old days. The first chapter carries a detailed log of all the legislation that has been passed at the World Conferences and also of all the legislation which has failed to get the required number of votes to be made into Earthprime law. The book is a perpetual record and the breakdown of the voting is kept secret and the Kings of the Kingdoms are not aware for twelve months who has voted for or against any piece of legislation; however, when you deal with certain people for as long as I have then it's quite easy to guess who's voted with you and who's voted against you."

Lady Guinevere succumbs to her Sovereign Prime's story and begins to take a keen interest in her King's words. "So although it's not yet logged that the King of Asia abstained in the second vote at the last World Conference, you still know it was him?" she asks.

And the Europan King smirks whilst portraying an all-knowing demeanour which has been gained from his many years of experience within the political arena. "The vote to return to an economy-based system should have been lost by three votes to two, but thankfully the King of Asia abstained. He is not a happy man after losing the valuable technologies onboard the Starship Zx12 which his Kingdom alone had developed and I thought that he may have sided with Bern, however he did not betray me and he did not betray his ideology; he just sent the necessary signal to me that he was deeply unhappy at the loss of the mission to the stars. The King of Asia holds the key to the resources we require for a successful Starship Zx class Space Program, yet I fear that it will take a while for me to get him back onboard," the King forthrightly replies.

"This is all very recent political history, so why do you need to look up these pieces of legislation in your book when you're already aware of the politic derived from their outcome?" Lady Guinevere asks her King.

The King of Europa hesitates and then comes to a momentous personal decision. "I'll tell you something now which I've not told a living soul before," he offers tentatively.

Lady Guinevere can see that her King is reaching out to her and is ready to put his trust in her and with her curiosity peaked she puts her monarch at ease. "What you tell me will remain between the two of us and be left within this room, my Lord," she says in reply.

The King nods in agreement as he returns to the open pages of 'The Ancient Book of Life' and settles back into his chair. "My father, the old King, would tell me the most wonderful stories when I was young about the old world and the events of the new history; stories of the Moon landings and of spacecraft that once travelled through our solar system and sent back pictures of far-off lands and galaxies, about the failed manned Mars missions and the building and rebuilding of various Moonbases. There was always one event which captured my imagination and that was the mission undertaken by the HMS Neon-Lit City; I think it was because it happened in my lifetime. I was fifteen years old when I stood next to my father and watched the great ship blast off. The spacecraft was a lot bigger and heavier than the Starship Zx12 and I was lucky enough to be introduced to the crew of eight shortly before its launch: the four old men and their four young wives who would live out the rest of their lives in space whilst escaping our brave new world. I can vividly remember one detail from the introduction that I had to the ship's crew and that was a single name badge," he says.

The King stops his story short and abruptly rises as he spies a bottle of whiskey and two empty glasses at the top of one of his bookshelves. He picks up the two glasses in one hand and the bottle in the other and places them upon his conference table, unscrews the cap and half-fills both glasses before finally returning to his seat.

Lady Guinevere says nothing of his dalliance as she wishes for her King to regain his full flow, and he soon obliges her. "I spent my formative years gaining my qualifications through the Europa Spaceprime Academy and I once asked my father to fast-track me onto Spaceprime astronaut training; he refused of course. We then lost the signal to the HMS Neon-Lit City. I was distraught; it felt like I'd lost a close friend, yet my father was strangely reticent about the loss of the ship. For a number of years, the Europa Spaceprime went through the motions of trying to communicate with the missing Stargazer class vessel and yet my father always appeared somewhat unconcerned about not finding the ship. Shortly before his death, I told him that once I became King I'd send out a mission to the stars to search for the HMS Neon-Lit City. By now he was ravaged with cancer, a frail shadow of his former self who knew that his time had come. He came up close to me shortly before he died and gripped both of my shoulders with firm hands and said, 'My son, I am so proud of you, but unfortunately you seem to be more like me than like your mother and I'd prefer it if you let the past be. Wherever the

HMS Neon-Lit City is berthed in space, it should be left there to rot.' He died two days later," says the King in recollection.

He returns his attention to his half-filled glass, sipping gratefully at his whiskey whilst Lady Guinevere sits trying to make sense of it all.

"Your father never wanted you to seek out the HMS Neon-lit City, why?" she asks.

The Europan Sovereign smiles, before he admits, "A question that I've been asking myself for the past few decades: why?"

Guinevere senses that her King is holding back. "There's more isn't there?" she asks in hope.

The King of Europa places his glass upon his conference room desk and places his index finger on top of 'The Ancient Book of Life', then continues. "This book contains the clues as to why the HMS Neon-Lit City mission was given the go-ahead in the first instance. The Kingdoms' Spaceprimes were in their infancy so why, with a Spaceprime motto of 'When the lives of the peoples of the Earthprime are complete, we shall look to the stars', why was the mission given the go-ahead at all? The peoples of the Earthprime Kingdoms were rebuilding their lives and rebuilding their cities and it was not the right time to send a mission out into the void. I have personally checked through all of the documented votes within 'The Ancient Book of Life' and for two consecutive years, the Kings of Americas, Asia and the North tried to pass the required legislation for a mission green-light and for two years they won the vote: three to two, with the Kingdom of the South and my father voting against the resolution. However, although the vote was won to send a ship out into the void, my father had the right of veto as his was the only Kingdom where a viable launch could be made: all the space-ports in the other Kingdoms had been destroyed during the Third World War, but Europe of old had its own launch site within the old

English nation from where they'd launched Moonbase missions in the early part of the twenty-first century – the site where the Europa Spaceprime Mission Control and Europa Spaceprime Academy complex is situated today."

Guinevere savours her alcoholic hot embers before attempting to forge insight. "So how did the HMS Neon-Lit City mission get the go-ahead?" she asks.

The King of Europa shakes his head slowly from side to side. "I can only guess at the next part of the story as the only fact that I have is written in this book," he replies placing an index finger upon the historic legislative record.

The Sovereign Prime turns the pages of 'The Ancient Book of Life' to the legislative year of 2100 and an obscure bill which had been passed at the turn of the century. "The vote to build a Starship and blast it out into the depths of space: votes for: five. Votes against: none," the King of Europa uneasily quotes. "I can only guess from this act that the Kings of the Kingdoms had met in secret and my father and the King of the South were given the real reasons as to why the HMS Neon-Lit City mission had to be undertaken," the Europan Monarch states as he reaches for a truth which he has spent his whole life searching for.

Lady Guinevere is clearly taken aback by the revelation. "I thought that this was a civilian mission. What do you think the mission was really about? What is onboard the HMS Neon-Lit City?" she asks.

"Those are good questions indeed, my child; the answers to which I am still striving to find and which I'm afraid, with the demise of the Starship Zx12, will not now be found during my lifetime. Whatever is onboard that vessel, my father did not wish for me to learn the truth and unfortunately for the truth, the old Kings are all deceased and in their vow of silence they've taken the truth to their graves. I believe that all of my fellow Kings are unaware of the importance of the HMS Neon-Lit City mission," he says as he reaches for the remains of his whiskey and enjoys the heat that is generated by the final remnants of his drink.

Guinevere is intrigued by the mystery surrounding the HMS Neon-Lit City and is not prepared for her King's story to be at an end – she is sure there is something else, something that her King is not divulging, something that he's not telling her, so she reaches forwards, picks up the bottle of whiskey and refills his empty glass. "My Lord, there's something that you've not told me," she says in her quest for an absolute truth.

The King of Europa takes another throat-burning sip and speaks shakily in his reply. "I sent Captain Jonas Dean to his death out of my own morbid curiosity. There are no families of the crew of the HMS Neon-Lit City to appease – that was a cover story that had been invented by my father and his fellow Kings, thus adding further mystery to the lost HMS Neon-Lit City mission and I have little choice but to keep up the premise of inherited propaganda."

Europa's Monarch pauses as Lady Guinevere sits stunned into silence by his latest disclosure.

The King wavers about continuing before giving out a heavy sigh of release and unburdening himself. "I wish that I'd never remembered that damn name sewn upon the female astronaut's cloth as to this day I would have been none the wiser," he says.

Lady Guinevere upon regaining her composure probes her King further. "Why is her name relevant?" she asks.

Europa's Sovereign head falls silent.

"My lord, what else is there to tell?" Guinevere says as she pushes for answers.

The King of Europa lifts his glass of whiskey and swigs back its contents until his glass is empty and he replies, "Guinevere, over the past few decades I've searched in vain to find out the names of the eight astronauts onboard the HMS Neon-Lit City but all official records of their existence have been wiped. I've interviewed the retired staff who worked within the Europa Spaceprime Mission Control during the time of the mission and they've all told me the same story. It was only the old King of Europa and his loyal General, General Rose, who had access to the communications to the Stargazer class vessel; the mission control centre for the voyage of the HMS Neon-Lit City was a closed environment. I believed, as the rest of the peoples of the Kingdoms of the Earthprime believed, that their mission was to set up an observatory in space and map the stars; yet when I was ordained King and I looked more closely into the lost voyage of the HMS Neon-Lit City, I became intrigued by the secrecy that enshrouded the space-flight. I recalled being introduced by my father at pre-launch to one of the wives undertaking the expedition, a striking woman whose harsh angular features and shock of black hair made an instant impression on me, a young lad of fifteen. To this day, I still recall the name sewn upon her lapel – C.J. Smith."

The King of Europa allows Lady Guinevere to register the name he has spoken; Guinevere does not speak during the lull as she's hopeful that her King will continue.

And Europa's King ventures forth with story's course. "I didn't have anything else to go on but a stitched name that I'd witnessed as a boy, yet shortly after my coronation I undertook an investigation to search all Earthprime civilian records to find any record of the existence of a C.J. Smith, but to no avail. For many years I searched in vain and I'd almost given up hope of finding her when finally I stumbled upon a record that had been filed away right under my very nose: a Europa Spaceprime Academy passing out certificate; a single document which my father had failed to erase. Jayne Smith had graduated on the 21st September in the year of 2104 and was immediately promoted to Captain of Europa Spaceprime Special Projects; I managed to access her academy photograph and it was most definitely the same woman – those angular features and that shock of hair were unforgettable to me. C.J. Smith: Captain Jayne Smith of the Europa Spaceprime; the voyage that had been undertaken by the HMS Neon-Lit City was no civilian charter, it was a military operation – but for what purpose we will now never know."

The King of Europa has shared his troubled mind with Lady Guinevere and the woman who has been entrusted with the truth leans across the conference table, picks up the drinks cap and screws it tightly onto the half-drunk bottle of whiskey.

*

At the head of the valley below, Europa Spaceprime Captain Jonas Dean views the three groove channels under Ganymede's night sky which is permanently dominated by Jupiter's storm planet. But he'll not be walking through the grooves and up towards the plateau's rise anytime during the next twenty-four hours as his onboard computer has confirmed to him that today is Christmas day.

Where the valleys converge, Jonas unfurls his Kingdom's flag upon a pole which he has planted into the rocky terrain before taking a step backwards and saluting as the flag hangs limply from its mast. "I lay claim to this Moon on behalf of the King of Europa," he says whilst looking around nervously in case an apparitional Ice Queen decides that she's not amused by his claim.

To record the historic event, Jonas takes out his camera and photographs the silver flagpole that is flying the flag of Europa, a single gold star upon a dark blue background, which is planted upon an alien world, before he heads back to his Starship to celebrate Christmas alone by breaking out double rations and a whole bottle of fresh water. He eats his rations and drinks half of his bottled water – his dry pack food is still as bland as it's always been, however, his water tastes like nectar and is a welcome change to the crystallised offerings which he has got used to.

Jonas has been awake for a week since his enforced hibernation and after spending his first twenty-four hours checking over his Starship and regaining his strength fully, he has decided to stay upon Ganymede for the foreseeable future as no human being has ever set foot upon Ganymede's surface and this is an opportunity that's too good to pass up.

Revived by his hearty meal and, in the name of scientific discovery, Captain Dean sets about putting his plans into action.

Firstly, he unloads three Nanosec boxes and then unpacks his Geiger counter, three cameras, one video recorder and a specialised barometer which he hauls to the hatch of the Starship Zx12.

A fully-suited Europa Spaceprime spaceman opens his Starship's hatch, climbs down his ship's ladder to the Moon's surface and starts his work by carrying the three Nanosec boxes and positioning them upon the surface of the Moon about fifty metres due south from his Starship. He then strides back to his ship and opens up an external hatch, from which he takes out three long lengths of cabling and diligently walks the exposed cable-lengths to his three Nanosec boxes. At his Nanosec box cluster site, he individually opens up each box, types his security code into the keypads and plugs each of the three cable-lengths into the boxes' vacant single socket points until all three of his activated boxes are glowing red.

After his Nanosec box set-up procedure, he carries his three cameras, his video recorder and his barometer past his activated

Nanosec boxes and up the incline rise to the top of the ridge, stopping only at the ridge's summit to gaze down into the valley below, where the barren landscape of the desolate land always takes his breath away.

He sets up his three cameras on three individual poles and points them down into the valley below in three different directions; Jonas programmes his cameras to take a picture every thirty minutes – his cameras are able to hold one thousand pictures each on their data cards and his experiment will take just over twenty days to complete.

He then sets up his video camera and points the lens in the direction of Jupiter. Jonas thinks long and hard about how to conduct his observation exercise and decides to film a fixed point where Jupiter currently resides in the sky; he has one thousand hours of recording time and is acutely aware that an awful lot of his video stream will contain the black emptiness of space, but he'll get some great footage when Jupiter, Io, Callisto or Europa cross the camera's path and he calculates that his experiment will last for just over twenty days.

Finally, he places his Geiger counter and his barometer between his three cameras; they also have their own data cards and Jonas will endeavour to gain a twenty-day record of atmospheric pressure readings and radiation level readings.

Captain Jonas Dean of the First Order of the Spaceprime stands proudly behind his recording instruments – his act of frontier science – before he returns to his Starship, where on his cockpit console array, his main computer flashes three warning messages.

NANOSEC TECHNOLOGIES
Warning – Nanodrone activation imminent

NANOSEC TECHNOLOGIES

Warning – Nanodrone activation imminent

NANOSEC TECHNOLOGIES

Warning – Nanodrone activation imminent

Dean types in his security code for the first programme and sets the Nanosec Nanodrones a very simple task: he programmes the billions of microscopic Nanodrones to journey south from their box, so as to spread out equidistantly over the area of the groove valley until the Nanodrones are all in their individually fixed positions, whereupon they'll then be able to transmit a signal between themselves and a signal back to the main computer onboard the Zx12; the signal data will allow his Starship's main computer to map the contours of the groove valley terrain.

The second programme that Jonas activates assigns the Nanosec Nanodrones from his second box to journey south over his groove valley control area and spread out equidistantly: the Nanodrones from his second box are programmed to transmit a continuous signal back to the Starship Zx12 with a rolling Richter scale reading; the Nanosec Nanodrones from his second box will monitor seismic activity within his control area.

Jonas types in his security code to activate his third box and programmes the Nanosec Nanodrones to journey south and search for rock samples within his control area; once a single sample's composition is identified it will be logged within the Starship Zx12's main computer; only one Nanodrone will be able to find a rock sample of singular composition which means that all of the other Nanodrones will have to continue searching until they find a sample that is of suitably different composition to the samples already

Nanodrone flagged; Captain Jonas Dean will then be able to use the data log to collect the differing rock samples at their flagged Nanodrone co-ordinates.

To celebrate his scientific endeavours, he reaches for his half-drunk bottle of water and drinks generously.

*

Hubert Snow checks his solid silver Spaceprime watch; time check: 2303 hours. He glances once more at the public viewing gallery. It's Christmas day night and for the first time since the loss of the Starship Zx12, Kira Yu has not appeared at her designated hour and Snow is engulfed by loneliness as he sips at the coffee that he had ritualistically made upon the hour.

Kira Yu and Hubert Snow have never spoken, yet the fact that she always arrived at the Europa Spaceprime Mission Control in the final hours of the day meant that someone else apart from himself harboured the belief that Captain Jonas Dean could still be alive.

Christmas is a tough time for Hubert Snow as he has no significant other – the Europa Spaceprime is his life.

Jonas Dean had been one of their own, yet people being people were beginning to forget and move on with their own lives and Hubert Snow's high expectations had begun to wane.

"Attention," General Thalt's clear command; the order shouted into Snow's ear.

The able Cap-com shoots to his feet with his coffee mug to hand.

"At ease, son," Thalt says.

Snow's shoulders relax. Why, he was asking himself, was the General here at this time on Christmas day night?

"Snow, in recognition of the fact that you've requested to be assigned to permanent nights for a year when you could have been assigned to do other duties, I've sanctioned a request that was made to me yesterday," Thalt says, appearing entertained by proceedings.

Kira Yu steps out from behind General Thalt carrying a large tray upon which, on a regulation Europa Spaceprime plate, a gravy-ridden turkey breast steams next to roast potatoes and an assortment of seasonal vegetables.

"Thank you Hubert," is all that Kira says and then leaves Snow speechless as she places the tray upon his workstation desk, before withdrawing to the public viewing gallery.

"I'm sorry Snow, I couldn't find any crackers, but enjoy your meal," Thalt remarks before making his way out of the mission control arena.

Hubert Snow reseats himself at his console clutching his coffee as he looks up at the soundproof glass public viewing gallery to where Kira Yu has retreated; he raises his mug to Kira who nods an acknowledgement.

And Hubert Snow eats heartily whilst a ringing continuous static discharge fills his ears.

*

Twenty days have passed since he set up his off-world science camp, yet Captain Jonas Dean is far from bored. He steps down the ladder of his Starship with a hand-held visual display map of his control area to hand which flashes fifty-seven flagged locations that his Nanosec Nanodrones have marked as rock samples requiring collection.

As well as his visual display map, Jonas also carries a golden gavel and a sack full of small specimen bags that can be individually sealed when he's collected each composite sample of Moon rock.

Jonas had done all of his preparation work before undertaking his journey into the control area: he'd labelled the specimen bags one to fifty-seven and he'd also numbered each flagged Nanodrone site accordingly onto his visual display map.

Jonas now walks out upon Ganymede Moon, following his pre-planned route to collect his Nanodrone flagged rock samples. Thankfully, his specimen bags are water resistant as he's surprised to find that well over half of his flagged samples are ice-encrusted and tainted by diverse levels of toxins.

It takes Jonas seven hours to walk his defined route and when his task is complete he's satisfied with his day's work. He is surprised and slightly relieved that although his journey has taken him part of the way down the groove valley, none of his collection points have been situated near to the high plateau – he is intentionally steering clear of the hallowed ground of the apparitional Ice Queen.

Once he has stashed all of his collected rock samples in the storage compartments within his Starship, Jonas retrieves the data-cards from his three cameras, his video recorder, his Geiger counter and his barometer. He stores all of his data-cards back onboard his Starship – he'll have plenty of time to view the imagery and process his frontier information at a later date.

His final task is to take down his cameras and collect his remaining recording equipment and store it all back onboard the Zx12.

Captain Jonas Dean then makes the journey back to the unfurled flag of his Kingdom, where he stands resolutely proud at the head of the groove valley, full of pride for the pioneering work he has undertaken and at having fulfilled a lifetime's ambition – he has stood upon a world where no other has, mapped the land, collected samples and recorded invaluable data and imagery.

"This is my reason for life," Jonas shouts into the valley's central groove; his cup of ambition has not emptied, but instead has grown fuller.

Jonas shouts once more with vigour, his voice carrying through the valley below, "I'll complete my mission and then I'll take my Starship beyond the great ringed planet."

And there's no reply.

*

Kira Yu rushes down the deserted corridor which leads to the Europa Spaceprime Mission Control whilst checking her solid silver Europa Spaceprime watch before swiping her glass door pass and entering the public viewing gallery; time check: 2212 hours. Why she's in a hurry does not make any sense, yet in her own mind she's late – these final two precious hours of each and every day are not hers, they belong to Jonas Dean. Upon entering the public viewing gallery, Kira realises that tonight, she's not alone.

Josiah Dean eyes the oriental beauty upon her late arrival, watching her as she makes her way silently to where he's seated and out of courtesy he stands.

"Kira Yu," she says as she presents herself to the old man of the Europa Spaceprime.

Josiah Dean thrusts a welcoming hand forwards.

Kira's broad smile greets Josiah Dean as she grips his well-worn hand. She seats herself next to Jonas's father whilst the monotonous aggravating static invades both of their senses; Kira has become used to the static-filled communications tinnitus, subconsciously filtering the noise out to concentrate on her assignments whenever she's alone.

Tonight, she's not alone with the backdrop buzz. Josiah Dean also listens intently to its unwavering continuous discharge; the minutes pass by as Josiah Dean sits hypnotised by the static's constant course as he grapples with his own disquiet.

Kira sips at her coffee as she sits quietly next to old man Dean whilst watching Hubert Snow undertake his 2215 hours walk around the Europa Spaceprime Mission Control arena.

Kira's respect for Hubert Snow has grown over the past few months; he's a man of perpetual routine and he has found his routine during the months of long nights that he has worked within the arena.

At 2200 hours, Snow religiously makes coffee and for fifteen minutes he sits and sips at his beverage. At 2215 hours, the able Cap-com Hubert Snow leaves the comfort of his chair and undertakes his nightly walk through the mission control arena. Every night his walk takes him to different consoles and various workstations, where he stops and checks a figure or a configuration and on occasion sits and updates a protocol or runs a routine. At 2300 hours without fail, the able Cap-com Hubert Snow makes another coffee before returning to his desk, where he shuts his eyes, concentrates and listens intently to the communications hissing discharge, trying to hear a change in pitch or a fall in tone due to the changes he has affected. On occasions, he jumps out of his seat, hurries over to another console and alters a setting at a workstation before returning briskly to the comfort zone of his desk.

Months have passed since the demise of the Starship Zx12 and its Captain, yet Hubert Snow still holds on to the fading notion that Jonas Dean, Captain of the Starship Zx12, is still alive.

Kira watches Snow double-checking a motherboard at one of the mainframe computers, her respect for the able Cap-com growing with every passing night. Suddenly, the old man of the Europa Spaceprime who is sitting beside Kira interrupts the static's constant course. "I'm not sure why I've come here tonight," Josiah Dean says, unable to give Kira a reason for his appearance at the public viewing gallery.

Kira already knows the reason why Josiah Dean has attended the public viewing gallery as it's the same reason why she attends the viewing gallery each and every evening and it always weighs heavily at the forefront of her mind. Yet she chooses to remain silent, ignoring the comment made by Jonas's father, intent only on watching Hubert Snow attend to his nightly work.

Josiah Dean speaks once more to Kira, "I heard there was a young woman who visited this place between these hours."

Kira turns sideways to face Josiah Dean and asks Jonas's father, "Have you come here to see me or to wait for your son?"

To which Josiah Dean honestly replies, "My answer should be both, but I believe that my son is lost. I came here to see you, Kira."

Kira shifts uneasily in her seat. "Why?" she asks forthrightly.

"I know my own son and I also know that he was close to you. He'd often talk about your exploits together at the academy and I'd like to have gotten to know you better if Jonas was still alive today, yet such is the fragility of life that death eventually comes to us all. I'm his father and I'll grieve his death until my last breath is forced from my body, but you Kira Yu must not waste your life waiting for a ghost. My son would have been insistent on me coming and telling you this and he'd also want me to tell you to move on with your life," Josiah Dean says with his affective speech unprepared in advance.

Kira beams as she staves off laughter. "Jonas would also have told you that if he had come to see me to talk me out of waiting for him that I'd have been bloody-minded enough to ignore him," she replies.

For the first time since his only son's disappearance, Josiah Dean smiles generously. "He did actually mention that you were your own person and I do respect you for that," he says.

Josiah Dean doesn't pursue the subject any further and it's Kira who offers insight. "I know why you've come here tonight and it's the same reason that I come to this place every evening of every day," she says.

"Enlighten me," Josiah Dean invites Kira.

"It's because, like me, you cannot bare to think that you'll never see him again and it's because of this that you cannot move on with your life," Kira says, speaking her mind.

Josiah Dean doesn't answer; he doesn't have too, because he already knows that Kira Yu has spoken the truth.

After an awkward moment's quiet, Kira collects up all of her paperwork as old man Dean checks his solid silver Europa Spaceprime watch; time check: 2302 hours. "What about your last hour?" he asks as she rises and makes her way to the gallery's exit, to the glass door beyond which the constant thrash of incomprehensible static will sever to mute, from where Kira replies to Jonas's father. "Just for tonight, I'll let you take my final hour," she says to Josiah Dean as she swipes her security pass through the glass door reader, just as Hubert Snow makes his way back to his desk with a freshly made mug to hand. "Goodnight Hubert," she whispers quietly to herself.

*

"Initiate check of Zx12 hull integrity," Captain Jonas Dean states as he confirms the launch sequence. "Zx12, sealed and airtight, check; all equipment locked down, check; Zx12 to manual control; manual control online – All systems online, confirmed; all Hyperdrive systems online, check; initiate Full-Power sequence, full power online – Rerouting excess power to main boosters – Commencing take-off sequence – Countdown is on. Five, four, three. Ignite boosters. Two. Initiate thrust. One. We have lift-off of the Starship Zx12."

The Starship Zx12's engines thrust Captain Dean's spacecraft upwards and through the thin atmosphere of Ganymede Moon and Jonas begins to steer his Starship into the deep reaches of space. Jupiter's Galilean Moons fall away behind as a portent signal flashes upon his main computer console screen: the last known co-ordinates of the HMS Neon-Lit City which is lost to the Earthprime Kingdoms within Jupiter's orbiting asteroid field.

*

The technicians, students, operatives and general staff of the Europa Spaceprime Academy huddle around the various streaming digital vision feeds within the Spaceprime Central Academy complex.

Kira Yu stands between Doctor Grace James and Doctor Aileen Grey upon the second floor of the Europa Spaceprime Academy as they all watch as one the medical laboratory's digital vision feed screen.

The King of Europa appears on the feed screen. He's seated behind one of his many desks in one of the many rooms within his royal apartments and he's flanked by the two first ladies of the Europa Earthprime, with his three generals at attention behind: always a show of unity.

The Sovereign Prime of Europa faces the camera and he looks through the blank window at a watching world whilst appearing thoughtful and composed. "My fellow Earthprime peoples, I invite you all to join together with me for a service of recognition upon the hilltop off the beach at Atlantis Strand, where we shall gather in memory of Captain Jonas Dean. The memorial service will take place at 2100 hours on the 24th of February in the year of 2149. At the hilltop's summit, I intend to place a memorial stone in memory of Captain Dean and upon this day, each and every year, we will celebrate the life of Captain Jonas William Dean," the King states somberly before the transmission ends.

Kira stares at the blank screen and vows not to attend the memorial event as this would be an admission of Jonas's death on her part and Kira is not yet ready for closure. Before she can pass comment on the royal announcement, Commander Marks appears at her side. "The King requires your presence immediately," he says formally and without waiting for a reply he steadfastly marches out of the academy complex as Cadet Kira Yu falls in behind.

*

"Kneel as Kira Yu," the King of Europa decrees in a stern voice that echoes throughout the long hall.

Kira Yu kneels although she's unable to make eye contact with her Sovereign Prime.

"Congratulations Miss Yu, you have been assigned a five-year mission as a doctor upon the new Moonbase and your training will commence immediately. Do you accept your mission, Kira Yu?" the King of Europa asks whilst already aware of her nightly attendance at the Europa Spaceprime Mission Control.

Lost within her chaotic thoughts, Kira Yu stalls; this is not closure, it's just getting on with my life, she thinks as she resolves herself into accepting her assignment. "Yes, my King," she shakily replies.

"Then rise as Doctor Kira Yu," the Monarch at the heart of Europa's realm decrees as he formally completes the ceremony. Yet the King's mind also lies elsewhere – with the failure of the Starship Zx12 mission, Captain Jonas Dean's upcoming memorial service and the loss of respect of his fellow Sovereigns.

Lady Guinevere senses her King's mind wandering and steps forwards from out of the rank and file to slip her comforting hand into her King's palm as General Thalt speaks directly to a risen Kira Yu: "Doctor Yu, your assignment will commence immediately and you'll report to Commander Marks at Far Point on Atlantis Beach at 2200 hours on the 24th of February in the year of 2149."

Kira Yu baulks when she hears the date but General Thalt doesn't allow her time to think. "Do you have any questions?" he demands.

"No sir," Kira replies, resigned to her impending fate.

"Then you're dismissed," Thalt says as he salutes the promoted cadet.

Kira Yu forgets to return the ceremonial salute and instead turns on her booted heel to take the long walk out of the King's hall; General Thalt lets her indiscretion slide.

A concerned Lady Guinevere addresses the decisive General as Doctor Yu leaves the significant ceremony behind: "General, would it not have been wiser to assign Doctor Kira Yu after the closure of the Europa Spaceprime Mission Control?"

"No my lady," Thalt says and he's reticent with his answer. "This will focus her mind and prepare her for the mission which she's required to undertake. We will of course monitor and support her throughout the difficult times ahead."

All eyes fall upon the King as he solemnly speaks, "I envy her as her hope has not yet waned and she puts me to shame."

And the King of Europa tries desperately to draw inspiration from Doctor Kira Yu.

*

The Starship Zx12 is guided by its autopilot as it careers towards the HMS Neon-Lit City's last known co-ordinates. It has taken Captain Dean's spacecraft three weeks to traverse the empty space between Jupiter's Moons and the asteroid field which orbits the planet and which is now looming large through his cockpit window.

Jonas has not activated his hyperdrive for this journey to the HMS Neon-Lit City as he wishes to spend the long hours during the undefined days collating and reviewing all of the data he collected upon Ganymede Moon.

He had acquired a full set of comprehensive atmospheric pressure readings and Jonas thinks, from the radiation level readouts which he has extrapolated from his Geiger counter data, that it would have been a lot safer to have spent a lot less time outside the safe haven of his Spacecraft. Yet his suit's sensors hadn't registered any prolonged exposure to large doses of radiation and Jonas had placed his trust in his spacesuit, the garment having saved his life upon Ganymede's surface.

The data records have also shown that seismic activity was at its highest level within his groove valley control area and, from his Richter scale readouts, Jonas has been able to plot the fault-lines that crisscrossed the groove valley landscape which lay below the rocky outcrop.

The digital camera images which he captured he has used to map the terrain of his control area, however there's a problem with his image data. Sitting back in his cockpit seat, he reviews his three full sets of digitally enhanced images, and realises that one of his cameras has failed him, the one he had pointed down into the groove valley that led towards the plateau's rise; all of his images are blank.

"The Ice Queen's final statement from beyond my mind's eye," Jonas says aloud, scratching at the base of the beard which he has been cultivating since waking up from his enforced hibernation.

He begins reviewing his video stream, beholding Jupiter's perpetual world storms that fill his screen as the planet orbits through his recording, its complexion changing with every frame: it was as if the planet was alive.

He fast-forwards his digital streaming data before pausing his recording upon a grey mass of rock orbiting through his lens. "Callisto," Jonas confirms aloud.

For a second time, Jonas fast-forwards his digital video stream and he watches the dark void flash by frame by frame until he presses the pause button upon a captured image; he clicks forwards a few frames until he is happy with the image that is exposed in front of him: Io and Europa orbiting together, twin Moons of vivid distinct colour, passing side-by-side through the black night sky.

Jonas's eyes drift towards the encased blue stone on display upon his cockpit console and he thinks of what Kira might be doing at this moment in her life; his reflections cause him to pour out his innermost thoughts: "Although I've fallen off-mission by six whole months, I don't expect to find any trace of the HMS Neon-Lit City at its last known co-ordinates, but if, after the futile search, I decide to remain out here in space, then Kira and my family will eventually get on with their lives. The apparitional Ice Queen was right about one thing: I'll soon be nothing more than a forgotten memory of a distant past. To Kira, my family, the King of Europa and the peoples of the Kingdoms of the Earthprime, I've failed them all. I know only too well that I've especially let Kira down with my actions and what I've failed to say to her, but whatever her feelings are towards me, she has the intelligence and the resolve to move on with her life."

At that moment, proximity alerts from his cockpit console array break Captain Dean's train of thought.

Jonas looks through his main cockpit view at the dark shapes resonating in the distance; his Starship has reached the periphery of Jupiter's orbiting asteroid field.

Captain Jonas Dean switches his Starship over to manual control, slowing his vessel to a crawl; the main cockpit console lights up his target location and it will be a short journey to his plotted co-ordinates.

Jonas manoeuvres his Starship through the rock-filled field whilst using his proximity data, his view screen and his instincts as a guide to steering his ship.

His journey is slow and not without danger, but after a half day spent piloting his spacecraft through the asteroid field, he brings the Starship Zx12 to a full stop at his target co-ordinates: both Jonas's ship and the fabled Stargazer class vessel, the HMS Neon-Lit City, now share the same co-ordinates upon his cockpit command console computer.

The asteroids which surround his vessel on all sides are gently swaying as if caught in a slight breath of wind, yet Jonas can see nothing else through his view-screen but dark masses of ancient rock against the vast void.

He ignites thrusters in order to change his ship's aspect which allows the Starship Zx12 to undertake a sharp static turn. Yet before his manoeuvre can be completed, Jonas hammers down on his ship's brakes and gasps in awed disbelief.

On a large lump of rock below the Starship Zx12, a vivid single beacon of light shines brightly within the rock-infested field. Captain Jonas Dean uses thrusters to drop his Starship down towards the brilliant white wilderness light, edging closer to the great shadowy mass of rock from where the light is emanating.

Jonas stares in fascination at the single light source which is shining from a cylindrical glass-made structure that has been purposely built upon the summit of an asteroid; from within the reinforced glass-constructed observatory, he can quite easily make out a telescope and what appears to be a leather-bound couch.

Beneath the house of light, the wide expanse of the HMS Neon-Lit City is berthed and shackled to the asteroid in four places and a short covered walkway connects the ship to the manmade glass observation outpost that has been erected upon the summit of the ancient space rock.

"Still fabled but no longer lost," Jonas musters, overwhelmed by the existence of the rediscovered new-age craft.

Captain Jonas Dean lets the Starship Zx12 drift along the hull of the Stargazer class vessel and begins to hail the newfound ship. "This is Captain Jonas Dean of the Starship Zx12, hailing the HMS Neon-Lit City, over," he says through his ship's local comms.

Jonas repeats his hail once more, before calling time on the futility of raising life within a ghost ship; for well over forty years, the HMS Neon-Lit City has survived intact in space, but there can be no survivors as its crew would all be a long-time deceased.

He allows the Starship Zx12 to drift to the rear of the fabled craft where black scorch marks are clearly visible on a sizeable section of the Stargazer's hull. Jonas brings the Zx12 to a full stop, close to the Neon-Lit City's standard Europa Spaceprime docking station at the rear of its hull.

"I really have to go and take a look around," Jonas says as he uses his ship's thrusters to line up the Zx12 docking mechanism with that of the Stargazer.

Captain Jonas Dean hears the howl of grinding metals as he locks his Starship onto the old spacecraft, completing his docking manoeuvre before powering down his vessel.

He takes a short while to conduct the final checks of his Starship and to make sure that his spacesuit is functioning within required parameters before he places his space helmet over his impenetrable membrane.

With his greatest ambition about to be fulfilled, he steps cautiously to his Starship's hatch; poised at the docking door of the Zx12 and with his heartbeat increasing by over thirty percent, Jonas takes two deep breaths before entering the Starship Zx12's docking door code.

His Starship's docking door slides silently aside and Captain Jonas Dean steps into the breach between the two ships; within the recess, he types a command into the control panel upon the sleeve of his spacesuit and the historic HMS Neon-Lit City's docking door code flashes up within the visor of his space helmet.

Jonas enters the code into the fabled craft's docking door panel. The composite steel door grates its disapproval as it slides aside and

Captain Jonas Dean finds himself standing rigid within the space between the two spacecraft with a laser weapon pointed directly at his chest.

"State your name and purpose soldier," a female voice says, her form hidden within the shadows of the great ship but her weapon in full view.

Jonas has no other choice and states, "My name is Captain Jonas Dean of the Starship Zx12 and I'm here under the direct orders of the King of Europa to seek out the HMS Neon-Lit City."

The laser weapon drops to the female astronaut's side and the woman whose face holds carved angular features under a shocking mass of grey hair steps out of the shadows, dressed in an old-fashioned Europa Spaceprime uniform. "My name is Captain Jayne Smith of the First Order of the Spaceprime and Captain of this vessel. Welcome aboard, Captain Jonas Dean," she replies.

Satellite City

There's a heap of junk in deep space, out by the Milky Way,
It's anchored to an asteroid; I'm going to dock my ship today,
It's sheltered against the lunar winds blowing through the spatial seas,
A Neon-Lit City swaying gently in the breeze.

At Satellite City, the sun will never shine,
At Satellite City, you can have a feel-good time,
At Satellite City, the worlds revolve around you,
At Satellite City, the shooting stars surround you.

There's a hulk of rust in deep space, tied to a lump of rock,
I've docked my brand new Starship upon its fabled lock,
Around the belted boulders and within the ebb and flow,
Lies a ghostly floating shipwreck that badly needs a tow.

At Satellite City, the sun will never shine,
At Satellite City, you can have a feel-good time,
At Satellite City, the worlds revolve around you,
At Satellite City, the shooting stars surround you.

You can take the moving walkway out to the asteroid,
There's a round-glass viewing station erected for humanoids,
There are holographic programmes connected to your mind,
The gallery will magnify your perception of space and time.

You can see the nebula in all its glory here,
A vast array of swirling light from within this plastic sphere,
The future and the past combine within the void,
I feel so insignificant stuck on this asteroid.

At Satellite City, the sun will never shine,
At Satellite City, you can have a feel-good time,
At Satellite City, there's enough for you to do,
At Satellite City, you can get a room with a view,
At Satellite City, you can forget about tomorrow,
At Satellite City, you can drown all your sorrows,
At Satellite City, the worlds revolve around you,
At Satellite City, the shooting stars surround you.

CHAPTER 8

Born a Piscean

Captain Jayne Smith rests upon a retro plastic chair within the HMS Neon-Lit City's living quarters. On her lap resides a thick logbook which is bound in green velvet and in her hand she holds a pencil, with which she begins to write: Captain's log: 24th of February in the year of 2149. The Starship Zx12 under the command of Captain Jonas William Dean of the First Order of the Spaceprime docks with the HMS Neon-Lit City.

Smith closes her logbook after writing her entry and places her journal upon an easy table next to her synthetic chair.

Following his unannounced arrival, Jonas had given Captain Jayne Smith a tour of the Starship Zx12; Smith had been impressed by the technological advancements made by the Europa Spaceprime, but had been adamant that her ship was of a more robust build.

Jonas had also taken the opportunity to change into his recreational uniform, before following the Captain of the Stargazer through the hull of her vessel and into the living quarters of her ship.

The Captain of the HMS Neon-Lit City is now seated opposite the Captain of the Starship Zx12, both sitting upon antique Europa Spaceprime plastic chairs. Jonas's head fills with relevant questions, yet he bides his time before asking any of them and instead he says to his Europa Spaceprime equal, "Captain Smith, today is to be a double celebration as not only do we meet for the first time, but I can also announce that today is my birthday."

"Congratulations Captain Dean, and please, call me Jayne. We may as well celebrate in style as it's not often that I have a visitor," Smith replies under a straining smile which, although forced, has taken decades off her. She rises from her chair and disappears out of her pale plastic living quarters.

Jonas's eyes wander around the sparse living quarters which Smith has vacated on a whim, looking for any clues to temper his feelings of apprehension. There is something that does not sit right about this whole situation — the old story of four ageing men and their four young wives journeying to the stars on a civilian mission is looking to his eyes somewhat shaky as Captain Jayne Smith is quite obviously one of Europa Spaceprime's finest. However, his instincts are telling him that he is in no mortal danger, but more and more questions are beginning to stack up inside of him.

Captain Jayne Smith arrives back in her living quarters carrying two containers which are filled to the brim with precious fresh water. She pops the cap on one of the plastic bottles and offers it to Jonas as she speaks, "Here's to you, Captain Dean."

Jonas nods respectfully, takes hold of the offered plastic container and drinks heavily whilst remaining silent, awaiting her story.

"Forgive me Captain Dean, for it's been nine long years since I've conversed with anyone but myself," she says.

"Please, call me Jonas," he says and quietens once more.

Captain Jayne Smith draws herself forwards onto the edge of her plastic chair and begins to speak. "In the year of 2108, the HMS Neon-Lit City blasted off from the Kingdom of Europa with a crew of eight. We travelled for five years in a ship that was big enough for everyone to have their own space, but still it was a long time to be on the move. We had a galley stocked full of food, a water supply that would last us all for one hundred years and specialised battery packs which had been developed by the Europa Spaceprime that would enable us to power the ship for a century. The four male astronauts onboard the Stargazer class vessel were not all old men as two of them were in their mid-forties, however the two eldest male astronauts, Aaron Ames and Hans Reiger, died en-route due to the rigours and strains of spaceflight and both were buried in the void."

"How did the wives handle their deaths?" Jonas says as he couldn't help himself from asking the question.

Smith pauses before giving her reply: "Nobody on board the Stargazer class vessel was married."

"A cover story," Jonas says bluntly.

"The fact that you, Captain Dean, have travelled over a vast distance of space after such a long length of time to seek out this ship and her crew has earned you the right to hear the truth and there will be plenty of time for questions later," Smith says coldly in reply.

Jonas nods his agreement that there will be no more interruptions from his enquiring mind until after he's heard Smith's story. He takes another sip of bottled water and begins to relax as her husky tone ventures forth. "For five years we travelled and then in the year of 2113 we entered Jupiter's orbiting asteroid field and navigated our way through the densely packed rock-filled environment. It was my decision to attach the ship to Asteroid 4571, one of the larger floating objects within the cluster, due to its sheltered location within the field. This required work to be undertaken outside the ship – drilling hooks into the hard rock surface, weighing the ship's four anchors and tethering the HMS Neon-Lit City to Asteroid 4571. The whole process took weeks to complete and we lost one of the crew during this time when Astronaut Natasha Korlov was struck on her space helmet by an unverified object whilst on an operational spacewalk; she died instantaneously and was lost to us within the void."

Silence suffocates Captain Jayne Smith as she recalls Korlov's death and she sips at her bottled water to rid herself of the taste of relived bitterness. "I'm sorry Captain Dean, but after five years of voyage, all of the ship's crew had become close and her death hit me hardest of all. We were all space pioneers and we'd found a place that we could call our home," Smith states to a fixated Jonas Dean before she continues. "For two weeks we mourned her death and then drew a line under the tragedy and the five remaining crew set about their work. We detached the communications tower from the forward section of the HMS Neon-Lit City and tethered it at the peak of Asteroid 4571. This had to be done as our sheltered position meant that our communications signal was pretty ropey at times and by fixing it at the peak of the asteroid, the signal which was being sent back to Earth improved by forty two percent."

Captain Jayne Smith slides back into her plastic chair and perseveres with her history recital. "Our next mission was to build the observatory which would also be situated at the summit of Asteroid 4571. The two youngest male members of our crew were both trained astronomers and led the installation project. Kim Solo and Sebastian Franc spent weeks unpacking the observation equipment, the framework and the reinforced plastic glass. They spent weeks more ferrying all of the equipment across to the asteroid's surface, where they built the observation tower with love, care and attention to detail. They installed all of the latest holographic software available to the Europa Spaceprime at the turn of the century and they also installed the latest magnification technologies and finally, to give the viewing station a nostalgic feel, the guys added a pre-war sofa and an antique telescope."

Captain Jonas Dean is confused by the pioneering tale he is being told – as two of the ship's crew were most definitely astronomers, why was there a need for a cover story and especially one which wasn't too far removed from the truth? Another question raised that he wishes to ask, yet he keeps quiet as his answers are slowly coming.

*

Josiah and Evie Dean have decided to walk to the memorial service, although they could have driven the coastal road and arrived at their destination in a matter of minutes.

In the heat of the day, they set off along the beach at Atlantis Strand, and trudge over hot sands towards Jonas's beach house which is located two miles along the coast.

The thought of undertaking this journey has filled Josiah Dean with dread as closure is a state of mind that he cannot yet prepare for and will not gain for the rest of his natural life. Josiah and Evie Dean have talked at length about their son's death and have both agreed that they will never find the peace of mind that they crave whilst they were both still alive, yet they will struggle through their loss as best they can. The best way for them to remember their only son on the date of his birth is to walk to his treasured beach house retreat and recall their defining memories of his life, before journeying in the late evening up the hillside to join their King in the memorial service which he has arranged.

The sweat is pouring from Josiah Dean as he walks. Evie has dropped about fifty metres behind him, yet she does not mind, because she knows her husband well enough to know when he is lost inside his own thoughts: this is a day Josiah Dean will remember, a day that he needs to remember: a memorial day on the date of his son's birth; a day which will haunt his dreams to come.

Josiah mops his brow as he rests upon the hot sands in front of his son's beach house residence and waits for his wife. Only when Evie Dean finally catches up with the old man of the Europa Spaceframe does he take out the spare key which Jonas had given to him shortly before his tank assignment and insert it into the beach house door's lock.

The old wooden double-doors fall open and Jonas's grieving parents venture into their son's main living area. Evie Dean switches on a light which illuminates the dust gathering upon Jonas's books, bookshelves and upon his knee-high table.

"This won't do, I can't have my boy returning to a house left in this state," Evie Dean says stubbornly.

And Josiah Dean says nothing to appease his wife's belief, because if hope is all that Evie Dean has left, then who was he to take it away from her?

Rather than confront his wife about an uncontested truth that their only son would never return, Josiah Dean shies away to his son's bookshelves and begins to read all of the titles of his son's book collection; the older books carry memories of his son as Jonas has kept his teenage annuals, almanacs and comic books – they all have one theme in common and all touch upon the same subject: space adventure.

Pride courses through Josiah Dean's old veins on viewing Jonas's prize possessions: at least his son had followed his dreams and lived his life in pursuit of his aspirations; at least his son had had ambition.

Several family photographs litter the bookcases. Jonas had chosen to keep these pictures within the confines of the old wooden units, not replacing them with any of the books which are piled up in front of the shelves – none of Jonas's family photographs are casually stacked up in front of the old wooden bookcases.

Josiah nods his head in recognition as he is aware that Jonas's photographs of his family were once treasured by his only son who is now lost to the stars.

Meanwhile, Evie Dean is hunting for cleaning solution which she can't find in Jonas's living room. She passes through into the kitchen area, where she immediately freezes and stares intently at the old wooden table top. "Joe, you need to come in here," Evie Dean calls coolly.

Josiah Dean retreats from his thoughts of loss and joins his wife in the kitchen to find her rooted in front of Jonas's old wooden table, looking down at a wrapped package which lies upon the table top.

Josiah Dean leans forwards and picks up the package to read the short hand-written message that his son had scrawled upon its brown paper wrap.

It read: For my darling, Kira Yu.

Josiah holds onto the wrapped gift box, and he already knows what's inside as he owns an exact replica which has saved his life on two occasions.

Deep regret invades Josiah Dean's old bones, because his son has followed his dreams and pursued his ambitions at the expense of his heart's desire, and has left his coveted solid silver engraved Europa Spaceprime timepiece for Kira Yu.

Josiah Dean has a newfound purpose in his life: to make sure that Kira Yu receives her gift.

After all, it was his son's final wish.

*

Captain Jayne Smith is telling her story, the truth as she calls it, on her own terms and at her own pace. "All the time we were in contact with the King of Europa and General Rose," she states.

Jonas sips at his gifted water as more unanswered questions form within his mind. What were the old King of Europa and General

Rose saying to the Stargazer's crew? Why is this ship so significant? Out of respect for Captain Smith, he says nothing.

Jayne Smith moves her story forwards. "The next mission that was required to be undertaken was for Solo and Franc to attach the moving walkway from the airlock door of the HMS Neon-Lit City, which is situated directly adjacent to Asteroid 4571, to the roundhouse viewing station airlock door. Again, Solo and Franc unpacked the required equipment, spending weeks outside the ship to construct the conveyor and its covering until eventually the project was complete. I was stunned by their achievement as I didn't believe that either of the men had it in them to accomplish such a historic task, yet between them they had constructed the first manmade wonder of the known off-world system. In the months that followed, this ship became a contented haven and Kim Solo and Sebastian Franc filled their waking hours with the study of the stars, distant galaxies, nebula and the planets. Caitlin Harper and Penelope Lawrence-Reid, the two other female members of the crew, began to take a keen interest in astronomy and undertook their own studies. It was a good time to be alive onboard this vessel. Nothing ever lasts though, and at the beginning of the year of 2114 we received word from the Europa Spaceprime Mission Control that our communications signal was still prone to breaking up and I was ordered to dispatch two communications buoys outside the ship within the asteroid field to triangulate and boost our signal back to Earth; it was a simple enough task and was carried out with the minimum of fuss."

Smith hesitates as she orders the facts in her own mind. "The team's original mission was to hide away in deep space until we were ordered to return home. But our peaceful existence was destroyed in the Year of 2115," she says.

Jonas frowns as these were strange orders indeed that had been deployed by the new Kings of an Earth reborn out of ashes and dust.

Smith ignores Dean's expression as she divulges more of the story. "In the year of 2115, our mission changed unexpectedly as the King of Europa ordered the communications tower which was situated at the peak of Asteroid 4571 and the two communication buoys that we'd deployed to be destroyed: we were being cut loose and His Majesty the first King of Europa was giving us just forty-eight hours to prepare for the mission. We discussed his orders and their implications, and we all looked forward to our new life of isolation," Captain Jayne Smith says to Captain Jonas Dean who is still frowning.

The cover story is by now in tatters, Jonas thinks – it had been the old King's decision to sever communications with the HMS Neon-Lit City.

One question is nagging away at the back of Jonas's mind: why?

Captain Jayne Smith finds it hard to tell the next part of her story and her voice begins to crack under the strain of recalling the distant past: the day that the Stargazer class vessel's communications to Earth had ceased. "Solo and Franc scaled 4571's asteroid peak and set the explosive charges at the base of the communications tower, before they both then undertook a spacewalk to set the explosive charges to the communications buoys. As the countdown progressed to the cessation of our communications lifeline, all of the ship's crew listened to a recorded message from the King of Europa and we were all told in no uncertain terms that we'd done a great service to all of the Kingdoms of the Earthprime and to all of the peoples of the Earthprime," the HMS Neon-Lit City Captain states uneasily.

Captain Jonas Dean cannot stay silent any longer; the overall picture has gradually been built up and he has to speak his mind: "This was definitely not a civilian mission and it was also not a

Europa Spaceprime mission – this was a military mission on behalf of all of the Kingdoms of the Earthprime: Jayne Smith, Kim Solo, Sebastian Franc, Caitlin Harper, Penelope Lawrence-Reid, Natasha Korlov, Aaron Ames and Hans Reiger, representatives from all of the different Kingdoms of the Earthprime."

Smith nods her agreement, yet she won't elaborate and Jonas will have to listen a little longer to her narrative of the past. The Neon-Lit City Captain briskly picks up the thread of her story. "Kim Solo and I oversaw the detonations from the bridge of the HMS Neon-Lit City whilst Caitlin Harper, Penelope Lawrence-Reid and Sebastian Franc stood upon Observation Deck Number Seven, awaiting the destruction of the communications lifeline. I detonated all of the devices simultaneously: the communications tower at the summit of Asteroid 4571 disintegrated as planned, but the communications buoys didn't – one of the buoys fragmented into three large pieces upon detonation. Two of these fragments were sent hurtling into the side of Asteroid 4571 whilst the final fragment crashed through the reinforced glass of Observation Deck Number Seven, where the three crew members had congregated to watch the severance of the communications; all three died instantaneously and their lifeless bodies were sucked out into the sea of space," Captain Jayne Smith says as she recalls the memories of her day of distress; the day when she'd wilfully destroyed the Stargazer's communications lifeline. Visibly drained, Smith nods her head and is unable to face her equal.

Captain Jonas Dean can't blame his fellow Captain for carrying out direct orders from her King, and although he still doesn't have all of his answers, he is not without heart. Captain Jayne Smith has unburdened herself of her tragic tale. Jonas is still hungry for a greater understanding, but he knows that it is time to allow the Neon-Lit City Captain some respite from her story, so that she can regain some semblance of composure.

"Did you say that you have real food onboard?" Jonas asks, offering his fellow Captain an opportunity to adjourn from her story of past histories retold.

"I do have real food onboard, Captain Dean and I'm sure that I can even stretch to a bottle of wine, but firstly I'll show you to your quarters as I'm hoping that you'll stay for a few days. Then, after our meal, you can take the moving walkway out to the asteroid," Smith responds, grateful for the pause in her story that Jonas has offered.

*

A refreshed Captain Jonas Dean soon makes his way back from his allocated quarters to the ship's galley to dine with his host. Captain Jayne Smith serves up a hot meal of preserved meat which she alleges is refrigerated venison and a mixture of salads that have been grown within the confines of the Stargazer class vessel's Earth house.

Although the salads are edible, the well-preserved meat is tasteless but its memory is removed from Jonas's palate by two glasses of wine.

The conversation at the dinner table has been light as Jonas has intentionally steered clear of Smith's tale – there will be time enough to return to her story later.

Jayne Smith's imposed isolation had become complete nine years previously when Kim Solo, the only other survivor from that ill-fated day in the year of 2115, had died of old age, after he and Smith had spent twenty-four happy years together upon the Stargazer. Jonas allows his fellow Captain to eulogise about her long-dead friend and life partner.

After the meal, Jonas retreats to his allocated room which is on the asteroid-facing side of the Stargazer class vessel. His quarters are sparsely furnished yet comfortable and from the window of his cabin he's able to view the brightly lit observatory which is a manmade beacon of light upon an alien landscape.

*

Josiah Dean holds onto his wife's hand as they walk up the rolling hillside to the hilltop to where their King will be overseeing the memorial service.

Thousands of Europa Earthprime citizens are walking up the gentle slopes to the memorial setting, carrying torches to light their way as the dusk begins to settle over Atlantis Bay.

Josiah puts his hand to his breast pocket and feels through the cloth of his coat the outline of the package which had been left to Kira Yu by his lost son.

Jonas's parents already know that Kira won't attend the memorial service as her hope has not yet faded.

Josiah Dean smiles wryly to himself; Jonas sure knew how to pick them, he thought.

*

Kira Yu steps out onto the beach at Atlantis Strand at the furthest point of the long stretch of coastline and through multi-coloured pastel-shaded eyes she peers into the descending gloom to the hillside some two and half miles in the shoreline distance.

The flaming orange lights are dancing upon the slopes, where the peoples of the Europa Earthprime have turned out in force to remember her lost love.

Kira looks down and puts her hand onto the length of rope which is tied in a double fisherman's knot around her slim waist.

A wetsuited Doctor Grace James and Doctor Aileen Grey are standing beside Kira, also watching the distant lights parading upon the hillside. Ropes with double fisherman's knots are also tied tightly around both of their waists, binding their black Europa Spaceprime wetsuits which are emblazoned with the emblems of the Europa

Spaceprime and the Europa Earthprime.

Commander Marks grins at all three members of his elite medical team.

"Are you staring, Commander?" Doctor James asks icily.

"Yes ma'am," Marks retorts.

James's smirk is full of mischief. "Just this once, Oswald, I'll let you stare. Now do you have a briefing to give us?" she asks coolly.

Commander Marks wipes the smile off his face and begins to brief his wetsuited medical elite. "As you are all aware, the new Moonbase will be fully operational within the next twelve months and each of you will be assigned to the Moonbase on a five-year mission. However, your assignment for the next three months will be to spend time in the underwater habitat that is located one mile off the coast as there you will be able to walk around underwater at your leisure which is the best training that the Europa Spaceprime can provide to mimic the conditions for walking upon the Moon. Does anyone have any questions?"

It is Kira who speaks up. "Sir, does the habitat have any working communications?"

Marks visibly sighs with regret and Kira already has her answer; Commander Marks is about to let her down as gently as he can. He looks Kira directly in the eye as he replies, "I'm sorry, Doctor Yu, but the underwater habitat doesn't have any communications devices. I fully understand your reasons for wanting to keep in touch with ongoing operations and I can assure you that if circumstances do change then I'll put on a rather large wetsuit, cumbrously tread water out to the habitat unit and tell you any news myself."

"Thank you sir," Kira says in admiration of his direct approach.

Doctor Grace James, the Europa Spaceprime Special Projects Medical Officer, steps a pace forwards towards Commander Marks and plants a kiss upon his cheek.

"I'll see you in three months, Oswald," James says under a wicked grin.

Commander Marks blushes at Doctor James's flirting.

*

Captain Jonas Dean stands before an unimposing airlock-door which is sited asteroid-side of the Stargazer class vessel and presses the fat red button at its side.

The door slides aside to reveal the covered walkway swaying gently in the solar winds. He steps inside the airlock and presses a second fat button that is situated behind the airlock-door to start the conveyor and the moving walkway is set in motion.

Jonas steps onto the moving conveyer belt, holds onto the handrail and begins his short journey to the brightly lit observatory outpost. After negotiating the bridge which hangs over oblivion, he steps off the conveyor at the summit of Asteroid 4571 and presses the fat red button that is situated at the side of the roundhouse viewing station's airlock-door, thus enabling him to step inside the quaint observatory and marvel at the internal furnishings and the external view.

The circular structure is fitted with long unbreakable glass panels connected at one hundred and thirty-five degree angles by thin layers of plastic-coated composite metal. A mosaic of the solar system resides upon the floor, a golden telescope gives off a newly polished glow at the centre of the observation point and a comfortable scarlet two-piece leather chaise-lounge sits invitingly to the rear of the brightly lit outpost.

Jonas looks out through the white-lit plastic sphere and over the jagged rooftops of the asteroids swaying within the field to the stars above. Jupiter and his Moons reside in the backdrop and refracted swirling nebula lie beyond.

"God's view," is all that Captain Jonas Dean can say.

*

The King at Europa's beating heart holds court upon the hilltop overlooking Atlantis Strand and its bay beyond. At the summit, he lays his own personal wreath of green poppies at the base of a newly erected stone monument.

The two first ladies of the Europa Earthprime and the King's three loyal generals are in attendance at the monarch's side, as are Josiah and Evie Dean who are hand in hand beside their Sovereign Prime.

At the hilltop's peak, the King of Europa delivers his sermon to the congregated masses. "Thank you all," he says in a glorious overtone. "The peoples of the Europa Earthprime have gathered this evening in their thousands to celebrate the life of Captain Jonas William Dean. Tonight is a time for remembrance: remembering who we are and remembering where we've come from. Our dark past fades into history's distance and the dawning of a bright new era and a brand new day has emerged. We've all lost loved ones and our thoughts this evening are with Josiah and Evie Dean who have lost their only son to the vast reaches of the void. This night I will spend but a single moment of my short life gazing upon the Moon and the stars and it is Captain Jonas William Dean who will be at the forefront of my thoughts."

Upon the hilltop's peak the King gazes into the night skies beyond the newly commissioned stone monument, and the attending masses all look skywards into the black of night and all of their thoughts are for Captain Jonas William Dean of the First Order of the Spaceprime.

A shooting star streaks across the heavens, momentarily bright and then lost to the naked eye.

Could that be the Starship Zx12, the King of Europa silently reflects?

*

Kira Yu takes one final moment to look towards the distant hillside at the mass of orange beacons that light up the summit of the hilltop's peak.

"Celebrate his life," Kira says, full of regret.

She walks slowly towards the ocean to follow Doctor Grace James, who has led on point and who is fully immersed in the cold black sea, and Doctor Aileen Grey who has already followed James into the sea's swell, some twenty metres ahead of Kira, and who is also about to disappear under a breaking wave.

Kira walks out into the sea, holding onto the taut length of rope that shackles her to Doctor Aileen Grey with the waves breaking over her shoulders.

The cold waters are dark and uninviting, but the impenetrable membrane which covers her head protects her from the saltwater swell.

A sparkle of bright light flares within the heavens above and Kira watches the star's descent as it races across the night sky; a single shooting star which falls, burning itself out to a cinder as the uninviting waters take her in and Kira gives herself up to the sea.

*

Was this the decision that Jonas Dean had to make? Did a life full of self-fulfilment mean effectively hijacking the Starship Zx12 to travel the unknown universe and explore the breach beyond?

Captain Jayne Smith was dead to the Kingdoms of the Earthprime and also, since the death of Kim Solo, dead inside. She'd been institutionalised by the HMS Neon-Lit City and, unless her orders were reneged by a reigning Monarch of Europa, she'd remain with her ship, hidden away from an Earthprime populace within the asteroid field which orbits Jupiter.

Jonas vows that he will never succumb to the fear of being alone and the downward spiral of decaying self-confidence which would ultimately lead to regret: commitment and ambition are his only desires and the focal point of his motivations.

The opportunity has arisen for Captain Jonas Dean to sever the taut rope that shackles him to the Earthprime Kingdoms and to venture on alone; a space pioneer in full-flight.

Kira and his parents wouldn't understand, yet history once revealed would show the future Orders that he had completed his mission and without doubt, within the next century, the Second or Third Orders of the Spaceprime would rediscover the HMS Neon-Lit City and read through Captain Jayne Smith's logbook and his name would live on as legend.

The only truly regrettable downside is that Kira Yu will be dead and his parents will be long gone; he will never again see those who matter most to him.

Guilt infiltrates Jonas's thought processes, so he buries his guilt alongside his closed emotions and his unrequited desires.

You think too much, Kira had once told him.

Jonas Dean stands alone within the roundhouse viewing station, watching the asteroids drifting within the infinite void sea. "I do think too much as I talk myself up and I think myself down, but that's what happens when you're born under the star sign of Pisces," Jonas contemplates.

A portion of unbreakable glass refracts within the white-lit observatory outpost and Pisces is highlighted within space; its constellation is magnified and visible to Jonas's naked eye, a three-dimensional holographic image of the water sign having suspended itself within the centre of the observation point.

The constellation Pisces isn't easily visible from Earth and Jonas suddenly remembers that the technologies which had been installed by Franc and Solo are state-of-the-art and thought operated, and he marvels at the holographic image rotating above the solar system mosaic – the magnification is the clearest view that he has ever seen of the arrangement of stars.

Jonas is contented by the image set out before him and all thoughts of his mixed emotions dissolve as he stares at the enhancement of the Pisces constellation superimposed upon a framed pane of unbreakable glass and converted to hologram at the centre of the observatory.

A bright flash of a dying star dances across the refraction before it melts away into the vacuum of space.

Jonas makes a wish as after all, it is his birthday.

Born a Piscean

I see the shooting stars falling out of the sky,
I see the stars shine out for me,
I search the constellations;
I'm looking for the one: the water sign,
I was born a Piscean.

I'm going down again,
I've talked myself down,
I've thought myself down,
I've gotta turn it around.
A bottomless pit,
I can't see the top,
I'm falling, I'm falling,
I can't make it stop.

I see the shooting stars falling out of the sky,
I see the stars shine out for me,
I search the constellations;
I'm looking for the one: the water sign,
I was born a Piscean.

I'm going down again,
I've talked myself down,
I've thought myself down,
I've gotta turn it around.
A bottomless pit,
I can't see the top,
I'm falling, I'm falling,
I can't make it stop.

Spiralling upwards,
Well wouldn't you know,
I've come to terms with myself,
Feel my aura glow.
Out from the pit,
Free in the air,
Happy at last,
Until the next wave of despair.

I see the shooting stars falling out of the sky,
I see the stars shine out for me,
I search the constellations; I'm looking for the one: the water sign,
I was born a Piscean.

CHAPTER 9

Saturn's Rings

"It started with the Antarctica Incursions and this was the catalyst for the biggest fuck-up in the history of mankind," Smith states factually as she sits stiff shouldered within the Captain's chair upon the bridge of the HMS Neon-Lit City.

Jonas had slept for hours upon the comfortable two-seater within the observatory, the brightly lit lighthouse having brought him spiritual contentment for the first time on his long journey.

His recovery sleep had been broken by Smith's voice over the intercom. "Join me on the bridge and I'll finish my story," was all that she had said.

After the awakening message, Jonas had sat up from his slept-upon sofa to find that the observatory's reinforced glass panel surround had refracted in several different places. A dozen constellations, the mysterious midnight blue hue of Neptune, as well as Saturn and his shaded rings had all become magnified within the strengthened glass framework and were currently on view, whilst suspended above the house of light's mosaic floor, a holographic image had manifested itself from his mind: a single planet was rotating before his eyes. Jonas had dreamt and his dreams had been projected and magnified: the blue planet spinning upon its axis: Jonas had dreamt of Earth; Jonas had dreamt of home.

Washed, shaved and refreshed, he had made his way down the central hull of the fabled craft to the control hub of the Stargazer class vessel, where Captain Jayne Smith was already in attendance.

The hard leather-backed seat is surprisingly comfortable as he sits in the vacant First Officer's chair upon the bridge of the HMS Neon-Lit City, staring at the dark floating masses of rock from the panoramic view that the bridge of the Stargazer offers.

Jonas listens intently to the HMS Neon-Lit City Captain; in all of Earth's distant history, he has never once heard of the Antarctica Incursions.

Smith's harsh words begin to flow; the ship's Captain is speaking in a venomous tone. "In the year of 2030 and due to immense pressure from all of the old nations of the Earth, the Madrid Protocol was overturned," Captain Smith pauses to gather herself, choosing her words carefully. "The Madrid Protocol was a treaty that protected Antarctica's environment from oil and mineral exploration. The treaty had come into effect in the year of 1998 and should have lasted for fifty years to protect Antarctica's barren and fragile ecosystem, but the old nations of the Earth reneged on the treaty as they had all become desperate."

Jonas asks the obvious question; it fell from his lips, "Why?"

Smith's anger begins to grow in her reply and with every word which she expends. "The world's oil reserves were almost dry. The Middle-Eastern and European oil reserves were long since gone and the United States of America had tapped into the last of her oil reserves in Alaska and the Rocky Mountains. In the year of 2028, the Arctic reserves were mined and within twelve months the oil supply from the Arctic field had begun to run dangerously low which left Antarctica as the last of the great untapped oil fields. There was no agreement made between the nations of old on how to split up the huge expansive oil reserve, just an agreement to abolish the Madrid Protocol. And so the mining of oil from Antarctica became a free for all," she states.

Smith stands and begins to walk around her theatre of command with her hands clasped rigid and centred at the small of her back; her words become more and more agitated. "There was an oil rush between nations: men, machinery, rigging, ships, drills, every piece of known hardware required for the exploration and the mining of oil descended upon Antarctica. The fragile ecosystem was destroyed in a matter of days. Hundreds of oil wells were built in a matter of weeks on the icy isolated continent and off the coast of Antarctica. The nations with the most extensive and flexible resources built the majority of the oil rigs and they soon began raping Antarctica of its oil reserves," she says, venting her fury.

Smith looks out of her panoramic bridge view at the swaying asteroids within the cluster with her arms crossed in defence of her story and with her back to Captain Jonas Dean. "The old nations of the Earth soon found out that they were all drilling from the same massive oilfield and it didn't take long for them to realise that if one or two oil rigs from another competing nation were made inoperable then it would protect the oil supply for their sponsoring nation." Captain Jayne Smith's head bows low. "And so the Incursions began," she says.

Pre-war history is a blur to Jonas, yet he's fascinated by Smith's account and does not doubt her words.

Smith raises her head once more and continues with past histories retold. "It was the little things at first: oil rigs becoming redundant for a day or so due to technical glitches which upon thorough investigation turned out to be sabotage. Secret operations commenced and Special Forces were brought in by the various nations to deploy guerrilla warfare tactics. An all-out proxy war ensued and the multinational oil rigs began to be systematically destroyed, scarring a once iconic landscape. Helicopter gunships rained down their missiles and destroyers anchored off Antarctica's coastline opened up with their heavy artillery. The whole damn situation became so bad that some of the stronger nations began sending in their infantry and hiring mercenaries; seizing oil platforms and drilling from the captured rigs. All of the old nations showed their resilience during this, the coldest of all proxy wars, and when an oil platform was lost to an embattled nation, there was always a redoubling of effort and two more rigs were built to take the place of the one that had been destroyed, causing more and more armed reinforcements to be sent into the conflict zone to guard the new builds."

Jonas stands up from the First Officer's chair and makes his way to the Neon-Lit City Captain's side. "How did it all end?" he asks calmly.

Smith unfolds her arms and quietly states, "It just ended and in the year of 2036 the Antarctica oil reserves had run dry. Not only was the iconic landscape scarred beyond recognition, but the world was also irrevocably harmed as Antarctica's fragile environment also influenced global climate and weather patterns. The world was without oil and the climate change crisis had escalated."

*

Josiah Dean hasn't slept all night and has spent the small hours sitting upon the beach at his Atlantis home, looking skywards into the clear summer's night.

He checks the inside pocket of his jacket to confirm that the package which is addressed to Kira Yu has not left his side throughout the cool evening.

He has watched as the lit torches faded upon the hillside until the last glow had extinguished and as the dawn breaks free, he lifts his stiff aching body off the sandy beach, collects his keys and drives his solar-powered, battery-enhanced car through the Anglian desert; the shifting sands of the new desert surround him on all sides as he drives the desert trail to the Spaceprime Central Academy.

The world is a better place than it had been over a century ago his own father had once told him. And Josiah Dean has dwelt upon his father's words.

Jacob Dean had preached to his only son about the old world; a world that had gone to hell. Uncertainty had rippled throughout the nations of old when the world's oil supply had dried up: fuel and food had become scarce commodities, electrical blackouts had been an almost permanent fixture whilst poverty and disease had prevailed. The elitist state had grown and with that the emergence of the super-class society; the chosen few who did not starve, who did not grow hungry, who were never cold and always had access to the best medical facilities.

Josiah Dean's late father's words were engrained in his memory. "The world stood on the edge of an abyss when World War Three broke out," he had once said.

As tough as life could be in the twenty-second century, his father and his father before him had lived through far worse and Josiah was grateful for the rule and guidance of the Kings of the New Earth, yet nothing would ease his suffering. His only son: dead, whose memory would live on through the hearts and minds of the people who had known him and the people who had loved him. Kira Yu had known his only son; Kira Yu had loved his only son and it was a matter of utmost urgency for Josiah Dean to deliver his son's package to Kira Yu.

*

"Ship: schematic alpha one, on screen," Smith orders through the HMS Neon-Lit City's voice recognition software.

Jonas Dean watches the central vista as the overlay of the HMS

Neon-Lit City schematic appears as a hologram.

"As you can see from this basic diagram, the ship is split into sixteen sections: eight sections forward and eight sections aft. The Neon-Lit City has three distinct levels. The bridge is situated on the upper level which is also the level where the berths are located. The central level is where the living quarters, galley, engineering and observation decks reside. The lower level is the hold," Jayne pauses, allowing Jonas to cast his eye over the holographic blueprint.

Captain Jayne Smith adds one final statement to her overview of the HMS Neon-Lit City. "The hold is sealed," she says ominously.

Jonas faces his fellow Captain. "What is in the hold?" he asks in the hope that the answer will define his journey.

The question is left hanging in the conditioned air of the bridge as Captain Jayne Smith makes her way back to her seat of command. "Captain Dean, please take a seat," Smith replies whilst motioning to her equal with her hand for him to retake the vacant First Officer's chair.

Captain Jayne Smith stretches out her arms along the length of her leather-bound armrests. Captain Jonas Dean has waited long enough for the truth. "In the year of 2037, a series of extreme weather events occurred throughout the world. Super hurricanes ripped across the Atlantic and devastated the east coast of the United States of America. A deluge of monsoons flooded most of Europe's capital cities and the rift in the ozone layer expanded exponentially. Oil and gas were by now resources of the past and the economy was on the brink of collapse. During the early part of the twenty-first century, DNA medical cures for cancer, Alzheimer's and Parkinson's disease had led to a short-lived golden age of medical treatment, but a consequence of the breakthrough was that the world population exploded and the birth rate became ten times that of the death rate. A booming population and the emergence of a super-class society, where ninety-nine percent of new births were being born into abject poverty, had led to a greater consumption of precious finite resources which impacted the worsening climate. The Arctic ice caps had all melted away, sea levels had risen drastically and one-third of the British Isles was by now underwater. The old nations of the Earth failed to plan, they failed to invest and implement new technologies due to the pressures of the economy; the old nations failed to find lasting solutions to conflict and to come together for the greater good," Smith says whilst evoking past failures.

Jonas Dean shifts uncomfortably in his seat as the unknown history of the Earth is set out clearly before him and he holds his breath in his accepted knowledge that a worse part of Smith's truth is about to follow.

The grey-haired Europa Spaceprime Captain exhales an unburdening sigh and then delivers the final part of her story. "In the year of 2038, and with the Earth perched precariously upon a precipice, the old nations came together for the greater good. Their leaders, all members of the elitist classes, along with the greatest scientific minds on the planet met to discuss the way forward and to plan future policy. The scientists warned of future catastrophic climate events due to global warming, rising sea levels and climatic conditions. At a three-day summit, all of the world's leaders agreed to a plan of action and they called this plan the way forward: Project New Dawn."

In silence, Smith stands once more and walks slowly towards the panoramic view screen, where she takes in the bleak well of the deep void of space which lies beyond her asteroid infested haven.

Jonas watches Smith as she composes herself whilst sensing her final verbal onslaught.

Captain Jayne Smith breaks her silence and her voice cuts a swathe through the bridge of the HMS Neon-Lit City. "The implementation of Project New Dawn occurred on the 1st of July in the year of 2038. At 0729 hours, Greenwich Mean Time, solar radiation ripped through the ozone layer along the equatorial line. Millions died in the initial wave of the deadly solar activity. At 0731 hours, Greenwich Mean Time, over a secure communications line, the following message was received: 'Codename is New Dawn'. During the course of the next three minutes, acknowledgements flowed over the single secure communications line, all stating the same message: 'Codeword is New Day'. Undercover of a terrifying global catastrophe, at 0735 hours, Greenwich Mean Time, on the 1st of July in the year of 2038, Project New Dawn was initiated and nuclear war commenced."

Jonas Dean shuts his eyes and leans back into the leather of his chair. "They all gave up," he exclaims soberly. "All the leaders of all the old nations of the world, and all of their greatest scientific minds – and mass murder was all that they could come up with."

Smith laughs hysterically and shakes her head in disdain. "It didn't end there Captain Dean, because the leaders of the old nations thought that they were clever. The calculation of the warhead yield upon the planet was that it would leave ninety-eight percent of the population dead. The old nations' leaders all believed that they had a foolproof plan to be amongst the two percent of the population who would survive the holocaust event and hence lead the new fledgling society. The leaders of the elitist societies hid deep within their purpose-built nuclear bunkers with enough supplies to last them for a century. How wrong they all were; all of the old nations of the Earth had information on each other's secret bunkers, all governments knew everything about each other and trust had become a used currency. Come the new dawn, come the new day, everyone was striving for an edge. It was not the cities, nor the military headquarters, not the nuclear power plants nor the silos that were the main targets of the nuclear warheads; the alpha targets were the bunkers where the leaders of the old nations had sought their own sanctuary. The most powerfully ironic moment of the twenty-first century – in destroying the planet, the old nations' leaders also managed to destroy themselves. With so many warheads and conventional weapons aimed at the individual bunkers where the old leaders had chosen to hide, the targets that these weapons should have been destined for avoided termination. That, Captain Jonas Dean, is the reason why twenty percent and not two percent of the world's population survived the third great war," Smith says unmasking the past.

Captain Jonas Dean has tried to take in everything that Captain Jayne Smith has told him; his head is spinning by her revelations – that the Earthprime that had risen from the ashes of the Third World War had unbeknown been tirelessly striving to build a better life for its citizens and overcome the insanity of its hidden past.

Self-revelation strikes Jonas Dean. "The peoples of all the Kingdoms of the Earthprime need to be told the truth about their dark history: you must learn your lessons from the past, the old King used to say," he states to Smith.

Jayne Smith's lips purse. "So do you journey back to the Earth and set free the hidden truth? Or do you journey on, into the unknown, allowing the peoples of the Kingdoms of the Earthprime to live out their lives in ignorant bliss whilst remaining dead to all of the people who know you and all of the people who love you? Captain Dean, at some point in the near future, you'll have a decision to make," she says in reply to his reason.

"Déjà vu," Jonas Dean whispers under his breath.

*

The glass door to the public viewing gallery hisses as it slides open and Katherine Jenkins, the on-duty Cap-com, strides into the observation booth and stands alongside Josiah Dean who is viewing the stagnant monitors; the rasping static-filled public viewing gallery is sapping his inner strength with every moment that passes. "You've asked to see me?" Jenkins says with a little too much authority.

"I'll come straight to the point," Josiah replies calmly as he feels inside his jacket pocket. "I've something to give to Doctor Kira Yu and I'm aware that she attends this place at 2200 hours every evening."

"I'll stop you right there, Mr Dean," Jenkins says abruptly and then marches out of the viewing gallery, leaving Josiah Dean somewhat perplexed.

Katherine Jenkins returns moments later with a thin packet held tightly within her right hand. "Doctor Yu is on assignment for the next five months in preparation for a forthcoming mission and Cap-com Snow wanted to give her this," she says whilst holding out the item in her hand. "Hubert Snow is not the most forthcoming of men but we all know that his heart's in the right place and he's been trying to find the right moment to give this to Kira."

Katherine Jenkins hands the thin packet to Josiah Dean who places it next to the wrapped package inside his jacket pocket.

"I'd be obliged if you'd deliver the item to Doctor Yu," Jenkins says sincerely. "Apartment sixteen, New Buildings estate," Jenkins follows up as she winks at the old man. "And you didn't hear that from me," she clarifies with a note of caution vented harsh within her speech.

Josiah Dean dips his head in appreciation of the guidance afforded; the Cap-com Supervisor was certainly pushy and forthright, but her heart was definitely in the right place.

And with a wrapped package and a thin packet to deliver to Kira

Yu, Jonas's father ventures to the public viewing gallery's glass door exit. Yet before he steps through it, he turns back to face the on-duty Cap-com. "How far is it to the New Buildings estate?" he asks.

"If you take the coastal road: eighty miles," Katherine Jenkins offers courteously.

And Josiah Dean departs the public viewing gallery with his purpose augmented.

*

Captain Jonas Dean has regained his composure – after all, the events of the twenty-first century belong to a different time, a different mind-set; however, there are still questions to be answered and Jonas begins to pace the bridge with one question stuck firmly at the forefront of his mind and he asks it evenly, "What, Captain Smith, is in the hold?"

"I'd have thought by now that it would be obvious, Captain Dean," Smith says, having relaxed into the confines of her Captain's chair. "The lights went out on the world for fifty years until, in the year of 2088, new leaders emerged and began the process of organising the sparse populace. In different parts of the world, searches were undertaken by specialist teams to ascertain every available resource that was left upon the planet. It was during these searches that several bunkers were located – the underground shelters where the elitist classes had hidden during the Third World War. The bunkers were partially intact, but all life had been extinguished during the initial strike. The underground bunkers were initially located in three different Kingdoms: the Kingdom of the North, the Kingdom of Asia and the Kingdom of Americas. The partially intact bunkers held a minefield of information relating to the secrets of the pre-war world and the new leaders of the Kingdoms sent in their top historians to collate all of the information. The lead historian for the

Kingdom of the North was a man called Hans Reiger, for the Kingdom of Asia, Kim Solo and for the Kingdom of Americas, Aaron Ames."

"Historians – of course, this ship is a data repository," Jonas exclaims with awareness dawning.

The huge weight of Smith's responsibility has lifted off her ageing shoulders as her trouble has been shared. "During the decade which followed, all of the bunkers were located in all five of the new Kingdoms of the Earthprime. Every single document, disk, record and file relating to Project New Dawn was collected and eventually shipped to the Kingdom of Europa. The old Kings came together in the year of 2100 to discuss their find. The focus of the fledgling society was to rebuild the cities and give the peoples' lives meaning. History is littered with human atrocity on a grand scale: the death of the innocent during wartime, Nazi death camps and ethnic cleansing to name but a few. However, nothing could come close to the liquidation that occurred on the 1st of July in the year of 2038. The old Kings couldn't bring themselves to tell their peoples about the pre-planned annihilation, but they did agree that at some point in the distant future the truth would have to be known. So they commissioned a ship, the HMS Neon-Lit City, invented a cover story and asked the historians from around the globe if they'd be willing to undertake a mission to the stars to hide the information off-planet until such a time came when the Kings of a new-age Earth decreed that the peoples of the Kingdoms of the Earthprime were ready to hear about the dark past of the twenty-first century," Smith states whilst ending her recollection.

Jonas sighs wearily. "The great mystery resolved: the HMS Neon-Lit City is an archive ship that was sent into the void by the Kings of old to bury a past which had reviled them all. What is it that drives men to such madness as to intentionally slaughter the majority of the world's population?" Jonas says as he thinks aloud.

"Desperation and the thought that they would emerge from the Armageddon event as Kings," Smith says with a hint of sarcasm in her voice.

*

The House Manager of the New Buildings estate is steadfast in not letting Josiah Dean enter apartment sixteen as he thinks this old man stooping before him couldn't possibly be part of the great and virulent Europa Spaceprime.

Josiah Dean's story doesn't hold any water with the man in charge of the building, but he does offer to store the wrapped package and the thin packet until the good-looking young woman with the strange eyes arrives back at her apartment.

Josiah is having none of it and he appears somewhat confused, which is merely a ruse allowing him to make a great show of checking the time upon his solid silver engraved timepiece.

The House Manager immediately flinches and backtracks on the idea of non-admittance as he witnesses the unmistakable gleam of the Spaceprime's badge of honour. He mops away the sweat which has begun to break out upon his neck and brow with a soiled handkerchief, realising that Josiah Dean is clearly Europa Spaceprime and not to be messed with.

The apartment key and directions are quickly handed over as the House Manager has no intention of upsetting his bosses and losing his cushy number.

With a fixed grin of justification set adrift over his wrinkled features, Josiah Dean wanders his way to the apartment's stairway and begins to climb the dimly lit stairwell to the third floor. Finding Kira's apartment, he turns the key in the lock and steps over the threshold and into the sparse quarters of Kira Yu's sanctuary home.

He doesn't wish to stay long as intruding upon Kira's personal space he thinks is an invasion of her privacy, and so Josiah takes the wrapped package and the thin packet out of his jacket pocket and lays them both neatly upon the mahogany desk which is situated under a tall window with views overlooking communal gardens and the bay beyond.

Kira's desktop is immaculately kept: pens, paper, pencils and paperclips all have their homes and he leaves his two delivered items in clear sight, before he takes one last look at the view from Kira's window, Kira Yu's aspect; Kira Yu's escape, before vacating her apartment. After dropping off the key to the nervy House Manager, he leaves the New Buildings estate behind, satisfied that he has done the right thing by his lost son; his last wish finally fulfilled.

*

All the revelations have been exposed; the fog of mystery has lifted; his mission is complete – yet no-one will ever know.

Jonas, with a renewed vigour, spends the weeks that follow his enlightenment pacing through the arterial walkways of the iconic vessel, taking in every nook and cranny, photographing rooms, passageways and the encircling asteroids from the HMS Neon-Lit City's various vantage points whilst armed only with his hand-held camera. He respects the sealed hold and won't venture down to the lower decks.

Captain Jayne Smith has given him free run of her ship and, once he's undertaken his initial tour of the vessel, Jonas has begun reporting to the Neon-Lit City Captain on a daily basis as there's plenty of work to be done onboard the Stargazer class vessel: electrical and operational maintenance are the norm and are duties he can handle.

Smith has flatly refused to use any Nanotech technology to aid with the repair work as she prefers all maintenance to be carried out the old-fashioned way and Jonas doesn't mind as the manual work makes him feel useful and he throws himself into his new role as it keeps his mind and body occupied.

Every evening, after a hard day's graft, Captain Jonas Dean returns to the brightly lit roundhouse viewing station where he sleeps upon the comfortable two-seater, his quarters abandoned.

Captain Jayne Smith often joins him at the end of a working day and they talk over a bottle of wine or water.

Jonas has been a guest on the Stargazer for well over a month when, during the course of one late evening, he begins to reflect on his newfound knowledge within the brightly lit observation outpost. "What enables mankind to administer such an atrocity?" he asks Smith.

"Arrogance," she replies sharply.

"I'd prefer to think of it as desperation," Jonas responds.

"I'd prefer not to think about it at all," the Neon-Lit City Captain shoots back which causes Jonas to surmise: "The elitist classes developed a god-complex that percolated into their own decision making and they tried to save themselves first and screw the rest of the world's population and they all got what they deserved."

Jayne Smith lifts up her precious bottle of water. "I'll drink to that, Captain Dean," she says in full agreement.

Insight strikes Jonas. "These are the past events which we cannot alter and have no power to change. You need not stay here, Captain Smith. Your mission is accomplished and, since the death of the old King, your orders have quite obviously defaulted; there's nothing left to be gained by tending to this vessel until you take your last breath. Come with me to Saturn, his rings and beyond, where together we shall travel the unknown universe. My vessel is more than spacious enough to carry another passenger. And maybe at some point in the future, I can take you home to Earth." Jonas ceases his talking upon realising what he has spoken of – this is the first time since his journey commenced that he has even contemplated voyaging back to Earth.

Captain Jayne Smith replies openly. "Thank you for your kind offer, Captain Dean – it's the best offer I've had in the last nine years, but my place is with my vessel and I've grown so used to being alone. The HMS Neon-Lit City is a part of me, it's my home and my responsibility, and my mission will not be complete until I draw my last breath onboard this vessel attached to Asteroid 4571. Over the past nine years, I've embraced my own solitude and my memories are buried deep within the confines of this ship. This is the life that I choose and you of all of the people I know should understand that I will never abandon my mission on a whim or a flight of fancy."

Jonas Dean is at a loss for words: would he embrace his own solitude, before drowning within his impending self-imposed isolation? Kira's insight had unnerved him.

*

The one-mile trek to the underwater habitat had been uneventful for the newly promoted Doctor Kira Yu and her fellow medical officers.

Doctor Grace James had followed the compass bearing that General Thalt had given her and the three medical elite staff had trudged through the ocean's murky polluted waters to the three interconnecting domes which reside at the base of a central steel structure that rises vertically out of the seabed.

For Kira, this has been a new experience and sharing quality time with her two female work colleagues is an experience that she's beginning to enjoy. Grace James is a strong-willed mentor, whereas

Aileen Grey is a talkative and dizzy colleague and friend.

Kira spent the first month of her assignment listening to Grace's advice on all matters medical and hearing Aileen's long-winded accounts of her social life which, if truth be told, is a complete mess, a car wreck from start to finish; it seems to Kira that Aileen had an awful lot of loose ends in her social life before she undertook her assignment.

The Europa Spaceprime medical elite team arise early and work long hours throughout the day, yet it's the evenings which Kira enjoys when they all sit down together with a bottle of wine and talk.

For the past month, Aileen and Grace have led the conversation, reciting anecdotes, telling stories and talking nonsense, especially if one bottle has led to three. But on this particular evening, Doctor Grace James begins to probe. "You're always so very quiet, Kira?" she asks.

At times, Aileen can't help but take over the conversation and she exercises all of her self-control to remain silent as Kira fights her own conscience for an answer.

"I'm sorry," Kira says honestly. "I'm not used to being around people for twenty-four hours a day and this experience is completely new to me."

"Aileen and I aren't too dissimilar to you, Kira. We've both trodden a similar path to gain the careers we've aspired too. It can be a lonely progression, but I do admit that I admire the fact that both you and Jonas managed to survive the full term in the tank – I would have got out after a day," Grace says with a welcome smile of friendship drawn over her features.

"After an hour," Aileen remarks, at which both Kira and Grace laugh out loud.

The wine is beginning to kick in, as Kira considers, "Was I completely insane to see out the fifteen months? It never occurred to me to walk as I saw it as a challenge thrown down to me by the Europa Spaceprime, but in hindsight it could've killed me."

"It nearly did," Grace says, pouring more wine as raucous laughter mixes with the recycling air.

The wine has taken the edge off Kira and Doctor Grace James, seeing how relaxed and talkative she's become, decides now is as good a time as any to try and guide her fellow medical officer. "Kira, don't take this personally, but do you see your regular nightly visits to the Europa Spaceprime Mission Control as worthwhile? Jonas Dean is lost to us all. Do you actually believe that he's still alive? It defies rational thought," she says, asking the question as sincerely as she can, but knowing that the question posed will still hurt Kira and maybe even offend her.

Kira empties her glass and upon taking a deep breath manages her careful reply. "I've spent a lot of time with Jonas and I was lucky enough to get to know the real Jonas Dean. I'll go to my grave in the belief that he's still out there, somewhere in the universe amongst the stars. I know it's not a rational belief and I'm also aware that Jonas has spurned me for his own burdening ambitions, yet I refuse to and have never shed a tear over his loss. Life will go on; days, weeks, months, years and decades will pass me by and Jonas may never arrive home, but it'll not stop me looking up at the stars at night and believing that he's still out there; lost to us all within the spatial void."

Aileen begins to cry and Kira leans forwards to cradle her in her arms.

Grace James, with her composure choked, speaks quietly to Kira. "Aileen and I are so proud to be your friends, but as a friend I must tell you that until you begin to grieve you cannot gain closure and therefore you'll be unable to move forwards with your life. Only then can time heal your broken heart and raise your soul, and we'll both be here for you when that time comes."

Kira hugs Grace as Aileen tries in vain to wipe her tears away.

*

Captain Jonas Dean stays two months on the vessel of his childhood dreams before he decides to ship out.

The airlock doors which intersect the two great rocket ships of the Europa Spaceprime are set wide apart and Captain Jonas Dean awaits Captain Jayne Smith at the HMS Neon-Lit City's airlock door, where a final farewell will be bid between the two Europa Spaceprime Captains.

Smith appears from out of the shadows to where Jonas is standing at full attention and Captain Dean salutes his counterpart; his mark of respect. "Captain Jayne Smith, it's truly been an honour to have met you and gained an insight into and an understanding of our planet's history," he says proudly.

Captain Jayne Smith takes a short stride forwards and places a kiss upon Jonas's cheek. "You are most welcome, Captain Dean, although I do have to ask, purely out of curiosity. Have you made your decision?"

Jonas's gaze drifts downwards and he is unable to meet Captain Smith's eyes as he is consumed by guilt because of the answer that he's about to give. "Although I have acquired the knowledge that my King and the peoples of the Kingdoms of the Earthprime require to gain a greater understanding and to learn the lessons of the past, I believe that my mind is already set: I must journey on," he replies.

"Is this the final decision that you've definitely made, Captain?" Smith enquires.

"I've made my decision to navigate the Starship Zx12 into deep space and spend some time on my own planning out the next stage of my journey," Jonas replies although he feels unsure of his own direction – he'd expected to be lifted by his impending adventure, yet confusion and self-doubt reign.

"Where will your initial journey take you, Captain Dean?" Smith asks, recognising some of her own single-minded individualistic traits within her fellow Europa Spaceprime Captain.

"Saturn's gate," Jonas says with a far-off look in his eyes.

Jayne Smith's brow furrows. "I've never heard Saturn called that before," she remarks.

"Forgive me, Captain Smith, it's just something that someone once said to me. I believe that it's at Saturn that I'll make my final decision to journey on to the distant stars," Jonas states.

"And I'm sure that you'll make the correct decision, Captain Dean. Whatever you decide, I have something for you," Smith states, holding out her thick green-velvet-bound logbook. "This book contains the full mission log for the journey made by the HMS Neon-Lit City. A detailed history of the events leading up to Project New Dawn is recorded in this logbook and if you do decide to return home, then this information will be vital to the Kings of the new Earth," she says as she hands over the written record that she's kept for over forty years.

Jonas cradles his gifted treasure. "I cannot accept this Jayne," he replies. "I've always had every intention of travelling into the beyond and never looking back at what might have been or what could have been and if I should perish within the void, then this invaluable gift would be lost along with me."

"And there's the rub, Captain Dean. I'll probably not encounter another human being for the rest of my natural life and giving you the logbook is my decision to make; a final request," Captain Smith says unapologetically.

Jonas nods respectfully whilst holding onto the evidential logbook before he steps through the airlock door. Once onboard the Zx12, he turns to face his equal.

And with a straight back and stiffening shoulders, a poised Smith salutes him. "Good luck Captain Dean, and Godspeed," she says to the Europa Spaceprime spaceman.

Jonas Dean reciprocates her salute. His lasting impression of Captain Jayne Smith is of her standing to full attention; her vivid angular features are engraved upon his memory as the Starship Zx12's airlock door slides shut, thus isolating the two ships.

*

The Starship Zx12 drifts away from the HMS Neon-Lit City and Jonas takes one final look at the beacon of light that originates from the summit of Asteroid 4571, where Captain Jayne Smith's form is clearly visible within the observatory through the Starship Zx12's cockpit view. Jonas eases his Starship out of Jupiter's orbiting asteroid field and steers his vessel into open space to prepare for hyperdrive initiation; the historic HMS Neon-Lit City is once again hidden with its secret revealed only to him.

*

Captain Jayne Smith leans forwards upon the comfortable two-seater within the brightly lit roundhouse viewing station. The Starship Zx12 is gloriously magnified before her eyes within a refracted glass panel and Jonas's ship is visible at a full stop well beyond the asteroid cluster as an exhilarated Smith awaits in wonderment for Captain Jonas Dean to engage the hyperdrive onboard the Starship Zx12. "This, I've just got to see," she says with a wry smile forming across her lips.

And the smile breaks free over an ageing Neon-Lit City Captain's face as Captain Jonas Dean rips through the known system whilst set on his course to Saturn, where for one brief moment the Starship Zx12 occupies its rightful place in space and within a heartbeat the ship is gone; the vacuum void rippling outwards from the Starship's vacated position.

*

Jonas can feel the heady rush of light-speed on hyperdrive until his Starship commences its braking procedure and his metallic cockpit seat once again unleashes his body and places him back in command of his ship.

The journey from Jupiter's asteroid cluster to Saturn is longer than the journey from Earth to Jupiter and it will be one hell of a hop from Saturn through to infinity, Jonas thinks.

The imposing presence of the mysterious ringed planet captivates Captain Dean as Saturn's yellowish tinged hue dominates his cockpit view with its lack of colour due to an enshrouded planetary surface that'd not be giving up its secrets without a fight.

Jonas won't risk landing his craft upon Saturn's surface as the gaseous giant is in constant turmoil, where high winds prevail. Early twenty-first-century data had shown very little information about the surface of the great ringed planet which is further compounded by the huge force of the planet's gravitational pull. If Captain Jonas Dean did manage to land the Starship Zx12 upon Saturn then he'd almost certainly be unable to get off the planet's surface. So Jonas slips his Starship into a high decaying orbit, where already the severe gravitational pull has begun to take its toll.

Saturn may not reveal to him the mysteries of its surface composition, but Jonas Dean is far from concerned as he's travelled to the gas mass for an entirely different reason – Jonas's primary desire is to unravel the secrets of Saturn's rings; a precursor to his journey into the unknown.

He peers from his orbit vantage point at the hypnotic concentric rings which are coloured from black to light through several shades of grey; the defined particles, glistening within the lighter shaded rings, could be the debris from a stray comet or a captured Moon that had been crushed to a pulp and then spat out with unimaginable force.

Jonas sits in his cockpit seat within the confines of the Starship Zx12 for days on end, staring at Saturn and his glorious rings, contemplating his life and the journey which has led him to this majestic planet.

He thinks of his parents, his King, the peoples of the Kingdoms of the Earthprime and his colleagues within the Spaceprime core, and he thinks of Ashilla, the apparitional Ice Queen and her warning of the great ringed planet. But most of all, he thinks of Kira; especially Kira.

It's at this place that he will decide his own fate, his inescapable future, his destiny; here, at Saturn's gate.

Saturn's Rings

Yesterday I saw Saturn's rings, but I've never seen anything as
beautiful as you,
Yesterday it meant everything to be in your arms and for you to hold
me too,
But that was yesterday,
And today's another day,
And the ache inside my heart is here and set to stay,
And the loneliness I feel,
Seems oh so very real,
And embedded in the core of my soul.

I saw Saturn's rings; so beautiful,
I saw Saturn's rings; so wonderful,
I saw Saturn's rings, but nothing compares to you.

Tomorrow I'll see Saturn's rings, but I've never seen anything as
beautiful as you,
Tomorrow I'd give anything to be in your arms and for you to hold
me too,
Yet tomorrow is nearly here,
And tomorrow's another day,
And the ache inside my heart will finally fade away,
And the loneliness I feel,
Won't seem so very real,
And my soul will rise and I'll finally find a way.

I saw Saturn's rings; so beautiful,
I saw Saturn's rings; so wonderful,
I saw Saturn's rings, but nothing compares to you.

I wish that I could see Saturn's rings, but I've never seen anything as
beautiful as you,
I wish that I could give everything to be in your arms and for you to
hold me too,
I'm wishing upon a star,
And praying for the day,
The future that I hope for will finally come my way,
And the loneliness I feel,
Will finally be healed,
And I'll be in your arms once again one day.

I saw Saturn's rings; so beautiful,
I saw Saturn's rings; so wonderful,
I saw Saturn's rings, but nothing compares to you.

I saw Saturn's rings; so beautiful,
I saw Saturn's rings; so wonderful,
I saw Saturn's rings, but nothing compares to you.

CHAPTER 10

The Simple Life

The individual hairs stiffen upon the nape of General Thalt's neck. It has been another difficult forty-eight hours for Thalt and his fellow generals, and the King of Europa is livid at the way that the events of the day have unfolded.

It has been nine months since the loss of the Starship Zx12 mission. Two World Conferences have been held, and on both occasions the Europan Prime has valiantly fought to reinstate the Starship Zx class Space Program, but his fellow Kings have turned their backs on the Europan Monarch and the political tide has turned against him.

A cold shiver pricks the General's spine as he fixes his gaze upon Bern, the King of the North, who is grinning inanely, an event that makes Thalt deeply uncomfortable as the Northern King is renowned for his unhappy nature.

King Johnson, the King of Americas, is speaking and all eyes have fallen upon him except for those of the King of Europa whose hard stare bears into King Bern. Johnson's rough tone drills through the tetchy atmosphere which has been generated over the Pentagonal table. "My Kings, the voting is in. The first item of legislation put forward by the King of Europa would decree an extension to the backing of the Europa Spaceprime Starship Zx class Space Program with a particular emphasis on forthcoming missions to seek out the wreckage of the HMS Neon-Lit City and to seek out the wreckage of the Starship Zx12: votes cast: five. Abstentions: none. Votes for: one. Votes against: four."

The Europan King's cold eyes do not leave Bern's as the vote is read out: the Europan Monarch's right hand is shaking involuntarily, swollen anger welling up inside of him.

The King of Americas reads out the terms of the second vote. "The second piece of legislation put forward by the King of the North is as follows. I, the King of the North, decree an immediate shutdown of the Europa Spaceprime Mission Control, to put an end to the false hope which has been generated by the Europan Kingdom after the loss of the Starship Zx12 mission: votes cast: five. Abstentions: two. Votes for: two. Votes against: one. And I hereby decree that the first motion has failed and that the second motion is carried."

The King of Europa arises unsteadily onto ageing legs; his right hand shakes spasmodically as he leans forwards over the legislative pentagonal star with stern eyes fixed upon the King of the North. And the Europan King speaks directly to Bern with his anger released. "It's a nasty game of pure politics that you play Bern. You seem to forget too easily the dark past of the twenty-first century and why the old Kings established this forum in the first instance. In those early days, hope was all that the old Kings could offer the citizens of the fledgling Earthprime Kingdoms. The old Kings embraced hope, fostering it willingly and nurturing it unconditionally. I will not sanction the second motion which has been passed today and turn my back on the expectations of my people. I hereby announce that I acknowledge the Kings' decision with regard to the second piece of legislation, but formally use my power of veto to disregard the decision that has been made. The Europa Spaceprime

Mission Control for the Starship Zx12's mission to the stars will remain online until the 17th of August in the year of 2149," the Sovereign Prime of Europa decrees.

General Thalt's pride bursts out as a broad smile as he watches King Bern's mood darken. The King of Europa doesn't wait for any response and, flanked by his three generals, he marches to his perimeter holding room with the two first ladies of the Europa Earthprime trailing in his wake. Lady Anne of Europa is the last of the Europan executives through the holding room door, whereupon she drops the heavy bolt to seal the antechamber.

During the course of the following forty-five minutes, the Europa Earthprime hierarchy gather their thoughts and make arrangements to leave for Spaceprime City whilst their Sovereign, who's usually so vocal after a world meeting, is lost within his own thoughts, where one solitary question is invading his regal sense of virtue; Bern's choice of words within the second piece of legislation had cut him to his core: was he selling false hope?

*

Kira Yu welcomes her regular period of nightly relaxation with her two medical colleagues. Her mornings are spent outside the underwater habitat, trudging along the ocean floor through the polluted claustrophobic seawater, and her afternoons are spent reading tutorials, medical theory and performing practical surgery on a plastic dummy under the watchful eye of Doctor Grace James. It's the evenings when she feels most relaxed and at ease with herself, and more open than at any other time of her life, as Kira has found friendship with like-minded people. Jonas's demise seems a lifetime away and his memory is beginning to slide away from her.

Kira has often questioned Jonas's decision to take his mission to the stars and she begins to question her own resolve as self-doubt creeps over her soul.

Doctor Grace James has coolly watched the change in her newest recruit. Over the passing days, weeks and months, Kira Yu's demeanour has become more positive and her personality has begun to shine through which has manifested itself as Kira carrying herself with greater confidence.

The plan which has been set in motion by Commander Marks, General Thalt and Doctor Grace James is simple enough: Kira Yu's acceptance of Captain Jonas Dean's death, because if Kira can accept Jonas's death then the Europa Spaceprime will be able to move forwards with its future objectives.

There is a lack of trained workers to undertake the most basic of tasks and each individual Spaceprime operative is a valuable asset. The remote launch of the medical staff to the new Moonbase, which will take place three days after the planned closure of the mission control for the Starship Zx12's ill-fated mission to the stars, is imperative and Doctor Kira Yu needs to be ready as the Europa Spaceprime values her expertise.

Commander Marks, General Thalt and Doctor Grace James had to get Kira Yu away from her nightly rendezvous at the Europa Spaceprime Mission Control and the training mission was too good an opportunity to miss.

Grace James watches Kira Yu and Aileen Grey who are deep in social discourse – it's time for the Chief Medical Officer to steer the conversation once more.

Doctor James sits upon her usual seat within the living area of the underwater habitat and infiltrates their rapport. "So, what'll you do when you arrive home Kira? Will you continue to attend the Europa Spaceprime Mission Control after your shifts have finished or will you look to your future?" James says in a balanced manner.

Kira replies whilst wavering at the thought of looking too far into her future. "I'm not sure anymore. I feel so detached from the outside world and Jonas's loss seems such a long time ago; maybe Josiah Dean is right."

"What did Jonas's father say?" Grace asks, seizing the moment and plotting future's course.

A distant Kira replies, "He told me that Jonas would have been insistent that I not waste my life waiting for a ghost."

This was it; an opportunity to end Kira's vigil and Grace does not waste her words: "Josiah Dean is right, of course – Jonas wouldn't want you to spend your time thinking about what might have been and holding onto the past for too long. Kira, you must move beyond this whole situation."

Kira resigns herself to considering a life without Jonas. "I'll endeavour to think about my future actions during the final weeks of our stay in the habitat," Kira promises.

Doctor Grace James holds out her hand and Kira takes a firm grip. "Whatever you decide Kira, you'll have my full support," she says in reply, before silence kills their conversation: Grace has often tried to put herself in Kira's position, but Kira's predicament is impossible.

*

Although Kira's enforced absence from the Europa Spaceprime Mission Control had initially deflated the diligent Cap-Com, Hubert Snow is no longer alone.

The mission clock shows two hundred and eighty-one days, and although Hubert Snow has habitually followed his nightly routine, the unchanged static discharge is still protesting an end-of-mission outcome. Snow glances up at the empty public viewing gallery as the midnight hour arrives and the two hundred and eighty-second day commences.

Two cups of freshly made coffee reside upon Snow's desk, where his view remains unchanged: static monitors, lack of data, dead life sign readings and the barren map of the known system.

General Thalt picks up his coffee as he sits informally beside his able Cap-Com. Since delivering the news to Kira Yu that she was to be placed on assignment for three months, Thalt has made a point of visiting Hubert Snow during the small hours of the day after he has finished his late evening paperwork; it is part of the deal that he made with Commander Marks and Doctor Grace James – able Cap-com Hubert Snow is also deemed to be a vital Europa Spaceprime asset and his initial irritation at General Thalt's nightly presence quickly evaporated.

General Thalt has waived protocol during the midnight hours and this has had the required effect of relaxing Snow.

Thalt rarely says much during his nightly visits, but he has become particularly non-commutative these past few nights since arriving back from the latest World Conference.

Hubert Snow decides to try his luck with his General and he is aware that only a direct approach will lead to answers. "General Thalt, is there anything that you'd like to get off your chest?" he asks.

The General quietly sips at his coffee and after further thought replies, "Are you sure you want to know, Hubert?"

It is the first time that the General has called Snow by his first name and Hubert Snow is intrigued by Thalt's thaw as here is a small chance for him to gain an insight into the machinations of the Europa Earthprime hierarchy. "I don't have anything else planned this evening General, Sir," he says.

Thalt speaks. "Times are tough, Hubert, and a few days ago the King attended the World Conference and for the third session in a row our King tried in vain to raise the necessary backing and resources for the continuation of the Starship Zx class Space Program whilst his allies deserted him; and to make matters worse, there was also a move to shut down the Europa Spaceprime Mission Control with immediate effect."

A thoughtful Snow asks the expected question. "What did my King do?"

Thalt laughs: a rare event indeed. "He vented his anger, rebuked his fellow Kings, stood his ground and turned defeat into victory," the Flight Director General conveys.

Hubert Snow feels enormous pride for his Sovereign Prime; a towering presence of the new-age.

General Thalt rises from his chair and stands proudly in front of Snow's console, looking out at the information-free monitors; with his back to Hubert Snow, he asks: "Hubert, do you think that Captain Jonas Dean is still alive?"

It's still an easy question for the able Cap-com to answer and he speaks clearly to the back of his General's head: "Sir, Captain Jonas Dean has been buried on the premise that the communications are down and therefore there's no signal emanating from the Starship Zx12 thus rendering all of the monitors within mission control dead. If Captain Dean's communications are down and his hyperdrive's not functioning then it could take him years to get back to Earth."

"Wouldn't that be something," Thalt mutters: more to himself.

"General, Sir, the control centre for the Starship Zx12's mission to the stars must remain open and manned indefinitely," Hubert Snow admonishes defiantly.

General Thalt shakes his head in abject defeat. "That is impossible Hubert, because unfortunately in our brave new world, politics still defines our direction. The King of Europa would become politically impotent if we didn't take the decision to close the Europa

Spaceprime Mission Control after twelve months. I'm truly sorry Hubert as I too would like to believe that Captain Jonas Dean is still alive and travelling through distant galaxies to unknown lands, but my rational thought and ordered mind tells me that Captain Jonas Dean perished shortly after the completion of the Hyperdrive mode of his mission," Thalt says, hinting at regret.

In silence, the General reseats himself next to the able Cap-com, hearing only the incessant static which prevails.

*

Tashi Chi sits resplendently to the left of her host at the King of Europa's consultation table in one of the many rooms within the King's royal apartments. Attaché Chi's sharply cut blonde hair has been manoeuvred into a tight bob and not a single strand has defied the cut whilst her intelligent hazel eyes have never left her host King as she's always watching and searching for weakness within the Monarch of Europa: this woman demands respect and she gets it.

The King of Europa is always careful of what he says and how he reacts in the presence of the Asian attaché. "I'm truly honoured and somewhat surprised at your visit, Miss Chi, and so soon after the last World Conference," the Europan King says whilst fully aware that this is the most important meeting he has had since the loss of the Starship Zx12 mission as it is at this meeting that the politics of future World Conferences will take their shape.

"Thank you for seeing me at such short notice, your Majesty," Tashi Chi says rather too pleasantly. "I always look forward to my visits to these shores to enhance the bond between our two great Kingdoms."

The King forces a smile: she is good, he will have to begrudgingly admit that to himself. Tashi Chi is attempting to lull him, a wily old fox like him; but all that matters is the Asian King's offer – and it will soon come, all he has to do is to remain patient.

Tashi Chi always enjoys sparring with the King of Europa; he knows the game better than she does, but there is little to gain by prolonging the small talk. The King of Asia's offer is immediately delivered by the Asian attaché who is acutely aware that her host King will not relish what she has to say: "Your majesty, I have been instructed by my King to offer you the following terms: immediate shutdown of the Europa Spaceprime Mission Control in agreement with the motion passed by all of the Kings of the Kingdoms at the last World Conference. The King of Asia also wishes that all future planned Zx class Starship missions are dropped and concentration of all assets and planet resources are diverted to the ongoing Moonbase project as the Kingdoms still need to take radioactive materials off-planet and bury them upon the Moon. In return, the King of Asia will stand at your side on all other issues which are raised. Would you like to take some time to discuss our recommendations with your advisors?"

"No," the King of Europa says flatly to the ice-cool attaché.

Tashi Chi frowns in response as the King of Europa is always so careful with his decision making and has often sought his own counsel on such matters. "I'd ask His Majesty to carefully consider the offer which has been made and not to make an emotional decision," she says in a pressing tone.

All hope for Captain Jonas Dean, the Starship Zx12 and the fate of the HMS Neon-Lit City is beginning to ebb away from the King of Europa's heart, yet the Sovereign Prime's shoulders begin to rise and fall as a guttural laugh escapes him.

The Asian attaché is stunned at being negotiated off-balance and is sent into a state of mind-shock as she has never before witnessed such a display at such an important meeting.

The King of Europa upon regaining his composure finds his voice and liberates his passions, "Miss Chi, I truly admire your skills of negotiation and I fully understand the consequences of my actions here today."

The great King pauses. "Three promises," he says as he bites down hard on his words.

"I don't understand," Chi replies, somewhat confused at the deal remaining uncut.

"One: the promise that my father, the old King of Europa, made to the families of the HMS Neon-Lit City crew. Two: the promise that I made to Captain Jonas Dean that if anything should happen to him then I'd do everything in my power to send out another mission into the known system to find him. Three: the promise that I made to his father, Josiah Dean, that I'd continue to search for his lost son. My reply to the King of Asia is a resounding no and the decision that I've made is purely emotional," states an animated Sovereign Prime.

The Asian attaché, still reeling from the Europan King's outburst, stumbles through her reply. "I'll deliver your message to my King, but you must understand that today the political landscape has irrecoverably shifted and the World Conferences will be a very difficult place for you in the near future." And without even thanking her host or waiting for him to reply, Tashi Chi, the Asian attaché, sweeps out of the Europan King's chambers.

Lady Guinevere enters the room as Chi departs and rushes to her Sovereign's side. "Your majesty," she says and waits for him to say something; anything.

The King of Europa has fallen into a catatonic silence and stares at the far wall of his consultation chamber.

Guinevere presses, "Your majesty, is there anything that I can do; is there anything that you need?"

The King's eyes never leave the consultation chamber's whitewashed walls as he mutters under his breath, "What we need is a miracle."

*

For the second time in six weeks, Captain Jonas Dean uses thrusters to reposition the Starship Zx12 into a higher orbit. He has spent the previous weeks analysing the data which he collected from Ganymede and reading through Captain Jayne Smith's logbook in great depth and detail and he is now attempting to focus his mind on the forthcoming decision which he has to make; a decision that is on hold.

And he has waited; patience learnt from Kira Yu at the academy. For six weeks he has calculated the effect of the rapidly decaying orbit upon his Starship and the window of opportunity is now upon him.

With his membrane reattached and his space helmet fixed firmly into position, Jonas stands at the airlock door of the Starship Zx12 with a jetpack strapped securely over his broad shoulders and tightly secured around his waist.

He falls forwards into the weightlessness of the vacuum void and drifts away from his Starship, to be swiftly caught up in the engrossing planet's gravitational riptide as it sweeps him in towards Saturn.

Jonas activates his jetpack thrusters to aid his plummet towards Saturn and his rings. He is travelling at an alarming speed on this, his first journey of the many that he has planned and the one which will be the most arduous and the most dangerous. He's rushing in towards Saturn, adjacent to the debris-ridden rings, and past the huge dark expanse of the particle-ridden 'E' Ring.

The minutes stretch into the passing hours as time becomes an irrelevance and Captain Jonas Dean feeds upon life-enhancing liquids. He's alone with his own thoughts and his own memories as he falls through the iconic isolation of an alien concentric landscape, descending onwards past the defined 'G' Ring whilst perpetually freefalling towards the giant gaseous beast.

Life's dreams lived, and Jonas begins to reflect on his life; his past, and only after contemplation could he decide on his own future fate. Jonas Dean is proud of his indoctrination into the Europa Spaceprime and his ambitions are being fulfilled beyond all of his hopes and wildest dreams whilst he's armed only with the knowledge that his own King would gladly trade places with him in a heartbeat.

The seclusion doesn't frighten him as he grew up alone, a prerequisite for the peoples of a post-nuclear age. But there had always been two people he could depend upon: his father, a Europa Spaceprime hero, and his mother, a rock and his anchor. All of his early memories are of long lazy days spent upon Atlantis Beach.

Jonas is accelerating to velocities beyond which any human has travelled without the protection of a hull whilst dropping down into Saturn's awaiting arms, plummeting past the 'F' Ring, the days falling by as he hurries past the captivating hallucinogenic formations with his speed unchecked.

The Keeler Gap passes him by and Jonas enters the particle-deficient Encke division, dropping forth to the brightly lit 'A' Ring.

An otherworldly luminescence lights up the 'A' Ring as he passes alongside the brightest of Saturn's rings, its luminosity illuminating the monochromatic landscape.

On and on he plummets, through the Huygens gap until the debris-ridden 'A' Ring gives way to the huge expanse of the Cassini Division: the wide gulf of empty space which lies between Saturn's 'A' ring and 'B' Ring; the photo-negative ringed landscape set out before him and falling away behind: a black void sea between two concentric coastlines.

Kira fills Jonas's thoughts as he swims through the empty space of the Cassini Division as he remembers for the first time in a long time how they'd first met at the academy; her storm-ravaged hair, her attitude and her style. His feelings had been nurtured, before he'd lost his ability to think only of himself within Kira's eyes of dual colour, where together they'd survived the tank, they'd completed their training and they'd honed their skills. It was his ambitions which had become focused, therefore sweeping away any chance that they may have had of a future together: soul mates lost.

Downwards Jonas plummets through the vastness of the Cassini Division, hurtling in towards the defined edge of the 'B' Ring with only regret filling his heart.

Jonas sweeps onwards, tumbling past the luminous glow of the 'B' Ring, falling further and further into Saturn's gaseous mass whilst thriving on self-administered liquids; time blurs as the hours merge with the days. And still Jonas falls with his mission exceeding all of his hopes and expectations; the Starship Zx12 is without doubt the pride of the Spaceprime fleet and its hyperdrive is a technological marvel. The data which he'd collected from the Moon of Ganymede is a new-age treasure haul and finding the fabled Stargazer class vessel, the HMS Neon-Lit City, and unearthing the hidden revelations of the past has been a truly humbling experience.

It is Ashilla's words, the words of his mind spoken, and all of the events of the past which have led him to Saturn and his rings, and it is here that he will make a rational, coherent decision and define his destiny.

Captain Jonas Dean is falling, falling, falling, further and further, forever onwards he plunges through the Maxwell Division and into the darker shaded 'C' Ring. The monochrome environment remains unchanged as he falls rapidly through the Guerin Division and into the vicinity of the 'D' Ring, the final ring before the planet with the huge imposing gas giant overwhelming his view. Once he has satisfied himself that he is well inside the 'D' Ring, he initiates the reverse thrusters on his jetpack to slow his descent.

Captain Jonas Dean of the First Order of the Spaceprime eventually comes to a full stop, adjacent to the final ring before Saturn's mass, where he manoeuvres himself using partial thrust into the particle-laden field and enters the rock-filled environment which, as with all of Saturn's rings, contains an array of particles, dust and rocks of differing shapes and various sizes.

Jonas finds the largest boulder in his field of view within his section of the ring and boldly reaches out for the ancient rock and tethers himself to the jagged mass; from this shackled position he leans forwards into the ring and picks out a small sample of floating debris.

Jonas holds the specimen in his gloved hand, brushing off its icy husk to reveal the weathering stone inside, wondering to himself: Is this the debris of a Moon, a comet or an asteroid that had drifted too close to the gaseous beast? Is this a rock sample from Saturn himself which had been rejected by the great unnatural forces in constant turmoil upon the planet's surface? He tags and bags his sample and collects a dozen more of differing shapes and various sizes.

Once he's satisfied with his haul, Jonas types in a command message on the sleeve of his spacesuit and the Starship Zx12's automatic thrusters initiate, sending his vessel to his debris-ridden location.

Jonas untethers himself from his temporary home and, using his jetpack thrusters, powers his way through space to the airlock door of his Starship.

The Zx12 is falling perilously close to Saturn's gravitational point-of-no-return as Jonas hurriedly enters his cockpit seat and manually manoeuvres his craft into a higher orbit whilst silently hailing his first completed freefall along the length of Saturn's rings a resounding success.

*

Whilst spending her last evening at the underwater habitat, Kira comes to a momentous decision; the culmination of five months of soul searching.

Kira and Grace, having stowed all of the vital training equipment within the underwater environment, are making final preparations for their one-mile sea walk to the beach at Far Point.

"Grace," Kira says with eyes glazed over, "I've made my decision."

Doctor James places a comforting hand upon Kira's shoulder and waits for her to express herself.

"I've decided to no longer attend the Europa Spaceprime Mission Control. The closure order will be signed within the next two months and I must refocus and prepare for my own Moonbase mission. Jonas made his own decision regarding his future and there was no place for me within his plans," Kira says whilst full of regret and unsure if her decisive stance is the right course of action.

Grace draws Kira close and holds onto her tightly. "If you wish to talk to me again then kick down my office door," she whispers.

Kira's multi pastel-shaded eyes begin to fill and her threatening tears are swiftly wiped away. "I will not shed a tear for Jonas Dean or this godforsaken situation," she emphatically thinks.

*

Commander Marks is left cursing the decision that he has made. "Bad planning," he mutters irritably to himself as he pulls out his handkerchief, mops his brow and runs the damp cloth around the back of his neck.

It is 1200 hours sharp, and the midday sun is beating down from its highest point within a clear blue sky and unfortunately for Marks he is in full dress uniform. He had thought of sending one of his operatives to pick up the medical team from the designated rendezvous point at Far Point, but decided instead that he'd have to personally attend the midday sands of Atlantis Strand as he wouldn't trust a junior operative to relay to him the hidden message.

The estimated time of arrival has passed and his medical team are overdue. Commander Marks resists the temptation to use his short-range tracer unit to map the exact underwater locations of his medical team which he could have used to trace the signals transmitted from the microchips embedded within the backs of their wrists. The hidden message will soon become clear when his Europa Spaceprime medical operatives emerge from the ocean's depths.

The wheels had been set in motion by Marks; the Commander had made an unofficial agreement with Doctor Grace James that if she'd made progress with Doctor Kira Yu then she'd place her on point duty for the return journey from the habitat.

*

The stressed rope which is tied around Kira's waist relaxes and with her compass bearing checked, she moves onwards in slow motion through the gloomy ocean waters at the bottom of the seabed with her line stretching once more to take up the strain.

Over the previous five months, Kira's medical knowledge has become honed and she's as ready as she ever could be for her impending Moonbase assignment.

With the beach at Far Point closing in, the rocky ocean floor soon gives way to a bed of sand and Kira Yu pushes her way purposefully forwards, the polluted murky waters clearing with every stride that she takes. Kira bends her knees and leans her shoulders into the slight sandy upslope as the deep blue sky shimmers through the roof of the ocean's surface.

*

Commander Marks sits, sweating profusely in full-dress uniform, staring out at the ocean to a single derelict wind turbine situated one mile offshore.

During the early part of the twenty-first century, sixty working turbines would rotate, capturing the winds and turning them into efficient energy. They had also had a secondary use as at the base of each of the sixty steel windmills there had once been three interconnecting habitats erected upon the ocean floor which could be accessed by a service-shaft from the surface: one hundred and twenty homes had once lain beneath the ocean waves and all but a single habitat had been washed away during the previous century.

Marks had often thought that he should have let the students use a motorboat or a dinghy to get to the rusting wind turbine, but it was an integral part of the training to order his operatives to undertake the walk.

Commander Marks lifts himself off the hot sands as a single membrane breaks through the ocean's surface and he views the three wetsuited female forms wading through the breaking surf towards his position; the lead figure has an effortless poised gait, her shoulders are relaxed, and she has a purposeful stride. The Commander squints at the three emerging figures and knows instantly that it can only be Kira Yu who is on point.

No joy fills his heart at seeing Kira leading the elite group over the sands although it indicates that Doctor Grace James must have made considerable progress with Doctor Yu. Over ten months have passed since Captain Jonas Dean's demise and it is time for Kira Yu to move on, Thalt, James and Marks had all agreed, and yet he still feels discomfited about having to tell Kira Yu that after her five-month assignment, the situation regarding the Starship Zx12's mission to the stars has not changed and never will change; the Commander has accepted this and Kira Yu has to accept it too and move on with her life.

*

Commander Marks accompanies the medical triumvirate back to the Spaceprime Central Academy to debrief the team after their underwater mission. Kira's mind wanders as Marks talks of remote shuttle launches, the Moonbase layout and Europa Spaceprime objectives.

Kira feels a sense of relief when her Commander eventually dismisses them all for the weekend. She almost runs out of the briefing room towards the academy's exit with only a cursory glance as she passes by the glass door entry for the Europa Spaceprime Mission Control public viewing gallery: Kira Yu is making changes to her life and she has chosen to head home.

*

It is late afternoon when Kira finally arrives back at her apartment within the New Buildings estate. She is feeling ill at ease after her laborious journey along the pot-holed coastal road, a trip which she had regularly taken during the small hours of early morning since Jonas's loss.

Over the past five months, her routine has changed and she has become determined to follow this through into her daily life: make changes and move on, she has vowed.

Kira places her key into the apartment door and steps inside her sanctuary, where she immediately feels the afternoon heat trapped inside her home. She begins to fling open the windows within her apartment: one in the main living area and another in the kitchen, before making her way to the bedroom to open the solitary window at the side of her bed. Finally, she moves out of her sleeping quarters and heads for her desk which is situated just off her main living area and in front of a tall window which can be pushed ajar, allowing the afternoon breeze to take the edge off the inner heat. The tall window never gets opened – instead, Kira stands over her desk, looking down upon a wrapped package and a thin packet. Ordinarily, she would have opened them without any thought, yet Kira hesitates as on the larger of the two items, clearly inscribed in black ink, are the words: For my darling, Kira Yu.

An avalanche of mixed emotions sucks the air out of Kira's lungs.

"Waiting for a ghost," Josiah Dean had once said.

The words are haunting: the black-ink handwriting is recognised. "Jonas," Kira stutters in disbelief, unable to bring herself to touch the handwritten package. Instead, Kira gathers up the thin packet and carefully picks at its wrapping; the brown paper wrap falls easily away to reveal its contents although she is unaware that Hubert Snow is the sender.

There is no writing at all on the data storage media and Kira turns the thin plastic unmarked case over in her hands before taking out the compact disc from inside.

She places the disc upon her oak carved desk and turns away, folding her arms as she paces the floor of her cooling living area. Kira is moving on with her life and her first tentative steps have already been taken, yet the compact disc holds her attention, and the inscribed package that has been anonymously delivered has unnerved her.

What to do? Kira thinks. Get rid of the deliveries? And yet Kira's inquisitive nature would never allow her to take that option. Save them for a rainy day? Well it probably won't rain before her remote shuttle launch and there's no way that she's going to spend the next five years upon the Moon whilst wondering what information the two packages contain.

"To hell with it all," Kira says stubbornly as she makes her decision and picks up Jonas's handwritten package and the unmarked compact disc before opening up her desk drawer and pulling out her retro compact disc player.

Kira leaves her cooling apartment behind and walks out into the afternoon sun and to the rear of her apartment where communal gardens lie, fronted by lush green lawns and bordered by vividly coloured maturing flowerbeds with tall conifers imposing upon the setting to provide the necessary shade.

Kira sits upon an old wooden bench which is situated at the head of the gardens, overlooking the neatly trimmed lawns to the picturesque setting of the bay beyond.

The wrapped package that is decorated by Jonas's own hand lies to her side on the old wooden seat as she carefully places the compact disc into her player. With her earplugs lodged, she waits through the silence; the muted pause draws on until a single recognised voice breaks free over the airwave.

And Hubert Snow speaks with authority: "Extract from the pre-flight sequence of the Starship Zx12's mission to the stars launch procedure."

There's another short noiseless pause before Snow's languid tone returns. "Cap-com to Zx12, you're T-Minus four minutes and fifty seconds to launch. What is your status, over?"

"Zx12 to Cap-com," Jonas replies to Snow and Kira buckles at the voice from beyond the grave. "All systems are functioning within required parameters. We're a go-flight from Zx12. I repeat we're a go-flight from Zx12."

Another short pause until Jonas's voice breaks through once more. "Zx12 to Cap-com," he says quietly.

"Cap-com receiving Zx12," Snow replies whilst sounding

concerned at which Kira frowns.

"Hubert," Jonas says with Kira listening intently.

"Yes, Captain Dean," Snow replies.

"Hubert, if anything should happen to me, tell my parents that I love them, and tell Kira." And Jonas pauses for what appears to be a lifetime as Kira holds her breath.

"Tell Kira: It was always Delta," Jonas Dean declares.

The silence intervenes through her headphones and Kira sits motionless, too afraid to stop the recording as she's unable to bring herself to cut off the quiet.

Tears are flowing readily from her softly tinged eyes, stalling at her high cheekbones, before overwhelming her visage.

Kira's world crumbles; the changes which she's making, the new life which she's striving for and her Europa Spaceprime Moonbase assignment all dissolve from her focus as she realises that Jonas Dean had loved her and that he'd not told her to protect her from the situation which she now found herself in. Yet Kira Yu didn't need protecting; Kira Yu didn't want protecting; and still Jonas had lied to cushion the blow of a mission failure.

Kira is unafraid now as there are no longer any regrets from her past – she had loved him and finally she knew that he had loved her too.

The brown paper wrap falls away from Jonas's inscribed package and Kira, with her tears still stinging her eyes, opens up the small box which is identical to the one that she already owns.

Jonas's solid silver Europa Spaceprime watch sits inside the black case; a token of his affection, his respect, his love: a final gift.

Kira removes the timepiece and turns it over in her hand to view the engravement upon its back plate: "J W Dean".

Choking back her tears, Kira is about to replace the watch in its custom casing when she notices a neatly folded parchment tucked away into the corner of the base of the grey rocket insignia box.

Kira sets the watch back into its case, unfolds the note and begins to read; over and over, she reads the passages as a torrent of tears flows freely from her eyes of powder blue and ochre brown, utterly lost in her disbelief that Jonas, a structured, rigid, militaristic man, could have written such a piece.

Kira's heart is pounding through her chest; Jonas's words having conveyed to her the true depths of his feelings; the title of his piece, the significance of his words, personal only to her.

No longer can she read the passages, but only stare longingly at the parchment's title: a world that she had craved with her lost love as Jonas has conveyed his inner thoughts within his writing; words that he couldn't speak on the day that they'd spent together upon Atlantis Beach.

The note falls from Kira's hand as she slumps back onto the old wooden bench and the afternoon breeze whips up the discarded parchment and carries it onto the kept lawns.

The onshore blowing winds are gusting through the branches of the tall conifers, creating a cacophony of sound within the communal gardens, yet all Kira can hear is the sound of her breaking heart.

And with the winds dropping to slight, all that can be seen is Jonas's handwritten parchment, fluttering face upwards upon the lush grass lawns, the title of his work clearly readable: a life that Kira Yu had wished for; a life that Jonas Dean had turned away from: the simple life.

The Simple Life

I've had fleeting passion; I've had some pain,
I've lived my life and I've had a little fame,
I'm a work in progress not a masterpiece,
And with you beside me, I'd feel complete.

I'm not the man that I used to be,
My scars from life are for all to see,
When I'm with you; you make me whole,
The only true guardian of my soul.

I want the simple life,
I won't ask for anything,
I just want a place in your heart,
For that I'd give everything.
I want the simple life,
I've got a simple plan,
But how could you understand,
I'm not a simple man.

I'm just a pencil drawing that'll finally fade away,
Yet I'll never keep from fading whilst my love grows day by day,
If I could hope to see you for a moment of your time,
I'd tell you that I love you and pray you would be mine.

I'm not the man that I used to be,
My scars from life are for all to see,
When I'm with you, you make me whole,
The only true guardian of my soul.

I want the simple life,
I won't ask for anything,
I just want a place in your heart,
For that I'd give everything.
I want the simple life,
I've got a simple plan,
But how could you understand,
I'm not a simple man.

I want the simple life,
I won't ask for anything,
I just want a place in your heart,
For that I'd give everything.
I want the simple life,
I've got a simple plan,
But how could you understand,
I'm not a simple man.

It's not a simple life.

CHAPTER 11

Cause: Solitude

Jonas Dean stands proudly upon the bridge of the Starship Zx12 with Saturn's menacing grip still pulling him into its heart; the depleted nose cone of the Starship Zx12 is continually pointed into Saturn's mass whilst his vessel's high orbit decays rapidly. Although his pioneering task is complete, Jonas's mind remains unmade.

During the course of the two months which followed Jonas's first venture into Saturn's halo, his jetpack-aided freefall had been repeated for all of the rings surrounding the gaseous giant. Having initially travelled to the 'D' Ring, each subsequent descent had taken him to a ring further away from the planet's deadly gravitational grip; each journey he made had been less arduous and therefore less dangerous.

Captain Jonas Dean had also despatched a Nanosec probe to the surface of Saturn; the probe had been lost within a matter of minutes of its landing, yet the core data collected by the probe's Nanodrones had been sent back to the Starship Zx12's computer almost immediately upon its impact.

His Starship's computer now holds vital data about the geological makeup of the Earth-sized planet's flux surface, as well as information from his already acquired rock and debris samples from each layer of every defined ring of Saturn. If ever Captain Jonas Dean returns home, then the scientists of the new Kingdoms may just have the unparalleled opportunity to unravel the age-old mystery of Saturn's rings.

The days and weeks have slipped by without a definitive decision from Jonas. Over and over, he's played through the differing scenarios in his mind: one hundred hops, two hundred hops, one thousand hops – the permutations are endless; his exit point blind, the danger is intoxicating and Jonas Dean knows he would thrive on the onslaught of jeopardy.

How could he journey back to Earth, to a utopian Earthprime society which had been born out of gross horror? How could he think of travelling back to his own planet, armed with the knowledge of what mankind was capable of? Jonas had spent a lifetime preparing for the moment that is at hand – the great journey will be undertaken within the next few days, this is his preferred course of action. However, doubts remain and Captain Jonas Dean of the First Order of the Spaceprime is working his way through them.

*

The Europan King sits alone in one of his many offices within the royal apartments, behind a shut door which is constantly locked as he doesn't wish to be disturbed by any member of his loyal court. Since his meeting with the glamorous, hard-headed Asian attaché, Tashi Chi, the Sovereign Prime of Europa has divorced himself from all of his official duties, avoiding his generals at every turn and detaching himself from the first ladies of the Europa Earthprime. The King of Europa is lost and alone.

And his dream will die in less than three weeks: the inevitable closure of the Europa Spaceprime Mission Control will see an end to his Starship Zx class Space Program. He will have failed in his promise to Captain Jonas Dean; he will have failed in his promise to his father, Josiah Dean; and if a promise had been made to the families of the crew of the HMS Neon-Lit City, then he will have failed them too. A catalogue of failure is all that the King of Europa will have to show for his progressive direction and steadfast endeavours.

Courage and resolve he has had in abundance during his balanced decision-making and he has been unrelenting in his course of action as he steered a steady course through the political quagmire. He has felt nothing but burning pride and immense satisfaction in his actions and his responses to those who have challenged him; never once has he deviated from his path. And yet fate's sleight of hand has deceived him.

This particular warm and clammy evening, and for the first time for as long as he can remember, the King of Europa feels nothing but shame.

The memo lies exposed upon his desk; the neatly typed Europa Spaceprime document, a despatch from Commander Marks. The King slips on his reading glasses to read the note once more.

DOCTOR KIRA YU CLEARED FOR MOONBASE ASSIGNMENT

Hope has been the cornerstone of his reign, and his father during his long tenure had also given it willingly and unconditionally. Kira Yu was the embodiment of hope, but this hope had been clinically severed by the King's own loyal troupe as his people had conspired to manoeuvre her away from her own personal calling. To the King of Europa's own detriment, he had allowed it to happen on his watch.

Foresight has told him that the political landscape will be treacherous and unforgiving three weeks hence and he is unsure whether he will have the stomach or the will to realign himself with his fellow Kings now that the balance of world power has shifted.

The Sovereign Prime bangs a fist angrily upon his desk. "I'll not let hope fade away and die," he shouts before rising and, with a newfound bounce in his step, unlocking his office door and walking out of his royal apartments and into the late evening air. His destination: the public viewing gallery at the Europa Spaceprime Mission Control.

*

Kira Yu has regained her grip on the actuality of her reality and a semblance of self-control. She gathers up all of the precious items which had been anonymously delivered to her before returning to the cooling environment of her apartment. She places Jonas's solid silver Spaceprime watch and the compact disc on a shelf and puts the well-weathered ochre brown stone that she had collected on Atlantis Beach upon Jonas's handwritten note. "You've less than three weeks, Captain Dean, before I jet off to the Moon," she says, speaking directly to her newly acquired memorial.

And with her energies rising on hope's acquittal, Kira gathers up the keys to her solar-powered, battery-enhanced car – an eighty-mile journey lies ahead of her along the starlit coastal road.

*

General Thalt is prowling around the meeting table which is situated at the centre of the private conference room that lies deep within the heart of the Spaceprime Central Academy complex. "And what of Doctor Yu?" Thalt asks, his question directed at Doctor Grace James who is examining her nails intently.

"That's the second nail that I've broken in a week – I really do need to take a break from this perpetual career and get myself a manicure," James responds, choosing to ignore the General's question as Thalt has received the memo and already knows full well the current situation as General Thalt reads everything.

"Grace, you know that you can't have a break from the day job –

you're lifting off to the Moon in three weeks and I'm sure that your nails will have already grown back by then," Commander Marks says whilst amused by the way that the Senior Medical Officer for Spaceprime Special Projects has sidestepped the General's direct question. The General will ask again as he always does.

General Thalt's tone softens unusually. "Will Kira be attending the public viewing gallery this evening?" he asks.

James and Marks stare in disbelief at their General and his question is immediately forgotten. It's Commander Marks who gets his reply in first: "Kira! General, you called Doctor Yu: Kira. You never call any of the Europa Spaceprime elite by their first names. I've never once heard you refer to me as Oswald or Doctor James as Grace." And with a grin rampaging over the Commander's face, Marks lightly taunts, "Are you going soft in your old age, General?"

General Thalt doesn't rise to the Commander's challenge as he casts a formidable eye over his Europa Spaceprime colleagues. "I'm uncomfortable with our current situation. Our King is politically paralysed and I fear that once my assignment has finished in three weeks then I'll be on diplomatic missions for the foreseeable future, pounding my head against a brick wall. The Moonbase mission must not fail as it's the first opportunity which this Kingdom will have to show that we're still capable of running the off-world projects; however, these issues do not bother me – what will be, will be. But I am uncomfortable with myself. I've sat these past five months with Hubert Snow, staring at blank monitors and listening to endless static friction. Hubert Snow and his unyielding belief that Captain Jonas Dean and the Starship Zx12 are still out there, lost within the spatial void. We were wrong to steer Doctor Kira Yu away from the Europa Spaceprime Mission Control as hope still resides within Doctor Yu and Cap-com Snow. I've learnt a valuable lesson during these past five months and that is to not look too deeply into the future; live for the moment, live for the day, all that matters is what is happening at this precise point in time. We have a mission to the stars in progress so, with due respect to you both, I'll take my leave and sit with Hubert Snow awhile, where no doubt I'll hear his views on the ways of the world whilst listening to an infuriating relentless static drone."

Thalt leaves his Spaceprime colleagues gaping in awe as he strides out of the private conference room.

"Awesome," Commander Marks comments freely.

"He had me at pounding my head against a brick wall," Doctor James states, full of praise for her General.

They both arise in unison and Oswald Marks speaks to Grace James directly: "It looks like we're in for a long night," he says.

"I'll get the coffee and meet you at mission control," James replies enthusiastically.

*

Hubert Snow is attending to his usual nightly business at the Europa Spaceprime Mission Control: relaying feeds, adjusting frequencies and testing differing scenarios. Yet upon this night, he is thriving on motivational impetus as he's playing to an audience.

Thalt, Marks and Doctor Grace James had arrived at 2200 hours: Kira's time. The initial cordiality had evaporated as soon as Commander Marks had begun to eulogise over past events, all of which had distorted details and humorous overtones. Chaotic laughter fills the Europa Spaceprime Mission Control arena and even General Thalt has laughed which is a rare event indeed.

Hubert Snow listens to the recital of past escapades whilst grateful for the company and the support that he's getting from the Europa Spaceprime elite.

After amending a setting at one of his local workstations, Snow replaces his headset and listens for any changes within the static flow over the communications feedback.

After all of these long months, he's still caught up in his single-minded objective to get the job done efficiently, effectively and to obtain the desired outcome, and yet static's course remains constant.

Hubert Snow slips off his headset after another failed reconfiguration to find to his great surprise that his Europa Spaceprime Senior Officers have quietened.

They have all risen as one and able Cap-com Hubert Snow follows their line of sight, slowly turning his head up towards the public viewing gallery where the King of Europa sits magisterially in the front row of the soundproof gallery, confidently staring out at the banks of redundant monitors.

Snow's eye is caught by the glass door to the public viewing gallery as it slides open to reveal Doctor Kira Yu. She steps into the breach and without flinching at the sight of her Commander in Chief she crosses the short distance to her King and seats herself at his side.

No words are exchanged between the King of Europa and Doctor Kira Yu, and Hubert Snow can quite clearly make out the hint of a smile upon the King's face.

Snow picks up his empty cup and shatters the concentrated focus of his Senior Officers: "Would anyone like a coffee?" he says.

*

The waves are defined by the moonlight and beat their steady rhythmic drum as they break over the sandy beach. Josiah Dean listens to the sounds of the ocean as he sits upon Atlantis Strand, alone under the Moon and the stars.

For Josiah Dean, all hope has been extinguished. Although torn apart inside, he's still drawn to the night-time sands in his wish to constantly search the midnight skies as he waits for a sign to rekindle his lost hope; and yet the empty moonlit night holds nothing for him to cling onto.

Evie Dean watches her husband from their beach house veranda. She knows that these past few months, Josiah has undertaken a nightly ritual of peering into the deep dark firmament as he waits for their only son to find his way home. Her husband is suffering through his loss and they are both acutely aware that the Europa Spaceprime Mission Control will soon be mothballed, although Josiah has refused to attend the mission control arena and impose upon Kira's nightly vigil as Kira's hope has shamed him and he has chosen instead to follow his own routine.

Evie Dean walks out onto the sandy beach to take up her rightful place beside her husband who instinctively places an arm around her waist. Together they gaze into the starry night as they wait for their only son to find his way home in their continuing search for hope's existence.

*

Captain Jonas William Dean is constantly fighting a losing battle to anchor his Starship at the gates of infinity with his vessel's depleted nose cone at all times pointing into the gaseous colossus of Saturn.

It has been almost a year since his departure and life back on Earth will surely have moved on; Captain Jonas Dean will also move on with his own life, never looking back and without any regrets.

There has never been any doubt within Jonas's mind of his direction as he fixates upon a single point within infinity beyond Saturn and his rings, where the deep well of space is calling to him invitingly; his choice of destinations is endless: point and engage the hyperdrive; a space pioneer in full flight.

His mission is already a huge success and no burden of guilt will weigh upon his broad shoulders about the opportunist nature of his circumstances; the rest of his life will be one long great adventure. Kira wouldn't understand and his father had always bowed to his strong-willed nature – he of all people would understand Jonas's decision to travel into the unknown universe. He also knew his King well enough to know that granted a similar opportunity he'd do exactly the same.

Queen Ashilla's taunting words of warning do not frighten him. "I'll live my half-life to the full," Jonas shouts ironically into the void and beyond the planet which is enshrouded by gas. With his eyes locked hard upon a dark point in space beyond Saturn's mass, and his ambitious nature burning away inside of him, Jonas's pivotal decision will soon be made.

All that he has to do is point and engage the hyperdrive – and yet Jonas stalls. What is he waiting for: enlightenment? Jonas has to be sure; patience learnt from Kira Yu at the academy. His ambitious nature has driven him to this point in space, at this moment in time, and surely his ambitions will propel him forwards; a few more days, a few more weeks will make no difference as time has become an irrelevance.

The burdensome weight feels heavy upon Jonas's broad shoulders; not the weight of his guilt, nor the weight of his expectations: Captain Jonas Dean is burdened by the weight of his own driving ambitions.

*

For the King of Europa and the Europa Spaceprime elite, time passes swiftly; all Moonbase Project decisions and other Earthprime matters have been placed on hold until the Europa Spaceprime Mission Control closure notice has been served.

Time races away for the Knights of the Spaceprime as it rushes headlong towards its inevitable conclusion, yet for Captain Jonas

Dean time crawls as indecision gnaws away at him, having once been so certain of his chosen path.

Jonas is in conflict with himself – his ambitions for an ongoing adventure are raging away inside of him, but lingering doubts still remain; a need to share the unearthed truth, a need to unburden himself of the past histories that he has gained.

Time has slowed as Jonas thinks through his impending actions, trying desperately to resolve his issues to clarity, yet always the waters of thought grow muddier.

For Captain Jonas Dean, time is almost at a standstill.

*

Upon the perceived final day of the Starship Zx12's mission to the stars, Hubert Snow arrives at 1800 hours for his last shift. At some point during the evening, he expects to receive the mission control closure order: signed by his King and acted upon by General Thalt.

Snow strolls into the familiar domain of the Europa Spaceprime Mission Control at Spaceprime Central, where Chief Communications Officer Katherine Jenkins greets the faithful Capcom from behind her console.

Snow smiles easily as Jenkins rises from her workstation. "No change," she says above the din of prevalent static.

Hubert Snow nods an acknowledgement. "Have you been reassigned?" he asks tentatively.

Looking somewhat tired and drawn, Katherine Jenkins replies, "Not as yet, although General Thalt has ordered me to take a month's leave."

"We'll catch up in a few days then," Snow states.

"I hope that we will, and thank you Hubert, it's been a great pleasure working with you," she says, leaning into Snow and kissing him upon his cheek. "You could be in for a short night as my guess is that the Europa Spaceprime hierarchy will shut us down at midnight," Jenkins comments, giving Snow a heads up.

The able Cap-com Hubert Snow is already aware of the forthcoming scenario. "I think that you're probably right as it'd look politically bad if the powers that be dragged this whole process out; we'll be shut down before the last minute of the day," he states, cementing Jenkins's intuition.

"Good luck Hubert," Jenkins says, already walking to the mission control security door without looking back at the situation that hasn't changed for one whole year of her life of service and which, as far as Katherine Jenkins is concerned, never will change. The Chief Communications Officer leaves the mission control environment with the heady static discharge ringing forever in her ears.

Hubert Snow settles in for the evening and begins to follow his nightly procedures. With his coffee cup to hand, Snow analyses the data for the previous twelve hours from the short-range listening devices which are operational upon the Moon. Afterwards, he reviews all of his communications feed data as he looks for breaks in the static flow or anything untoward. During the early part of his evening shift, Hubert Snow reads "The List": with no long-range telescopes operational upon the planet due to all of the world-famous observatories being destroyed during the Third World War, the only way that anyone can actually see into the vast depths of the Solar System is by using a telescope. This hindrance has necessitated a reliance upon amateur enthusiasts from around the globe who gaze into space and, if any unusual sightings occur, contact the Spaceprime Central Academy which alerts the Europa Spaceprime Mission Control of the anomalies which have been found in the night's sky and this spatial void anomaly information is then added as a log entry onto 'The List.'

Finally, during the early part of the evening, Snow updates the mission log with his findings. The entry which he makes on the final evening of operations is the same as all of the entries that he has made for the previous twelve months.

MISSION STATE: UNCHANGED

And Hubert Snow clings onto his fading hope.

The King of Europa is seated amongst his beloved tomato plants as the final hours of the Starship Zx12's mission to the stars fall away; time is running out for the Europan regent who is politically cornered and has few options.

Lady Anne appears at his side with a single sheet of paper grasped within her hand. "My Lord, the closure order as requested," she says formally.

"Stick or twist," the King states cryptically to his closest confidant.

Lady Anne frowns. "I don't understand, my lord," she says.

The inevitability of the final night of operations had led the Europan King to look to his future. "Anne," he says gruffly. "Do I stick and ostracise the Kingdom of Europa from the world's decision-making process for the foreseeable future, or do I twist and try to cut a belated deal with the King of Asia?"

Without hesitation, Lady Anne answers, "We twist of course – we've no other choice, and it's not a decision that we have to make; it's the course of action which we must follow. But that is tomorrow's issue, my Lord, as you must sign this document immediately."

The King receives the formal closure order from the First Lady of the Europa Earthprime and, without reading any of the text, he signs away Jonas Dean's lifeline: if his Europa Spaceprime astronaut at any point in the future tries to contact Earth by any means possible then there will be no-one listening.

"Leave me alone awhile Anne for I'm an unworthy Monarch and not fit to reign: I've just signed away three promises that I'd vowed to keep and I already loathe my own self-pity," the King of Europa says, full of broken desperation.

"I'll attend to you in one hour, my Lord," says Lady Anne, concerned by her King's state of mind.

The Europan Sovereign bows his head, unable to make any sense of his newfound situation, where only his confusion reigns.

*

Lady Guinevere is in residence within the study room of her private apartment, where she has never before witnessed Lady Anne so flustered.

"I'll kill him myself if he does anything stupid," Anne of Europa says through gritted teeth.

Guinevere has never heard the King's aunt speak of His Majesty in such a manner. "What can we do?" she asks, concerned by the events that are unfolding.

"As of tomorrow, we must keep him busy and fill his mind with Earthprime projects and the forthcoming Moonbase missions," Lady Anne replies with her mind working through the closure notice procedure as she speaks. "The courier is en-route with the closure order for General Thalt's eyes only and tonight we'll plan Europa Earthprime projects: new buildings and power plants to harness renewable energy; the continuation of the Kingdom of Europa's clean-up process to improve our environment; projects that will enrich the lives of our peoples and make better use of the limited resources at our disposal. And when there's nothing more left to plan, then tomorrow we'll make busy our King, but tonight we'll let the man grieve for his is the grief of all of the peoples of our great Kingdom."

*

Doctor Kira Yu has completed her final inventory checks of the medical supplies which will be accompanying her and her fellow medical officers on the remote shuttle launch to the newly built Moonbase.

The digital reading upon her solid silver Spaceprime watch gives her the correct time and Kira has five minutes to get to the Europa Spaceprime Mission Control as this night will soon become her final agony. She privately fears for her own emotional state during the forthcoming two hours if all of the rumours are true, which they usually are: the King of Europa will shut the Europa Spaceprime Mission Control at midnight. Upon this, her final night, Kira Yu will not be late.

Her medical colleagues have gathered around her and it is Doctor Grace James who finally speaks on behalf of them all: "Time to go Kira, the final wake for Captain Jonas Dean awaits you. We are T-Minus three days from our Moonbase launch and we'll deal with final issues tomorrow, for tonight, Kira Yu, our thoughts will be for you," Grace James says as she double-checks her solid silver Spaceprime watch, before returning her gaze to the dual-coloured eyes of the Doctor. "It's almost time, now go" she urges.

*

At 2200 hours precisely, the glass door to the public viewing gallery slides open and for one final time, Kira Yu crosses over the threshold of barrier glass into the soundproof public viewing gallery, where a continuous buzzing static still hums its defiance.

Ignoring her usual seat, Kira stands with her arms crossed defensively before the glass partition as she surveys the now too-familiar surroundings. The scene that she witnesses before her is an intimate canvas, a portrait which she has viewed frequently over the previous twelve months, and yet something is quite clearly amiss.

Kira frantically darts her dual-coloured eyes around the Europa Spaceprime Mission Control arena as she tries to process the missing information in her mind until her eyes fall upon the anomaly; the changed event.

Hubert Snow is still; the resilient Cap-com sits unmoved at his desk, where he's staring blankly at redundant workstations, the dormant map of the known system and the flatline medical monitors that have found their perpetual role, showing Captain Jonas Dean's life sign readings.

Hubert Snow, a man on a mission, can no longer bring himself to check one final algorithm, one last setting or try one more reconfiguration; the frantic static continues and able Cap-com Hubert Snow is lost within its continuous ebb and flow.

Snow has given up and all hope has gone.

*

Jonas's mission has been ongoing for one year; the first of many, Dean thinks. His decision is almost made and his Starship is prepped for hyperdrive initiation: point, engage hyperdrive, destination.

His parents will be forever in his heart, a heart which Kira owns, whilst the sealed compartments of the Starship Zx12 contain an archive of information and artefacts: the prize-data which he has collected from Jupiter's Moon of Ganymede, Captain Jayne Smith's HMS Neon-lit City logbook and the samples that Jonas has extracted from all of Saturn's defined rings. The Starship Zx12's main computer also holds invaluable information about the geological make-up of Saturn's surface, the mapped terrain of Ganymede and all of the hyperdrive statistical analysis.

It doesn't matter to Captain Jonas Dean that he is taking the information which he has acquired with him as nobody from the First Order of the Spaceprime or the Kingdoms of the Earthprime know what riches are held onboard his Starship and it will probably take centuries before the HMS Neon-Lit City is rediscovered and people realise that Jonas's mission has been a historic success.

Jonas catches sight of his encased powder blue stone: Kira's stone. He has spent all of his adult life preparing for this moment in time and never once thought that his own judgement would ever become clouded by the calling of his heart.

"Kira," Jonas mouths her name; a faint whisper. "I cannot think straight and this decision should have been easy," he says, frustrated by the compressing turmoil that is trapped within him.

And for the first time in a long time, Jonas remembers the note that he had left within the case of his treasured Europa Spaceprime timepiece; Kira will have read his message by now and surely she will have destroyed the parchment: but what if?

He is almost certain that his opportunity for a fulfilling life on Earth has long since passed: unless.

The powder blue stone keepsake is fully filling his view: a distant memory from a past that he has long since lived.

I mustn't look back, he thinks. "It's not in my nature," he shouts and the echo reverberates around the inner hull of his Starship.

Could he possibly contemplate sacrificing his life's ambitions for Kira Yu? If he were to return home, then surely he will feel nothing but regret at not fulfilling his destiny.

Point, engage hyperdrive, destination: that's all there is to it; a simple decision made and acted upon, yet still Captain Jonas Dean needs more time.

*

Jayne Smith, Captain of the fabled Stargazer class vessel the HMS

Neon-Lit City, relaxes upon the comfortable two-seater within the brightly lit spatial lighthouse.

During the months that have passed by since Jonas's departure, she has watched the Starship Zx12 through her observatory's enhanced refracted glass. Smith has setup a permanent magnified view of Saturn within the observatory and she continually views Jonas's vessel being pulled in by Saturn's deadly gravitational grip and Captain Jonas Dean guiding his Starship to a higher orbit every few weeks.

Whilst onboard the HMS Neon-Lit City, Jonas had worked mainly on her ship's life-support systems by day, before retiring to the roundhouse viewing station where he'd slept upon the comfortable two-seater and it was upon the chaise-lounge that he'd dreamt; his dreams played out as holographic images: his dreams recorded.

Captain Jayne Smith has replayed at speed the recorded holographic images of Jonas's dreams to gain an insight into his soul's direction and she already knows what decision Captain Jonas Dean will take, because why else would she have allowed her own personal logbook to leave the HMS Neon-Lit City?

Smith flicks through the saved holographic recordings, seeing that every recorded image is similar except for the final optical reproduction: the blue planet is spinning upon its axis in each recorded image, showing Earth from an altered angle or a changed perspective, apart from the final image which has been captured in frame and Captain Jayne Smith cannot understand why this particular vision has invaded Jonas's dreams as it appears to be out of place: rotating twin Moons of Jupiter, side by side: the powder blue Moon of Europa dominating a foreground aspect with the slightly eclipsed, subtle ochre colouration of Io orbiting behind.

With the Starship Zx12 visibly pointed at Saturn and his rings, Smith raises herself off the two-seater to stand proudly within the centre of the observation outpost with her gut telling her that Captain Jonas Dean's time to decide has come.

Captain Jayne Smith smiles confidently at the spatial distortion which has been amplified within the roundhouse viewing station. "Make your decision, Captain Jonas Dean," she whispers.

*

Titan: shadowing spectral guardian of Saturn; its mysterious veneer veiled. The Moon's titanic secrets are hidden beneath its atmospheric haze, where numerous protruding snowbound islets are surrounded by a boundless elemental liquid lake.

Upon one of the islands, the Titan Queen stands tall with her bare feet entrenched within frozen methane ice, wherefrom the Ice Queen, Ashilla, raises her solid silver staff over her diamond studded silver crown as she peers through the atmospheric mists at the Starship Zx12 which is orbiting Saturn high above. "Make your decision, Jonas Dean!" she roars, causing elemental waters to swell and give rise to huge waves of liquid methane which rush outwards as a tsunami from her isle-bound position.

*

Time has run out for Captain Jonas Dean: for far too long, he has dwelt upon his decision, his mind blurring when he aches for impulse. "What is my purpose? My mission is fulfilled," Jonas thinks aloud whilst wracked with uncertainty. "The long hop into deepest infinity would not be a senseless, meaningless journey as I'd be pushing back the boundaries of time and space. But for what reward and where will it all end? Isolated and lost within the deepest reaches of the void with my enclosed existence empty, because of my own enforced solitary confinement."

And then upon an inkling, Jonas's divisive thoughts coalesce to a sudden epiphany and the great weight of his burdening ambitions lifts from Captain Jonas Dean's broad shoulders as realisation hammers home with a certainty of which he speaks aloud: "Why should I settle for living a full half-life when I can live a full rounded existence? Why would I wish to become institutionalised by my own impending solitary isolation? Captain Jayne Smith has embraced her own solitude, yet I still have that choice to make, so why would I choose to be lonely, friendless and lost?"

All Jonas Dean's past beliefs evaporate as a calling to home defeats his own burdensome ambitions; the conflicting battle of self-doubt that has raged within his mind dissipates and his soul begins to rise.

His cup of ambition is full to the brim and overflowing, yet it is intoxicating desire which overwhelms his soul as Jonas realises that his ambitions lie elsewhere: Kira Yu with her hypnotic eyes of brown and blue, and his parents – the foundation stones of his life; the great treasure haul onboard the Starship Zx12 and his ability to set free the hidden truth regarding Earth's dark past.

And at Saturn's gate, Captain Jonas Dean of the First Order of the Spaceprime makes his decision.

Cause: Solitude

I thought the road through life was paved with gold,
Some people say that I'm brave and I'm bold,
I played the system and a man I was made,
Some people say that I'm bold and I'm brave,
I don't want to wake up when I'm old one day,
And regret I didn't treat the world in a better way,
I know I'm not going to an alter place,
At least I managed my own fall from grace.

I chose to fly away,
And spread my wings today,
Not another year,
Wishing that you were near.

I don't wanna live my life in solitude,
I don't wanna live my life alone,
I don't wanna live my life without any pride,
Cause: solitude is not a place to hide.
I don't wanna live my life in solitude,
I don't wanna live my life alone,
I don't wanna live my life until I run out of time,
Cause: solitude is not my state of mind.

I thought the road through life was easy to take,
But I was hell-bent on making mistakes,
I wouldn't listen to advice that was made,
I found that I was wishing for a life that I craved,
My split decision could go either way,
My new path through life won't wait another day,
I've got to make a decision that lasts,
My head's been turned by events from my past.

I chose to hide away,
I couldn't face another day,
I lived the year,
Wishing that you were near.

I don't wanna live my life in solitude,
I don't wanna live my life alone,
I don't wanna live my life without any pride,
Cause: solitude is not a place to hide.
I don't wanna live my life in solitude,
I don't wanna live my life alone,
I don't wanna live my life without any pride,
Cause: solitude is not my state of mind.

CHAPTER 12

New Dawn, New Day

Captain Jonas Dean's heart begins to sing and he listens to its beating song calling him home.

"I'll give myself a chance of living a full life and who knows what the future may hold, but at least I'll allow myself the fullest of opportunities to reach out and grasp happiness and contentment," Jonas asserts with his mind set and his direction defined. The Europa Spaceprime spaceman will no longer play dead and will no longer feel dead inside as he prepares for his return to Earth.

The compartments onboard the Starship Zx12 are locked down in readiness for Jonas's final journey and for one final time he stands upon the bridge of his ship, beholding the glorious view of Saturn and his magnificent rings whilst locking the memory down deep inside of him.

"It's time to go home," Jonas says, finally at peace with himself.

*

Within Captain Jayne Smith's refracted image view she watches the Starship Zx12 powering up its reverse thrusters and breaking free of Saturn's gravitational grip.

Jonas steers his Starship through a one hundred and eighty degree turn, before coming to a full stop with the depleted nose cone of his vessel pointing towards Earth.

Smith stands at the centre of the brightly lit roundhouse viewing station with her hands gripped and tightly locked at the small of her back. "And so Captain Dean, your decision is made," she says, defining the moment. "Home to all of the people who know you and to all of the people who love you: Jonas Dean, defender of the Earthprime, hero of the Spaceprime, a legend that lives."

*

Upon Titan's mysterious world, the freezing waters of the Moon's endless lake are still once more. And with heady rasping laughter, Queen Ashilla throws her arms aloft, whereupon the liquid methane which had been becalmed within the great boundless lake is thrown high into Titan's haze to replenish the mists, before falling back to the arcane Moon as precipitated methane snow.

And through the unnatural blizzard, the Ice Queen of Titan's Moon calls out, "Your destiny is known only to me, Jonas Dean."

*

General Thalt, who has the reputation of an ordered man, sits at his desk within the depths of the Spaceprime Central Academy complex watching the digital clock which resides upon his office wall eating away at the final moments of the Starship Zx12's mission to the stars.

The General's ongoing paperwork is neatly stacked in four piles upon his desk: incoming, outgoing, Moonbase and other. His incoming pile is almost empty; the documentation has been administered and placed within his bulging outgoing tray. The Moonbase project is proceeding according to plan and he resolves himself to look at any final issues after receiving the scheduled update from Commander Marks and Doctor Grace James which will occur upon the morning that follows the closure of the Europa Spaceprime Mission Control.

The tray marked other holds one single file: a file which has held a permanent place upon his desk for the past twelve months, a file that will no longer be there by morning.

General Thalt reaches for the single file and places it neatly upon his desk in front of him; the file is clearly labelled Mission to the Stars and the Flight Director General leaves it intentionally unopened and waits.

*

Kira has been upon her feet for almost an hour, listening to the constant frenzy of the monotonous static, whilst during the past sixty minutes, Hubert Snow has remained indifferent, staring blankly ahead: killing time.

Kira watches with her arms folded as Hubert Snow finally takes to his feet, his hourly breaks as regular as clockwork.

Hubert Snow is always aware that at this hour in the evening, Kira Yu is watching over him and, with his coffee cup in hand, the able Cap-com trudges slowly towards the kitchen area, unable to glance in her direction, acknowledge her existence and let her see his defeated eyes.

The final mission hour commences and Kira can only watch the dormant monitors, disabled workstations and the life sign readings of the deceased; a captured view that will invade her dreams for weeks, months and years to come.

The once-able Cap-com Hubert Snow has been disabled by events out of his sphere of influence and he returns to his workstation with his cup in hand, where he sits motionless and still as the final hour begins to play out to a backbeat of dead static.

*

It will be a night like any other night for Josiah Dean, and his vigil will continue far beyond the enforced line that has been drawn in the sand by the Europa Spaceprime hierarchy. The memories of his only son he holds vivid and rich at the forefront of his mind as he sits upon the sands of Atlantis Strand, listening to the sounds of the ocean under dark skies; the black seas merging with the night as the foam-tops escape from broken waves, freeing themselves from their watery rides.

The night sky's full Moon is a towering presence overhead, balancing low upon the silvery skyline and if Josiah Dean stares long enough at the brightening Moon then he's able to witness occasional flashes of brilliant white light as the new Moonbase reflects sunlight from its angular crystalline glass structure.

Progress, Josiah Dean thinks; mankind's fascination with the eternal space that lies beyond Earth's atmospheric boundaries. Its perimeter had been penetrated in the mid-twentieth century and in the early part of the twenty-first century, a multitude of space stations had been built and lost which had been closely followed by the failed manned Mars missions. The hiatus had set in as the world collapsed into near darkness at the dawn of the Third World War until the early part of the twenty-second century which had brought with it the launch of the fabled Stargazer class vessel, the HMS Neon-Lit City. And then yet another failed mission, and it's this final failure that pains Josiah Dean most of all; the loss of the Starship Zx12, the loss of his only son.

Josiah Dean catches sight of a flash of portent light from the Moon's surface; yet another Moonbase, yet another failure waiting to happen, he prophetically thought.

"Damn your progress," the old man of the Europa Spaceprime whispers painfully into the night's sky.

*

The midnight hour is closing in and the King of Europa has surrendered to his silence. His entangled mind is unable to plot a course through the political maelstrom which lies ahead of him, but his choice is simple enough: if he chooses to venture on alone and continue with his Starship Zx class Space Program then it will leave his Kingdom severely weakened politically. The Europan King has only one viable option: he will have to sacrifice his space program to preserve his ideology. His mind is tumbling and turning as he allows for the interwoven strands of his logical thought to play their way out through their many differing scenarios and always the same conclusion is reached: Lady Anne had been correct in her assessment – a deal with the King of Asia will have to be sealed within the next twenty-four hours as there's no viable alternative and tomorrow's decision has already been made.

*

Lady Guinevere begs Lady Anne to allow her to attend to her King, and after due consideration Anne relinquishes her responsibility to her young precocious prodigy, understanding fully the direness of the present situation and knowing that the King of Europa will be more receptive to Lady Guinevere's coercion. Anne realises that dragging the Europan Monarch out of his deep depression will be a long and arduous process and knows that Lady Guinevere is a potent weapon within her arsenal.

Lady Anne of Europa is forthrightly blunt with the lady who will be allowed to attend as this is not a time for niceties. She duly informs Guinevere: "Get him through the remnants of the mission and we'll deal with the fallout in the morning."

*

Lady Guinevere enters the stifling environment of the King of Europa's outhouse, where she is greeted by her regent's solemn presence; a husk of a man she had once known who is redundant of all progressive thought.

The air-conditioned seating area's lamps scatter light into the glass-panelled outhouse and embolden the catatonic King's beloved tomato plants to cast out their long shadows.

There are only twenty minutes left until the midnight hour and the final grains of sand within the Starship Zx12 mission's hourglass have all but drained away.

Guinevere sits beside her King whose mind is still silently storming and lays her head upon his shoulder; the termination hour is upon the Europan Monarch and Lady Guinevere will be there for him after it's all over, suffering in his silence and immersing herself in his grief.

*

The firm knock that falls upon Thalt's office door causes the General to check his solid silver Europa Spaceprime watch and then double-check the digital clock which is shedding time upon his office wall; their times tally at twelve minutes to midnight.

"Come," Thalt says authoritatively with his prophetically anguished face watching the office door as it opens to reveal the King's own private messenger.

The messenger traverses the short space between the General's door and his heavily framed desk to stand before Thalt, where he doesn't salute because he does not have to as the King's own private messenger is Earthprime.

"General Thalt, for your eyes only," the messenger says formally and the sealed despatch is placed in front of Thalt upon his desk.

The Flight Director General waits until the messenger has made his way out through his office door, and only when the door is shut and the messenger's footsteps can be heard receding through the corridors of the Spaceprime Central Academy does Thalt unseal the confidential paperwork.

And the order is brief; the order is as expected.

I, THE KING OF EUROPA, DECREE: THE IMMEDIATE CESSATION OF ALL OPERATIONS IN RELATION TO THE STARSHIP ZX12's MISSION TO THE STARS.

And the despatched paperwork is signed by the King's own hand.

Even though he had known the order to be imminent, Thalt still takes a short moment to digest His Majesty's requirement – to carry out the order will mean the severance of Captain Jonas Dean's lifeline and the death of the Starship Zx class Space Program.

Opening up his desk drawer, General Thalt takes a determined hold of his rubber stamp; placing it between his thumb and forefinger, he raises the stamp high above his right shoulder before slamming it down hard onto the top page of the Starship Zx12 mission file, branding the paperwork in rich red ink – MISSION FAILED.

Thalt then places the dead file into his outgoing tray – he will find a home for the confidential paperwork after the shutdown of the Europa Spaceprime Mission Control.

At eight minutes to the midnight hour, the General rises and steps out from behind his heavily framed desk. He straightens his uniform and brushes off both of his shoulders with his right hand, a purely habitual act, before checking that his badges of honour which he wears with pride have remained unblemished. This will be a difficult task for General Thalt but it's only right that he should personally enforce the King's order as the able Cap-com Hubert Snow and Doctor Kira Yu deserve nothing less.

The Flight Director General exits his office door and makes the short journey to the Europa Spaceprime Mission Control.

The conscientious Cap-com Hubert Snow sits stiffly at his desk, facing the blank map of the known system. During the final hours of operations, his industrious nature has failed him as mission time is all but spent.

Over the humming static friction, his keen hearing takes in the familiar sound of the high-level security door opening to the rear of the mission control arena.

Snow is no longer alone within his theatre of operations and he can perceive his General's presence who has readied himself to play his part in the last formal act which is about to be played out.

Hubert Snow closes his eyes to hide his desperation; to shut out his despair. The Flight Director General will soon be at his shoulder and all that he can do is await the endgame whilst listening to the unabated static which is still flowing freely over the Starship Zx12's communications line and where silence is due to intervene.

*

Josiah Dean wraps the warm blanket over his ageing shoulders as the temperature upon the beach has dropped significantly during the past hour, the dusk having turned the clear skies to night. It will soon be time for him to retreat to his beach house sanctuary.

The chalk Moon is filling a cloudless night sky as Josiah stares out towards Earth's oldest companion.

Then, without any prior warning, the horizon explodes across the night sky as an intense corona of bright light ripples out in waves from its source beyond the Moon; shafts of diamond light splinter throughout the solar system as they are sent fleeing from their point of origin and Josiah watches the unnatural occurrence in awe of the cataclysmic forces that he is witnessing.

A sudden awareness begins to dawn on the old man of the Europa Spaceprime as his ageing legs lift him from the sands of Atlantis Beach;

his blanket falls away as he continues to stare open-mouthed at the zenith as the final remnants of flickering light sparkle in the heavens before they converge with the darkness of the near void.

Hope: found. "Jonas," the old man cries and Josiah Dean is running, his ageing legs pushing him through the fine sands in short controlled strides.

Not since his days at the Europa Spaceprime Academy has Josiah Dean moved so swiftly, his fitful laughter escaping him as he pushes his body beyond its years up the slight incline of the sandy slope to his beach house residence.

"Evie," he calls out to his wife who appears suddenly upon the veranda, watching her husband as he undertakes his final strides to be at her side.

Evie Dean has stood resolutely by her husband for almost half a century and after the loss of their only son, their conjoined lives have become emptier; yet upon this night, and for the first time since Jonas's loss, her husband appears revitalised.

"Tonight we travel, my love," Josiah enthuses to his wife.

Evie Dean senses a change in the course of events and yet fearing the onset of further pain and amidst her rising anxieties, she summons up the remains of her courage to search for an answer from her husband. "Joe, it's late, where are you planning to go?" she asks.

And boldly, Josiah Dean replies to his wife: "To the Europa Spaceprime Mission Control."

"Why?" she gasps, exasperated.

And under the Moon's filtering light, Josiah Dean delivers his reply: "My love, our son has come home."

*

The intensifying static growls its continuous flow unabated, crackling forth through the open communications channel, a surging torrent of harsh noise.

Kira Yu, with her arms folded, had watched General Thalt step through the high-level security door and now, at five minutes to the cessation hour, Thalt stands rigidly within the recess of the Europa Spaceprime Mission Control with his orders to hand. He is rooted to the control arena floor, watching the mission clock as the final minutes of the final hour of the final day run out.

Casting her eyes back to Hubert Snow, a beaten motionless hollow form with his head bowed low and his eyes closed, Kira is unsure whether she can watch anymore of this final inevitability.

Kira decides that she cannot face the demise of her hope. With a single tear, she turns away from the forthcoming tragedy, moving in an arc to the static-filled communications feed switch which she flicks to the off position, killing the communications line to the public viewing gallery.

The balcony room floods with silence as she turns her back on command and control: no longer can she watch the death of all hope.

Under laborious breaths, trying desperately to contain her inner suffering, Kira gathers up all of her belongings.

*

Decelerating out of hyperdrive, an exhilarated Captain Jonas Dean regains manual control of his vessel and flies the Starship Zx12 in low over the surface of the Moon.

Jonas hails the Europa Spaceprime Mission Control from the far side of the Moon in the full knowledge that the short-range receivers which are located within the vicinity of the new Moonbase will enhance his signal and bounce it back to Earth.

*

Kira Yu paces out the dozen strides to the glass door exit of the public viewing gallery.

I'll not look back, she thinks. I must move on with my life and the next stop will be a night sky's mass and maybe there I can find a new lease of life and begin to realise my own fledgling ambitions.

Kira fumbles inside her tunic pocket for the swipe card that Commander Marks had entrusted to her the morning after Jonas's loss, but her security card is not where it should have been. As she turns away from the glass door exit, Kira sights the plastic pass which she has discarded in error upon the floor at the front of the public viewing gallery.

Kira doesn't want to have to go back to fetch her means of exit, but she has no choice.

With her head carried low and her eyes averted from the changing circumstance within the control room arena, and focusing only on the swipe card upon the floor of the public viewing gallery, Kira re-crosses the balcony room and bends down to pick up the loaned access pass that she has forsaken in error. However, as she straightens, Kira glances out into the mission control arena to see General Thalt is striding purposefully towards a seated Hubert Snow without taking his eyes away from the mission clock.

*

Snow's eyelids snap open; it's over and General Thalt is standing at his shoulder, sharing his vacant monitors and placing the closure notice upon the able Cap-com's workstation desk. "I'm so sorry Hubert, but this is the way that it has to be. If you make some coffee then we'll begin the shutdown procedure," Thalt says in low monotone.

Snow nods in recognition of the decision which has been made by a higher authority. For twenty years, he has been loyal to his Europa Spaceprime masters; the victories have been sweetly celebrated whilst the defeats have been mourned. Yet the loss of the Starship Zx12 is the hardest defeat of them all as he mournfully accepts his decreed fate: that a ceaseless incoherent static tinnitus has beaten the able Cap-com; the final dance of the angry static, a constant drone over the communications flow.

*

Annoyed at her instinctive reaction, Kira turns away once more, and armed with her means of exit she hastily retraces her steps to the glass security door, having already regretted witnessing the unfolding event.

With her swipe card to hand, Kira stretches out her arm to run the plastic pass through the metallic card reader with her hand that is shakily hovering over the door-lock system reader. And yet she is unable to bring herself to perform the automatic release function as she stares in bewilderment at the barrier glass of the security door.

*

Grasping his white mug as he stands, the white ceramic cup emblazoned with the grey rocket emblem of the Europa Spaceprime, Snow turns away from the soon-to-be-evicted life sign monitors.

He walks in slow resignation towards the mission control's communal area as his mind begins to readjust his focus. Starting upon the morn, he will take some time to reassess his goals, his reason for life, his chosen career path, which he will almost certainly refuse to alter.

*

Without swiping the door lock release, Kira places her security pass back inside her tunic pocket; the glass door exit remains shut.

The corners of her mouth turn upwards towards her eyes of powder blue and ochre brown as an assured smile drifts across her face whilst her tunnelled vision doesn't leave the glass barrier exit – she's too afraid that if she averts her gaze then the apparition will be gone.

Kira tentatively pushes out her hand in front of her, placing it upon the transparent glass with her forefinger pointing directly at the spectral winking glow; the red dot which is flashing within the glass framework of the public viewing gallery security door, an unobtrusive dot whose meaning will change the course of the political landscape within all of the Kingdoms of the Earthprime.

Kira's heart leaps, pounding to the rhythm of the signal that is emanating from the Starship Zx12, and she briskly retreats back into the balcony room, where she hurriedly switches on the communications flow and the static's constant frenzy reignites.

Kira rushes to the front of the public viewing gallery to eagerly watch her pulsar of hope, transmitting its signal as a red flaring beacon upon the map of the known system. On an impulse, Kira bangs the palms of her hands against the soundproof window; the glass barrier shivers as Kira tries desperately to grab the attention of either General Thalt or Hubert Snow.

*

Snow walks to the communal area with thoughts of the future filling his head and to the constant crackle of backdrop drone, the unrelenting noise of fizz and buzz that will be his overriding memory of the past twelve months. "Will I ever again be able to sleep in silence?" the able Cap-com thinks as he undertakes his slow defeated walk, deliberately stalling General Thalt's orders.

The constant breaks, the static jumps and the floor of the Europa Spaceprime Mission Control arena willingly receives Hubert Snow's precious Spaceprime mug; the ceramic receptacle is greeted with glee by the hard surface as it shatters into irrevocable non-usage.

Hubert Snow's head shoots up to the monitors that are situated at the front of the control arena; his acute hearing alert to the anomaly sound.

Dead data is still being received by the life sign monitors but a single red dot is flashing at the far side of the Moon upon the map of the known system.

The static jumps for a second time and General Thalt's eyes begin to widen as his jaw drops and he looks away from the flashing red beacon to Hubert Snow's stationary presence with the breaking static signal leaping around wildly.

For the first time during the entire evening, Hubert Snow raises his head up to the public viewing gallery to where Kira Yu is frantically banging the palms of her hands against the shatterproof glass and shouting wildly.

Hubert Snow reacts and breaks out into a run: one workstation is in his direct path but it's the shortest route to his desk and the able Cap-com traverses the hurdle with his backside sliding over the plastic finish as he makes short work of the distance between his starting point and his General.

Snow calms himself as he stands directly over his console desk and places on his headphones, where in the fracturing static a signal is building.

General Thalt is but a mere passenger to the events which are unfolding around him and he allows his able Cap-com to do his job. Hubert Snow is still listening intently while his eyes are now transfixed upon the red flashing readout on the map of the known system; amending settings, trial and error, homing the signal to clarity, the faltering static losing its pitch and deadening to a hum as a calming communications channel signifies static's death.

Hubert Snow concentrates upon the soundless line of contact whilst shutting out his General's close proximity, before the calming peace of quiet gives way to a clear sound: a lost voice, an echo from the past who is calling out repeatedly over the airwaves.

"Cap-com, this is the Starship Zx12, come in, over. Cap-com, this is the Starship Zx12, come in, over. Cap-com Hubert Snow, will you please get your backside out of bed," the lost voice relays.

And with a widening grin, Snow replies coolly, "This is Cap-com to the Starship Zx12, it's good to hear your voice again, Captain Dean. What is your current situation?"

"Cap-com, I'm pleased to announce I've just broken the hyperdrive flight distance record yet again, however the Starship Zx12 is without its state-of-the-art communications tower as I appear to have lost that on the way. Snow, this is going to give me a problem if I attempt a re-entry into the Earth's atmosphere, but all other systems are working within required parameters," Jonas says thoroughly.

Is this just a fly-by or is Captain Dean trapped in space? is the able Cap-com's concerned thought. Hubert Snow decides upon delivering good news to his Europa Spaceprime colleague as he collates mentally all of the differing safe-return-to-Earth scenarios. "This is Cap-com to the Starship Zx12. Captain Dean, Doctor Kira Yu is at Mission Control," Snow informs Dean.

A quiet delay follows as Captain Jonas Dean fails to reply.

What are Captain Dean's intentions? Hubert Snow needs to find out as General Thalt would expect nothing less from his trusted Cap-com.

The question is direct as Snow knows of no other way. "This is Cap-com to the Starship Zx12. Captain Dean: what is your destination?" he asks.

The quiet continues until Jonas's confident voice cuts through the clear comms hush. "Tell Kira," Jonas pauses, before the Europa Spaceprime spaceman states, "Tell Kira, I'm coming home."

"Roger that, Captain Dean," Hubert Snow responds and his smile lights up the mission control arena.

"General," Snow indicates to Thalt. "I think that we may need to get one or two operatives in here."

General Thalt, with his pride restored in the Europan Kingdom's ability to manage off-world operations, replies, "Aye aye to that, Hubert."

And calmly, the Flight Director General walks the entire length of the mission control arena and presses a fat red button which is marked emergency and that is openly displayed on the back wall of the control hub.

*

The alarms ring out throughout the Europa Spaceprime Mission Control and the Europa Spaceprime Academy and the alarms are triggered in the city, which brings the peoples of the city out onto the streets, and the King's own royal household is also awakened by the loud repetitive tone.

*

Lady Guinevere is sleeping upon the King of Europa's shoulder within the King's outhouse which is immune to the shrill as Lady Anne's running footsteps clip off the marbled corridor floor in her hurried desperation to reach her regent.

Lady Guinevere stirs as the King of Europa turns to face Lady Anne as she enters his beloved sanctuary: she doesn't have to say a word as it's written all over her face and within her body language.

Guinevere awakens at the King's arising to greet the overseer of Europa Earthprime affairs. "Situation report, my lady," the Europan King says as he straightens his black tunic.

"The Starship Zx12 is reported at the far side of the Moon and in contact with the Europa Spaceprime Mission Control. Captain Dean is heading home, my Lord," she coolly replies with her enthusiasm contained within.

"I'm going to assume that Doctor Kira Yu is already on site, so find Josiah and Evie Dean, raise the generals and contact the Kings of the Earthprime," the Europan King decrees with his mind sharpening as his confidence returns. His progressive pathway is clearing as the political mire turns to stone and there's only one small detail that has been left unattended to and the King draws back his regal shoulders and holds out both of his hands to the first ladies of the Earthprime. "Let us go and bring our boy home," he says nobly.

*

"Here we go," Jonas shouts as he initiates full thrust.

Afterburners light up on the Starship's tail – the Europa Spaceprime Captain is in a hurry and the knowledge that Kira Yu will be waiting for him is all that matters to Jonas Dean.

His speed remains unchecked as his Starship hugs the grey rushing blur of contoured rock as he rides the tight gravitational camber around the Moon.

The Europa Spaceprime's new Moonbase comes into his rushing view on the slanting horizon and with the rapier speed of his thrust system fully engaged the new-age outpost disappears beneath him in a flash; its angular crystalline structure still under construction.

The G-forces are pressing down hard upon the Europa Spaceprime spaceman and indenting his facial skin. Under breakneck velocities, Captain Jonas Dean can feel the heady rush as he slingshots his Starship around the Moon, holding onto the tightening turn as he races for home, to a future that remains uncertain, but that doesn't matter to Jonas as this will be a new dawn for him and he will build himself a better life and Kira Yu will be part of it. He already knows that it will take some time, but worthwhile aspirations often do.

He will celebrate the new day upon planet Earth whilst surrounded by all of the people who know him and all of the people who love him.

And the Starship Zx12 breaks free from the adverse camber, shooting out into the straits of space with its booster rockets flaring.

Captain Jonas Dean is pushing onwards towards home with a resplendent Earthrise set out before him, bathed in sunlight and in all of its full glory.

New Dawn, New Day

New dawn, new day,
I'm contemplating life today,
All the chances I didn't take,
All the moves I should've made.

New dawn, new day,
I'm striving for a better way,
A better way to define myself,
A different path to follow.

New dawn, new day,
Planet Earth isn't far away,
I'm homeward bound and reborn anew,
Returning home into your arms.

The blue of Planet Earth against the black silk of the darkened night,
I realise that I fell short at many moments of my life,
I've seen new worlds collide,
I've seen the violent storms that can tear a world apart,
And now I see it clear,
I see it very near,
Planet Earth,
My heart it skips a beat,
And very soon we will meet,
On Planet Earth.

New dawn, new day,
I'll be on Planet Earth today,
I see a hurricane storming off the coast,
I feel nature's destructive power.

New dawn, new day,
Now I know I'm not far away,
I've re-entered the atmosphere,
Gravity has taken over.

I see a burning sun against the deep blue of the summer sky,
I realise that I fell short at many moments of my life,
I've seen new worlds collide,
I've seen the violent storms that can tear a world apart,
And now I see it near,
I see it very clear,
Planet Earth,
My heart it skips a beat,
And very soon we will meet,
On Planet Earth.

New dawn, new day,
I've crashed my Starship today,
I'm sat on top of the fuselage,
My life as I know it is at an end.

New dawn, new day,
My Kira is on her way,
I see a distant mass of people,
They've come to save the day.

I see a burning sun against the deep blue of the summer sky,
I realise that I fell short at many moments of my life,
I've seen new worlds collide,
I've seen the violent storms that can tear a world apart,
And now I see it near,
I see it very clear,
Planet Earth,
My heart it skips a beat,
And very soon we will meet,
On Planet Earth.

New dawn, new day,
That's what all the people say,
I'm living the first day of my new life,
I'm gonna live through the new dawn,
I'm gonna live for the new day.

Lyric credits

Jupiter's Moons
Competition (Lyrics only)   -   Finalist 2012 UK Songwriting

The History Of My Life
Songwriting Competition
(Lyrics Only)   -   Semi-Finalist 2012 UK

This Desolate Land
Songwriting Competition
(Lyrics only)   -   Commended Entry 2012 UK

Saturn's Rings
Songwriting Competition
(Lyrics only)   -   Commended Entry 2012 UK

New Dawn, New Day
Songwriting Competition
(Lyrics only)   -   Commended Entry 2012 UK

ABOUT THE AUTHOR

I'm a hobby writer who has over the past number of years written for fun and this is my first attempt at actually attempting to get anything into print.